KT-437-840

Dreaming of Venice

Dreaming of Venice

T.A. Williams

CANELO

First published in the United Kingdom in 2017 by Canelo

This edition published in the United Kingdom in 2018 by

Canelo Digital Publishing Limited
57 Shepherds Lane
Beaconsfield, Bucks HP9 2DU
United Kingdom

Copyright © T.A. Williams, 2017

The moral right of T.A. Williams to be identified as the author of this
work has been asserted in accordance with the Copyright, Designs and
Patents Act, 1988.

All rights reserved. No part of this publication may be reproduced or
transmitted in any form or by any means, electronic or mechanical,
including photocopy, recording, or any information storage and retrieval
system, without permission in writing from the publisher.

A CIP catalogue record for this book is available from the British Library.

Print ISBN 978 1 78863 156 3
Ebook ISBN 978 1 911420 92 7

This book is a work of fiction. Names, characters, businesses,
organizations, places and events are either the product of the author's
imagination or are used fictitiously. Any resemblance to actual persons,
living or dead, events or locales is entirely coincidental.

Look for more great books at www.canelo.co

Printed and bound in Great Britain by Clays Ltd, Elcograf S.p.A.

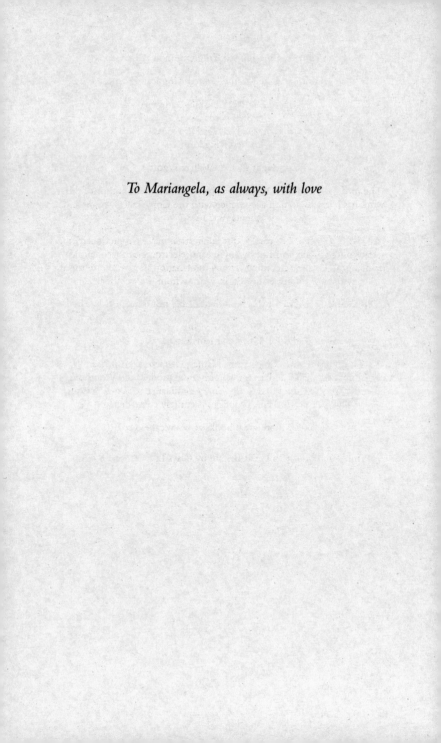

To Mariangela, as always, with love

Prologue

In London it was grey, wet and cold, yet in Penny's head it was a warm, sunny day in Venice. She imagined herself lounging in a shiny black gondola as a gondolier in a stripy shirt sculled along the Grand Canal. All the way past magnificent monuments, incomparable *palazzi* and some of the greatest art galleries in the world, she sat back and listened as he serenaded her in his melodious tenor voice. When they reached the Rialto Bridge and slipped smoothly underneath, onlookers waved down at them and smiled. Penny looked up from the comfort of her upholstered divan and smiled back. As daydreams went, it was pretty damn good.

An incomprehensible message over the station loud-speaker and a trickle of rain on her cheek brought her back to reality. She sighed, wiped the water off her face and glanced down the line, relieved to see the yellow front of the train approaching. At this time of day she knew she wouldn't get a seat, but at least it should be warm and dry.

As the train drew nearer, a woman appeared down the slope from the road. She was pushing a pushchair with one hand while helping herself along with a crutch held in the other. She looked even wetter and more miserable than Penny, who felt a sudden wave of compassion sweep through her. Here she was, cold, soaked and broke, but at least she had her health. Grim as things were for her at the moment, they could be worse.

But Penny didn't have much time for introspection. As the woman hobbled down the sloping path from the road, she lost her footing on the slippery surface, her bad leg gave way, and she let out a despairing squeal. The crutch slipped on the wet concrete and she toppled over, landing heavily on her side in a puddle. Penny watched in silent horror as the pushchair rolled free of the mother's grip and across the platform towards the line. The mother's squeal turned to a panic-stricken scream. The buggy slowed as it reached the edge and for a moment it looked as if it would stop, but as they all held their breath, the wheels kept on turning and the child, still secured in the buggy, toppled onto the tracks.

Penny was the first to react. Dropping her bag, she sprinted to the edge of the platform. The noise of the train was louder now as it rumbled ever nearer, but she didn't hesitate. She leapt down onto the line and grabbed the pushchair containing the child, lifting it up and almost throwing it back onto the platform, into the arms of a rapidly growing group of people. Behind her she heard the deafening blast of the train's horn and the squeal of steel against steel as the driver desperately applied the brakes. She scrabbled furiously at the wet concrete, trying to pull herself back out of danger. Hands gripped hers and she was whipped up and out of the way just in time. Out of the corner of her eye she saw the driver's face contorted in horror as the train slid past and screeched to a stop, two carriage-lengths further on. As she lay sprawled on the wet platform, panting for breath, Penny's eyes flicked down to the spot where she and the pushchair had been only seconds before. Any trace had disappeared in the shadows beneath the massive wheels.

She took a deep breath and looked up at the faces of the crowd that had gathered around her. Hands helped her to her feet as a cacophony of praise assailed her.

'Fantastic. That was awesome.'

'How incredibly brave.'

'You were amazing. You saved that little girl's life.'

Hands patted her on the back and cameras clicked. The child's mother was helped across to greet her, the little girl now clutched safely in her arms and apparently none the worse for her experience. The mother was crying her eyes out and all she could do was to throw her free arm around Penny's shoulders and collapse against her, mouthing the words 'Thank you,' over and over again.

Chapter 1

Next morning, it was still raining as Penny walked to work past the railway arches, carefully avoiding the potholes in the tarmac. A few days earlier she had made the mistake of leaving her only umbrella in the bucket by the entrance to the café, and somebody had stolen it. She knew she wouldn't have any spare cash to replace it until the end of the week and in consequence a dark blue line had formed on her thighs as the water running off her jacket soaked into her jeans. The flimsy hood was plastered down over her head, and her hair was damp underneath it, making her feel cold and miserable.

Her knees and elbows were still sore after yesterday's events at the station and her jeans now had a tear at the knee that had nothing to do with fashion. At the time, the excitement had been a welcome highlight in her humdrum life, but she had woken in the middle of the night bathed in sweat and shivering as she realised how close to death she had come. She had tried calling Rick in Australia to tell him all about it, but the line had just rung and rung. He had been in Australia for three months now and she really missed having him around. She had little doubt that he was at work, in some meeting or other, but it would have been reassuring to hear his voice.

When she reached the café, she pushed the door open and walked in, the smell of bacon assailing her nostrils as she did so. When she had first started the job at the aptly named Apocalypse Café, this had been a welcome smell, stimulating her appetite. Now, two years later, it was all she could do not to throw up.

'Here she is! The hero of the hour!'

Spiro's voice echoed across from the counter, making heads turn towards her all across the café. Behind him, Piotr peered out of the hatch from the kitchen and gave her a whoop. Penny felt her face flush as Jimmy came rushing across to give her a big hug.

'Well done you. You're famous, sweetheart. A total celebrity.'

'You're all over social media. They're saying you deserve a medal, Penny.' Spiro emerged from behind the counter and, ignoring her soaking wet jacket, enveloped her in a bear hug of his own. Penny felt the air whistle out of her lungs as his powerful arms lifted her off her feet and spun her around. 'Our very own Penny, a hero. You really do deserve a medal for what you did.'

'I just did what any normal person would do.' Penny did her best to hide her blushes as she made her way through the tables to the counter and into the back of the café to dump her jacket and put on her apron. Jimmy came in with her, took her wet jacket and hung it up for her, then tidied her hair with his long slim fingers, just like he did every morning. He perched himself on a spare stool and scrutinised her carefully, also just like he did every morning.

'You've got the most beautiful hair, you know, sweetie. You really should get it styled, specially if you're going to have to go to Buckingham Palace to receive an award for bravery. You can't just tie it up with a scruffy band like this.' His own hair, as ever, was immaculate.

'Fat chance of me ever meeting the Queen, Jimmy. Anyway, do you know how much a good haircut costs these days? Where am I supposed to find the money for that? I can't remember the last time I went to the hairdressers, or bought new clothes for that matter.' She gave him a grin. 'My underwear's so worn, it's transparent.'

'I've told you time and time again, just go on the game, darling. With a face like yours and a body like yours, not to mention your transparent underwear, you'd make a fortune.' He grinned back at her. 'If I was that sort of man, I'd be in the queue.'

'Jimmy, for the last time, would you stop trying to make me into a prostitute. Sooner or later I'm going to get my paintings accepted by one of the big galleries and I'm going to become an overnight sensation and it's all going to be fine. My hair can wait until then to be cut.' She smiled back at him. 'Besides, if I keep letting it grow, when I get really desperate I can cut it all off and sell it. That's as close to selling my body I'm going to get, thank you.'

'Such a waste.' Piotr was standing at the door. He glanced back over his shoulder to be sure Spiro wasn't listening. 'But what I not understand is why you work here in this shithole?' His colloquial English was improving in leaps and bounds, even if his vocabulary did tend to lack finesse. 'You could get job in high class coffee shop or champagne bar in West End, no problem.' He grinned. 'Maybe topless bar in Soho. You soon make lots money.'

'Listen you two. I'm happy here, thanks, with my long hair and fully clothed. Just give it a few more months and my paintings will be hanging on the walls of the rich and famous. Just you wait. Dreams really do come true, you know.'

'You honestly believe you're going to be the next Damien Hirst?'

'Damn right I do.' She tried to sound as confident as possible, but after three years trying to break into the London art scene, she was gradually losing hope.

'And, talking of dreams, what about the man of your dreams?' Jimmy was incurably nosey.

'The man of my dreams is ten thousand miles away, Jimmy. You know that.' She could hear the regret in her voice. Separation from Rick had been harder than she had thought.

'So Rick's still the man of your dreams, is he, Penny? You still think this long distance thing's going to work?'

She caught Jimmy's eye. He really did know her very well by now. 'Of course it's going to work. We're making it work.' She did her best to sound confident, but she knew it wasn't easy. As the weeks went by, it was getting harder and harder to find things to say to each other when she and Rick spoke.

Jimmy was reading her mind. 'They say absence makes the heart grow fonder but, in my experience, it's the opposite. Unless you see the person regularly, you start to forget them. You mark my words.'

'It'll be fine, Jimmy. You'll see.' Secretly, in her pocket, she was crossing her fingers.

'If you say so, darling. But you're a sensual woman and you have needs.'

'Needs? Who said I had needs, or I was sensual, for that matter? You've been reading too many women's magazines.'

'Of course you're sensual. A beautiful girl like you has to be. And now you're famous and a hero. So, what if some gorgeous man sees your photo on social media and comes looking for you? Might you be prepared to give him a try? Your boy's ten thousand miles away, remember.'

'My photo on social media…?' Penny didn't like the sound of this.

Jimmy caught her eye and explained. 'Spiro's been tweeting all morning, telling the world that he employs heroes and urging people to come here to the Apocalypse to meet you.'

'Oh, God…'

It was just after three o'clock when somebody did indeed come into the café looking for Penny, but it was a woman, not a man. Penny noticed her as soon as she came through the door. She was wearing gorgeous soft tan leather boots with heels, a stylish coat, and, unlike Penny, she had clearly been to a high class hairdresser very recently. Compared to the normal clientele of the café, she could just as well have come from another planet. Eyebrows raised and jaws dropped around the room as the woman went over to the counter to speak to Spiro. He beamed and waved across the room to Penny.

'Here, famous Penny, come over here. This lady wants to talk to you.'

Blushing once more, Penny did as she was told. The woman extended a manicured hand towards her and introduced herself. 'Hello, Penny. My name's Caroline

8

Moor. I saw your photo on Twitter. You're a very brave girl.' Her accent was very posh, but her smile was friendly.

Penny shook her head and repeated the mantra she had been using all day. 'I just did what any normal person would do.' She studied the woman more closely. She was probably four or five years older than her, maybe thirty or so. She was well-groomed and looked affluent. Penny suppressed a sigh of jealousy.

'Is there somewhere we could talk for a moment?' The woman was looking around warily.

'Er, yes. Are you a journalist or something?' Penny led the woman across to a table in the far corner and ran a cloth over a seat before indicating she should sit down.

'No, nothing like that, Penny.' The woman, Caroline, sat down tentatively, but avoided putting her arms on the table top. Penny nodded to herself. Although she knew that Spiro kept the Apocalypse spotlessly clean, the battered appearance of the furniture could be off-putting, especially to somebody wearing an expensive light-coloured coat. Caroline waited until Penny had sat down opposite her before starting to explain. 'No, I came to see you to ask if you might be interested in a job.' Seeing the surprise on Penny's face, she was quick to expand. 'Not a full-time job. You could still carry on working here most of the time, if that's what you want.'

Working at the Apocalypse certainly wasn't what Penny wanted, but a job was a job, and she had grown close to the boys, Jimmy in particular, over the months she had been here. She looked across the table. 'What sort of job?' She saw the other woman hesitate, shooting a wary glance around the room before replying. Her voice dropped to little more than a whisper.

'How would you feel about meeting me somewhere we can talk more freely?'

Penny began to get a bad feeling about this. Was this some sort of attempt to recruit her to the secret service? Or maybe the woman was some sort of pimp, trying to sign her up for a life of prostitution just like Jimmy and Piotr had suggested. Caroline must have seen the suspicion on her face as she was quick to reassure her.

'It's nothing underhand. Please don't worry. It's just that my employer is a very private person and I've been given strict instructions that what I have to say must be strictly between the two of us.'

Penny nodded. Although several tables separated them from the counter, Spiro was leaning forward nonchalantly, his good ear trained on their corner. Not a lot escaped him. She took another good look at Caroline. She looked trustworthy enough and she was very well spoken. Maybe if they were to meet in a public place there would be no harm in it. She nodded again and the other woman made a suggestion. 'Do you know the JC coffee shop below the Metropole Hotel halfway along Piccadilly?'

Penny nodded again. She knew it from having walked past it a good few times, but she had never dared go inside. The place had *expensive* written all over it, from the tropical fish in the massive aquarium by the window to the liveried doorman whose only job appeared to be to open the door for patrons of the establishment and to keep riff-raff out. Riff-raff which would no doubt include Penny, the way things were at the moment. She dismissed the thought and brightened up. Assuming they let her in, at least she was unlikely to be mugged, raped or kidnapped in a classy establishment like that.

'I know the place. I'm on the early shift here tomorrow so I finish at four. Would five thirty be all right for you? I could get there by then.' Caroline nodded, an expression of what could well have been relief on her face. Penny remembered her manners. 'Fine, I'll see you there, then. Now, can I get you a coffee or a tea or something?'

Caroline stood up rather too quickly and shook her head. Penny didn't blame her. Her own immune system had strengthened no end since working here, and she could well understand the other woman's reservations.

'No, thank you, Penny. Here's my card. If something comes up, just give me a call. Otherwise I'll see you in the JC.' She deposited a crisp new visiting card in Penny's hand and headed for the door. Penny watched her walk out to a black cab that had been waiting for her. As the taxi drove off, Penny found herself wondering just what this mysterious job could be. Nevertheless, there was no disguising the fact that it sounded interesting and, apart from the baby on the line incident, her life was sorely lacking in interest at the moment.

That night Penny found herself lying in bed dreaming of Venice once again. As so often in her dreams, she was travelling slowly up the Grand Canal in a gondola propelled by a tall man in a stripy jumper. All around her were gorgeous historic buildings, many housing extraordinary works of art, but the funny thing was that she wasn't concentrating on the buildings. She only had eyes for the gondolier. Frustratingly, though, every time she tried to see his face, he turned away from her, and all she could see were his broad shoulders and his mass of dark hair.

Chapter 2

Penny just about had time to rush home as soon as she got off work next day. Mercifully the weather had finally dried up after two or three weeks of interminable rain and, although her room was on the middle floor, sparing her the constant dripping that was driving the top floor residents to distraction, the whole house felt and smelt damp as a result. She jumped in the tepid shower to remove as much of the smell of all-day breakfasts as possible and changed into the only half-decent clothes she still had. She was lucky with the trains and it was five twenty-five when she emerged from Green Park tube station and hurried along to the JC coffee shop. The door was opened for her by the bulky doorman, his eyes ranging discreetly over her clothes as he did so. Somehow she had a good idea that he had worked out their provenance and cost down to the last 99p, although his expression gave nothing away. Mercifully, he let her in. She walked in and stopped on the mat, looking around for Caroline.

'Penny. Up here.' She caught sight of Caroline waving to her from up on the mezzanine floor so she climbed the glass and steel staircase and made her way across to the table she had chosen. As she got there she saw a *Reserved* sign on the table top. Clearly, this meeting had been carefully pre-planned. If she had expected to meet Caroline's *private* employer, she was to be disappointed. The only occupant of that corner of the coffee shop was Caroline. Today she was wearing a smart grey dress and an antique coral necklace.

'Penny, hi. Come and sit down. What can I get you?'

Penny glanced at what Caroline was drinking. It looked very much like a glass of prosecco. She pointed across the table. 'Thanks. I'll have what you're having if that's okay.'

An immaculate waitress appeared at her shoulder and Caroline caught the girl's eye. 'Another glass of champagne, please.'

Penny sat down, reflecting that people who dressed like Caroline and staged meetings in places like this would probably turn their noses up at anything less than champagne. She slipped her jacket off and was conscious of Caroline's eyes giving her a close forensic examination. Maybe she was a lesbian and this was nothing more than an elaborate chat up? She had nothing against lesbians, but it just wasn't her thing. She was just starting to compose a suitable polite put down when Caroline spoke up.

'It's quite uncanny.' She was talking to herself as much as to Penny. 'Quite amazing.' Her eyes were still ranging over Penny's body.

Penny's suspicions deepened. She cleared her throat and was about to speak when the waitress reappeared with her champagne. Caroline waited until the girl had left, then launched into an explanation before Penny could voice her reservations.

'I work for a very private family who keep a very low public profile. You've almost certainly never heard of them, although they're some of the wealthiest people in the country. Anyway, the thing is, we're looking for somebody to take the place of Olivia – that's my employer – at a number of conferences and meetings over the next few months.'

'Really? What sort of conferences?' Penny wondered if somewhere along the line the story had got out about her having an MA in Art History.

'The environment. My employers sponsor a number of good causes, mostly involved with research into climate change.'

Penny shook her head in bewilderment. 'But that's not even my subject.' Caroline looked up and caught her eye.

'Well, why don't you tell me all about you and your subject. What've you been doing since school? Have you always been a waitress at that… place? You're what, maybe 25 or so?'

'26 last month. I'm an artist. I did a degree in fine art at the Slade and then an MA in Art History and since then I've been painting and trying to sell my paintings.' She looked up at Caroline and smiled. 'So far without any great success, but I'm still hopeful. I've been working as a waitress for the last couple of years as well, to try and help make ends meet.' She spotted interest in Caroline's eyes; interest and approval.

'That's marvellous, Penny. You've got a degree, and a postgraduate one at that. One of the things we've been concerned about was whether you'd have the necessary academic and intellectual tools for the job. Clearly you do. That's excellent.' She picked up her glass and held it out across the table. 'Cheers.'

Penny dutifully clinked her glass against Caroline's and took a mouthful. She hadn't had champagne since her sister's wedding and this tasted delicious. She took another mouthful and let it slip slowly down her throat before speaking. 'But why me, Caroline? Surely you'd be better off with a scientist, an environmental specialist. I'm all right with Michelangelo or Titian, but I don't know the first thing about global warming.'

Caroline smiled back at her and Penny suddenly realised she rather liked her. 'Don't worry, Penny, I'm sure you'll be fine.' She glanced at her watch. 'Do you have any plans for this evening?' Penny shook her head. 'Well, if it suits you, maybe you might like to come along with me to meet my employer, and then I'll take you out for dinner. Anywhere you like. How does that sound?'

'That sounds great, but tell me more about the job.' She still couldn't get her head around why she, of all people, should have been chosen.

'If you don't mind, I'll leave that until a bit later. Once you've met Olivia it'll be easier for me to fill you in on the details. What I can tell you is what we're offering. We anticipate this occupying your time for one or two full days a month, mostly at the weekends, along with a couple of weekday engagements of just a few hours here and there.' She looked up at Penny. 'Would you be able to give us that much of your time?'

'Yes, but I don't see…'

'It'll all become clear this evening. In the meantime, I can tell you that we're proposing to pay you five hundred pounds a day or pro rata for the shorter engagements.'

'Ah...' A response didn't come readily to Penny. Caroline and her mysterious employer were offering her five hundred pounds each day for two days' work a month. That was a thousand pounds a month, maybe more, for what sounded like very little commitment. A thousand pounds a month! Suddenly a trip to the hairdresser, a visit to the dentist for the first time in years and maybe even a flight to Australia to see Rick loomed into range. She reached for her glass and drained it.

'Another one? I could certainly manage one.' Caroline emptied her glass and raised it in the waitress's direction, along with two fingers. 'So, do you reckon these terms might be acceptable to you?'

Penny resisted the temptation to throw her arms around Caroline's neck and kiss her. An extra grand a month would make an enormous difference to her life. She took a deep breath. 'More than acceptable, Caroline. That sounds most generous.'

'Excellent. Now, if you don't mind, tell me more about your background. I'd like to know as much about you as possible before we go to meet Olivia.'

They left the coffee shop at half past six and Caroline hailed a taxi. It took them to Notting Hill and stopped outside a huge white Georgian town house. Penny had no idea how much a house like this might be worth, but she suspected it would be well into eight figures. Caroline led her up the steps and rang the bell. The door was opened almost immediately by a middle-aged lady, introduced by Caroline as Janice the housekeeper. From behind her, a dark shadow appeared. Penny took an apprehensive step backwards as a big dog emerged from a doorway and came charging towards her. She relaxed as she saw it was a handsome black Labrador whose intentions, from the way his tail was wagging furiously, were clearly anything but aggressive. Then, unexpectedly, the dog suddenly skidded to a halt on the polished wood floor a few feet from her and subjected her to a long stare, his head slightly to one side, as if unsure who she was.

'That's just Gilbert. Don't worry about him, he's very friendly.' Caroline clicked her tongue and the dog came over to greet her. As she scratched his ears, Caroline gave Penny a smile. 'He's probably just confused.'

'Confused?' Penny didn't have time to dwell on this comment as the housekeeper ushered them into the lounge. This magnificent room was the size of the Apocalypse Café and Penny's bedsit put together. There was an intricately sculpted white marble fireplace with a collection of delicate oriental jade figures on the mantel-piece. The floor was polished oak and the furniture modern and elegant.

From Penny's point of view, however, the most inter-esting thing in the room by far was a painting. It was a wooden triptych, hanging on the far wall, that she recog-nised immediately as late medieval. When doing her MA, she had specialised in medieval art and she would dearly have liked to study this painting more closely. She felt a surge of excitement as she saw that it looked uncannily like the *Garden of Earthly Delights* she had seen in the Prado in Madrid. Surely, she thought to herself, this couldn't be a Hieronymus Bosch original. If it was, then it was worth more than the house, and probably the houses on either side of it as well. She was dying to go across and examine it more closely when another door opened in the side wall and two people walked into the room. Suddenly Penny forgot all about the painting. She could hardly believe her eyes.

'Penny, this is Mrs Brookes-Webster, and this is Olivia.' Although she was still trying to process what she was seeing, Penny couldn't help noticing the apprehension on Caroline's face as she made the introductions. She took a good look at the mother. The woman, probably in her fifties, was very attractive. She was wearing a very stylish, if deeply revealing, silk gown and her ears, fingers and neck were heavy with gold and diamonds. A powerful wave of very expensive perfume wafted into the room along with her. Her thick, black hair was piled up on her head in a style that could only have been done by a professional, and not a cheap one either. However, the expression on her face was far from welcoming. In fact, the way she was looking at Penny made Caroline's inspection of her in the coffee shop seem like a fleeting glance. But Penny's eyes returned almost immediately to the daughter. Caroline was dead right. It really was uncanny. Penny felt as if she was looking in a mirror. She and Olivia could have been twins.

The dog, by this time, had worked out who his mistress was and he trotted over to Olivia, who stroked his head as he took up position beside her.

'Good evening.' Penny held out her hand to Olivia and the girl reached out and took it, shaking it limply. She barely raised her eyes from the priceless rug beneath her feet and only just murmured a greeting. As welcomes go, it was weak, to say the least. As it turned out, feeble as it was, this proved to be a lot warmer than the reaction she got from the mother.

'Good God, Caroline, what's this supposed to be? *Pygmalion*? I know you have some funny ideas from time to time, but, really? How on earth do you intend to transform a nobody like this into Olivia?' Her voice was heavy with disdain and Penny had to stifle the urge to reply in kind. Sensing the hostility in the room, Caroline was quick to respond.

'But Mrs Brookes-Webster, surely you can see just how similar the two girls are.'

Penny, who was still doing her best to swallow the *nobody* remark, took a good look at the daughter. Olivia's hair was almost exactly the same shade of chestnut as hers, although it was a good bit shorter and had been cut and styled to perfection. The girl wasn't wearing an evening dress like her mother, but her expensive-looking deep red silk top was almost certainly out of the same designer stable as her mother's. Penny studied her for a moment. Caroline was right. It wasn't just their faces. Even their bodies were almost identical, their legs a similar length, making them pretty much the same height. She couldn't see the exact colour of her eyes, but they were light, as were hers. Unlike Penny, though, Olivia glittered with gold earrings, and her heels were almost as high as her mother's.

'Well, what's your name?' Not even an attempt at cordiality.

Penny returned her attention to Mrs Brookes-Webster and did her best to keep her voice level and respectful as she replied. After all, there was a thousand pounds a month and maybe a trip to Oz riding on this.

'Penny Lane… like the Beatles' song.'

The other woman gave no reaction. Instead she walked slowly all the way round Penny, staring at her closely as she did so. Finally she turned to Caroline and sniffed. 'Well, I still don't see why we need to go to all this palaver, but if this is all we've got, then I suppose we'll have to give it a try. But frankly, Caroline, I can't see it working.' She glanced across at her daughter. 'What do you think, Olivia?'

'I don't know, but I do think it's worth a try.' The girl wouldn't even meet Penny's eye. She looked as disinterested as she sounded, concentrating her attention on the dog. Penny could have slapped her and her ostentatious mother. The two of them were discussing her like a piece of meat. For a moment she was once more reminded of Jimmy's comment about prostitution. She was on the point of telling them what they could do with their job and leaving, when the mother turned on her heel and headed for the door.

'I have to go now, Olivia. I don't want to be late for the premiere. Are you sure you don't want to come?' Olivia shook her head. Mrs Brookes-Webster stopped at the door and turned back to glare at Caroline. 'I still think this is a mistake, Caroline. An expensive and unnecessary mistake.' And she left, not giving Penny so much as a goodbye.

Penny's returned her attention to Olivia, who was still standing with her eyes downcast, stroking the dog. After a few seconds that felt like minutes, Olivia finally raised her head and looked across at Penny. 'I agree with Caroline that this is something that's worth trying. It won't be easy, but it *is* worthwhile. Really.' With that, she turned and left through the same door as her mother.

The dog got up, glanced across at Penny for a moment and then padded out behind her.

After she had gone, Caroline went across to the door and checked that it was firmly closed before speaking. First she invited Penny to sit down. Penny shook her head and the two of them stood there uncomfortably for a few moments, digesting the scene that had just finished.

'Look, Penny, I'm sorry about that. I'm afraid Mrs Brookes-Webster can be a bit prickly at times. She's going to a big event tonight and she's probably just a bit hyper.'

'Prickly? I think the words you're looking for are downright bloody rude.' Penny caught her eye and only briefly hesitated before adding 'What a cow!'

'I'm sorry, Penny.' Caroline dropped her eyes. 'Anyway, as you must've noticed, the resemblance between the two of you is quite remarkable; like two peas in a pod. What we're hoping to do is to pass you off as Olivia on a number of business occasions as she hasn't been too well, and she's not really up to going out and meeting people yet. She's already missed a huge number of engagements.'

Penny shook her head. From the clothes and the surroundings, it seemed more likely that Olivia was just more interested in bling, glitz and socialising with her equally rich-bitchy friends. She shook her head a second time.

'We may look physically similar, Caroline, but God help me if I resemble people like this in any other way.' She turned towards the door through which they had entered the room. 'I'm sorry, Caroline. You're nice and I'm sorry to disappoint you, but I've still got some scruples, even if I am a *nobody*. I'm afraid I just couldn't bear to be associated in any way with those two. Thanks for everything. Thanks for the champagne, but I think I'm just going to go.'

'Penny, please, don't go.' Penny looked across and saw that Caroline was on the verge of tears. She paused with her hand on the door handle as Caroline went on. 'Please think again. There's an awful lot riding on this. Please wait. Listen.' Her voice became more urgent. 'This was all my idea and if it falls through, I'm going to find myself in big trouble.' She paused. 'Look, I've been authorised to go up to twice the original offer. Would that make a difference?'

A thousand pounds a day? Penny hesitated, the prostitution parallel still running through her head. What was that film where Robert Redford offers a million pounds in return for being able to sleep with Demi Moore? The lesson of the first part of that story was that money can buy anything, even love. If she said yes, surely she would be prostituting herself. Well, she thought to herself, not exactly prostituting in the sense of her body being violated, but to be treated the way she had just been treated was as close to violation as she wanted to get. Still, the pragmatic part of her brain reminded her that a couple of grand a month would turn her currently pretty shabby life around. And, she realised with a rush, just one month would get her more than enough for a return ticket to Sydney. She stood there, looking hard at Caroline, trying to make up her mind.

'What do you mean, there's a lot riding on this?'

Caroline glanced round the room again apprehensively. 'I can't go into detail for now, but all I can say is that Olivia and I feel it's very important for you to take her place. Hopefully it won't be for long; two, three months, maybe.'

Penny looked at her sharply, a sudden thought surfacing in her mind. 'Wait a minute, Caroline. Could this be dangerous? You're not looking for somebody to replace her because she's in danger of, I don't know, kidnap or something?' She was thinking fast. Kidnap would be a real possibility for people as rich as this. Once again her eyes flicked across to the painting on the wall. Anybody who could afford to hang something potentially worth tens, if not hundreds, of millions on their lounge wall would be prepared to pay handsomely to get their daughter back.

Caroline shook her head decisively. 'Oh my God, no. Not at all, Penny, it's nothing like that. I promise.' She looked sincere, but Penny still wasn't convinced. Caroline lowered her voice. 'Look, I can't go into detail at this point, but it's nothing dangerous. It's more a question of... call it internal politics.'

'Internal politics? Internal to what?'

Caroline hesitated. 'Family politics, does that help?'

Penny hesitated. She had clearly seen how unenthusiastic Mrs Brookes-Webster had been about the proposal. Maybe there was bad blood between mother and daughter. It didn't sound good, and getting caught up in the middle of a fight between mother and daughter was definitely bad news.

Caroline was looking more desperate as she tried again.

'Listen, Penny, honestly it's not dangerous, and I promise you're not going to get caught up in some sort of family feud. It's politics, that's all I can say.' Her voice became more persuasive. 'And besides, in order for you to play the part of Olivia, you'll need to have a total makeover; your nails, your hair, your teeth.' Penny reflected ruefully that she hadn't been to the dentist for three, maybe four years now. 'And you'll need a new wardrobe. I'll come with you and we'll buy everything from underwear to shoes to evening dresses. It'll all go on their account. And once you finish this job, you get to keep everything. Please, Penny, say you'll do it.'

'I don't know, Caroline. It all sounds very dubious and I just can't bear the thought of being in the presence of those two again.'

'But you won't need to,' Caroline rushed to reassure her. 'At least, hardly ever. Think about it. You and Olivia can't ever be seen together, so you'll have to be kept away from each other at all times, and you don't need to have anything to do with her. And apart from an occasional visit to a convention or a cocktail party, you don't need to worry about being in close proximity of Mrs B-W.' She paused, during which time she looked hard at Penny and evidently came to a decision. She lowered her voice. 'Listen, Penny, Olivia hasn't been well recently, and Mrs Brookes-Webster's been taking her place at business meetings.' Her voice now dropped to little more than a whisper. 'The thing is that Mrs B-W's not doing so well at it. She's been putting a lot of people's backs up and we need to try to redress the balance. By replacing Olivia you'll actually be replacing her mother as well, so you'll hardly see her either. Besides, Mrs B-W's going off on holiday for most of the month of November.' Penny was slightly encouraged by this, but still uncertain. Then Caroline delivered the coup de grace. 'And she's only home for a week or two after that because the Venice conference in December is when she goes on holiday to the Caribbean, so you won't have to worry about bumping into her at all.'

'Did you say Venice?' The name stunned Penny for a moment. All her life she had dreamt of visiting that most magical of cities. As an artist, she had been to Italy a number of times and she loved the country. She spoke the language pretty well and had visited Rome, Sicily and Tuscany, spending a whole year in Florence, but had never managed to make it across to Venice. Only as recently as the previous month she had confided to Jimmy that she would be prepared to sell her soul to the devil for the chance to go to Venice, and now here it was. And although Olivia and her mother were pretty grim, they weren't exactly the devil incarnate.

'Yes, it's a five day conference just before Christmas. It's an annual event. You wouldn't be busy all the time and there must be hundreds of amazing paintings there for you to see.' Caroline had evidently noted the spark in Penny's eyes when she used the "V" word. Now she didn't hesitate to capitalise on this bargaining tool. 'And we'll be staying in just about the very best hotel in Venice; one of the best in the world. Surely you'd like that?'

There was absolutely no doubt at all in Penny's mind that she wouldn't just like that, she would love it. The whole thing still sounded decidedly dodgy, but the combination of much-needed extra income that would hopefully allow her to fly across to see Rick, and the chance to go to Venice, outweighed her doubts. She took a deep breath and held out her hand. 'All right, Caroline. You've talked me into it. I'll do it.'

–

That night, Penny tried to get in contact with Rick in Australia to give him the wonderful news that she might, after all, be able to fly out to see him this winter. She waited until eleven o'clock, knowing that she should be able to catch him in what would be the early morning over there, before he left the house to go to work. She went onto Skype, dialled and waited. It took her a few tries, but she persisted, telling herself he was probably in the shower. Finally, just as she was beginning to despair, he answered. The screen cleared and his face appeared. From his bare shoulders, he had either just come out of bed or the bathroom.

'Penny, hi. How's things?' He sounded surprised and a bit flustered.

'Hi, Rick. I'm fine. What about you?'

'Good, good. How's the painting going?'

They exchanged a few snippets of news while she was making up her mind how to broach the subject of the very unusual job she had just accepted that would, hopefully, allow her to make enough for an air ticket to Australia. Somehow, trying to find the words to explain how it had all happened wasn't straightforward. She decided she had better start at the beginning, with the baby on the railway lines, but she could see he had something on his mind. His eyes were darting around uncomfortably and, clearly, he wasn't concentrating on what she was saying.

'Is everything okay, Rick? Are you all right?' He definitely didn't look his normal happy self.

She saw him glance over his shoulder and heard him clear his throat. 'Look, Pen, I've been meaning to call you.' He hesitated briefly. 'You see, it's like this. This long-distance thing, between us, it isn't working.'

'What do you mean, not working?' Penny suddenly felt cold. She pulled her dressing gown tighter around her shoulders and tried again. 'I don't understand, Rick. Why isn't it working?'

She saw his back straighten as he sat upright and concentrated. 'I mean, Pen, look, I'm awfully sorry, but I think I've found somebody else. I mean, I *have* found somebody else.' She saw him take a couple of quick breaths. 'I should have told you before. I'm sorry.' Penny just sat there, dumbstruck, as she listened to what he had to say, a numb sensation flooding throughout her body. 'I've started a relationship with somebody else, and it's going really well. So I suppose what I'm trying to say is that I think it's best if we break up, you and I.' He stopped, waiting for her reaction. It took her a while to find the words, any words.

'You're telling me you think we should break up?' Penny heard the quiver in her voice and he must have heard it too.

'Yes, but I'm really sorry.'

'Because you've found somebody else?'

'Erm, yes.' He glanced back over his shoulder again and Penny found she was beginning to put two and two together. Her feeling of dismay began to change to something else.

'And she's there with you now?'

'Erm, yes.'

'Well, you've certainly moved on bloody fast.' She felt a wave of anger rising in her and decided to terminate the conversation before she exploded. 'And you didn't even have the decency to tell me before you jumped into bed with her?'

'Erm, no.'

'Well, that's that, then, Rick. Goodbye.' She reached forward furiously.

'Goodbye, Pen.'

She managed to close the laptop without slamming it hard enough to fracture the screen, but she definitely gave it a hefty thump. She flung it to one side and lay back on the bed, doing her best to digest what had just happened. Here she had been, about to break the news to her boyfriend that it looked like she was going to be able to fly all the way from one end of the earth to the other in order to see him and, instead, she had found herself being unceremoniously dumped. She lay there for a good long while, her head spinning. Yes, she had always known it was going to be hard to keep a long distance relationship alive, but just as she had said to Jimmy so recently, she had been determined to try. And now this… Thought of Jimmy made her reach for her phone. She knew she needed to talk to somebody and she knew she could count on him. She and he had really bonded recently. If this had happened a year earlier there was no doubt she would have phoned her big sister, Diane, but now, Jimmy had become her default option whenever she needed comfort. He answered almost immediately.

'Hello, sweetheart, how're you?'

'Not so good, I'm afraid.' She gripped the bedcover in her free hand and clenched her fist, determined not to break down and start crying. Her resolve didn't last long.

'What's happened, poppet? Tell Uncle Jimmy all about it.'

'It's Rick. He's gone off with another woman.' Her voice tailed off. She knew she wouldn't be able to say anything else for a little while for fear that it might make her cry, so she lapsed into silence. But Jimmy and silence didn't mix.

'What, some Australian woman? For God's sake, is the man crazy? You're gorgeous, sweetheart, how could he do something like that?'

'I'm not feeling very gorgeous at the moment, Jimmy. I suppose it's like you were saying; absence makes the heart forget, not grow fonder.'

'Well, all I can say, Penny, is that it's pretty clear it wasn't going to work out anyway, if he can't even keep his hands off other women after, what, two or three months?'

'Three months and five days, but who's counting?'

'Do you want me to come over for a snuggle? I'm a very good snuggler, you know.'

In spite of the circumstances, Penny found herself smiling. 'I'm sure you are and thank you. But I think I'll just go to sleep. I'll see you tomorrow at the café and, thanks, Jimmy. You're a good friend.'

Unsurprisingly, Penny had an unsettled night, but she must have slept at least some of the time, as she had the Venice dream once again. This time the dream was less comfortable. One moment she was in a gondola, working the oar herself as the boat glided down a narrow canal between two beautiful old buildings, the next she lost her balance and fell into the water. All around her people were walking past or sitting enjoying the sunshine, but nobody noticed her, however loud she shouted and screamed. She splashed and splashed and splashed, but there was nobody to help her.

Chapter 3

One of the conditions of the job was that Penny was sworn to secrecy. This was done at a solicitor's office close to the Temple church in Central London, where she was summoned shortly after accepting the job.

She was ushered into the office by a stern-looking secretary and found herself in the presence of an even sterner-looking older man with a shining bald head. He was sitting behind a massive wooden desk, empty apart from a telephone, a gold fountain pen and a lone folder. As she came in, he stood up and came round to greet her, extending his hand in her direction.

'Miles Jenson. Do sit down. Miss Lane, isn't it?'

'Yes, Penny Lane.'

'Like the Beatles' song.' For a moment what could have been described as a smile crossed his face, but it disappeared again in an instant. 'Do take a seat, please, Miss Lane. It is Miss, isn't it?'

'Yes, I'm single.' Penny sat down as instructed and took a quick look around. The walls of the room were lined with oak panelling and the floor had recently been carpeted. The window looked out onto a windswept court three storeys below. Although it was still September, the trees were already losing their leaves and it looked bleak out there. Back inside it didn't look much more cheerful. Mr Jenson's fleeting smile had been replaced by a look of grim severity.

'I have here a solemn undertaking for you to sign, Miss Lane. You should read it carefully before you sign it. In brief, it's a formal, legally binding undertaking not to reveal the part you are playing in this little...' He hesitated, searching for an appropriate word, '...charade. As you will see from the wording of the document, the consequences of any breach of confidentiality would be serious, very serious indeed. I hope I make myself clear.'

'Quite clear, thank you, Mr Jenson. Would you like me to take the document away and come back once I've read it?'

'No, just take your time and read it here.' His eyes flicked up to a fine old wall clock. He was, no doubt, being paid handsomely for his time. Penny set down her bag and concentrated on the legal document in her hands. As she started reading, she was still turning over in her head the wisdom or otherwise of embarking on this very unusual course of action. She would have dearly loved to have somebody with whom she could discuss things. With Rick now out of the equation, she felt sure that Jimmy, for instance, with his innate common sense, would have been able to advise, but Caroline had made it quite clear that she was forbidden to reveal it to a soul, not even her mum and dad. And now, in case she were still under any misapprehension, this stipulation was going to be enshrined in law.

Penny did her best to ignore these thoughts as she read the document to the end. It was uncompromising. Any disclosure to anybody of what she was doing would result in legal action. She had little doubt that the full weight of the law would be brought to bear upon her, and if it came to a legal battle between her and Mr Jenson and his team, she had no illusions as to the inevitable outcome. Still, she told herself, Venice was Venice, and a grand or two a month was the lifeline she so desperately needed, so in for a penny, in for a pound. She finished reading and placed the document on the solicitor's desk. As he looked up and caught her eye, she nodded. 'That's quite clear. I agree to abide by the conditions laid down in this document. If you've got a pen, I'll sign it now.'

'Excellent.' Mr Jenson picked up the gold fountain pen, screwed off the lid and handed it to her. She signed and he added his own signature below hers. Finally he produced an old-fashioned rocking blotter from a drawer and ran it over the wet ink, before rising to his feet. He held out his hand once more. The meeting was over.

Penny stood up in her turn, stretched across the desk and shook his hand. 'Thank you, Mr Jenson.'

'Thank *you*, Miss Lane. And remember that this interdict applies even to your closest friends and relatives. Are we clear? Not even to your fiancé or boyfriend.'

Penny shook her head. 'That's not going to be a problem.'

The solicitor nodded approvingly. 'Excellent. Now, goodbye to you and good luck with this enterprise.'

Outside in the waiting room, to her surprise, she found Caroline waiting for her. As they walked out into the chilly autumn day together, Penny explained what had just transpired. Caroline nodded.

'I had the same thing yesterday. Janice the house-keeper and Arthur the chauffeur had to sign as well. You're a closely guarded secret, Penny.' She smiled at her and glanced at her watch. 'What are your plans this morning? Do you have to get back to work?'

'Not until four. I'm on the late shift now for the next few days.'

'So you're free for a few hours?'

'Yes. What were you thinking of?'

'Shopping, Penny, shopping.'

Their shopping expedition exceeded even Penny's wildest expectations. Altogether they spent over four hours in Harrods and some of the surrounding shops and boutiques. In the course of that time, Penny acquired an extensive new wardrobe at eye-watering cost, all paid for by Caroline's credit card. Penny found herself with several pairs of shoes, including stilettos, mules and some gorgeous soft Italian suede boots, any one of which probably cost as much as all the shoes and boots currently stuffed under the bed of her rented room. They even bought a selection of underwear, some fancy but, thankfully, most of it comfortable and, unlike most of her stuff, non-transparent. A brace of mind-bogglingly expensive designer dresses and a selection of tops and jeans, all bearing well-known labels, filled more and more bags. One small bottle of Olivia's favourite perfume cost more than Penny earned in a week at the café. A warm winter coat, not dissimilar to the one Caroline was wearing, completed the ensemble. They had so many bags they had to be assisted out of the last shop by the same shop assistant who had initially turned up her nose when she had first seen Penny's modest outfit. Now, no doubt thinking of the commission she had just earned, she was all sweetness and light.

Penny slumped down in the back of the taxi alongside Caroline and glanced across at her, reflecting that retail therapy appeared to be surprisingly good at taking one's mind off two-timing pigs in the Antipodes, at least for a few hours. 'They don't believe in doing things by halves, the Brookes–Websters, do they? We must have spent more than I've earned in a year of working at the Apocalypse Café.'

Caroline smiled back at her. 'You've got to look the part and the fact is that this is the stuff they wear. If you turned up at a conference in your old clothes, somebody might smell a rat.' Penny was reminded of the very real rat she had seen running down the corridor just outside the door to her room the other morning, and shuddered as Caroline carried on. 'And while on the subject of making you look convincing, there's a trip to the salon to fix up.'

'Hair salon?'

'Hair, nails, a full facial for a start. I'll try and get something booked this week.' She caught Penny's eye. 'The problem is that it'll have to be a different hair salon from Olivia's usual one. If she suddenly turned up with hair twice as long as it was last week, they, too, might smell a rat.'

'Could you stop talking about rats, please, Caroline. I think I've got one living in my house.'

'Ugh. Anyway, what we're going to have to do is to book you in somewhere and produce a photo of Olivia as she is now. We can say it was your old style and you want to go back to it. Are you free any morning this week?'

'Yes, I think so. I'm waiting to hear from a couple of galleries, more in hope than in expectation, but I imagine they'll give me a few days' notice. That is, if they get back to me at all.'

'Great. I'll see what I can arrange and I'll give you a call as soon as I know.'

By now the taxi was approaching Penny's far from glamorous lodgings. She stared out of the window at the down-at-heel surroundings and reflected on the vast chasm that existed between her lifestyle and the Brookes-Websters'. She turned back towards Caroline. 'I'm not making a huge mistake, am I?'

Caroline shook her head. 'Not at all. You're actually doing something very positive and important. It may sound a bit over-dramatic, but the work of the Foundation is of massive importance to the whole world.' Seeing the look of uncertainty on Penny's face, she expanded. 'Really. It's vital that the research continues, and your taking Olivia's place will make a real difference.'

Penny shook her head. 'If you say so. When do I start to find out more about the Foundation?'

'Very soon, Penny.'

–

Somehow, Caroline managed to make the hair appointment for the very next day. When she phoned with the name of the salon, Penny almost fainted. She was going to have her hair done by the same people who did the hair of countless footballers' wives and girlfriends, as well as members of the more traditional aristocracy.

'Your hair's being done by Gaston and I've sent him a couple of shots of Olivia's hair. I've booked you in as

Olivia Brookes and he's promised to get you looking just like that.' Caroline hesitated for a moment. 'I told him you've been away on a gap year and you haven't been looking after yourself, so you might do well to invent a cover story in case he's one of the chatty ones. They reckon they should be able to cut and style your hair, do your nails, and give you a full facial in the course of the morning, so you should be able to get to work in the afternoon all right. I've given them the card details so you don't need to pay a penny. All right?'

The morning at the salon passed in a crazy blur. Penny didn't know whether to be excited, appalled or terrified as the full weight of an expensive makeover was lavished upon her. As Olivia had magnificent long nails, Penny found herself on the receiving end of some expensive false nails that were duly painted the same shade of bright red favoured by Olivia, or at least her mother. The facial, consisting of a never-ending succession of perfumed creams and lotions, accompanied by soothing background music, left her feeling remarkably relaxed. But the sense of relaxation only lasted until she was led to the hair stylist, Gaston. As her lovely long chestnut brown hair began to tumble onto the floor all around her, she came close to weeping. She had had long hair her whole life and losing it felt like losing an old friend; albeit a very scruffy, damaged old friend with no sense of style, if Gaston's commentary as he snipped away was to be believed.

Penny did her best to relax as the stylist did his work. Finally, after quite a while, Gaston declared himself satisfied and a menial was summoned to remove her gown. A mirror was held up for her to inspect the results of his labours and as Penny saw the transformation he had worked, a shiver went down her spine. It was strange and rather spooky, like looking at somebody else. As she tilted her head from side to side, she half expected the face in the mirror to start speaking to her. She turned towards Gaston, truly astounded.

'Gaston, that's amazing.' Remembering her act, she added. 'I look just like I did a year ago. You couldn't have done it any better.' She meant it. Although Gaston didn't know it, now, as a result of his efforts, she and Olivia no longer looked just like twins. Now they looked like *identical* twins and it felt really quite scary. Somehow, this visit to the hairdresser had cemented her part in Caroline's plan even more firmly that her signature at the bottom of the legal document in the solicitor's office. This was it now. She had passed the point of no return.

At four o'clock that afternoon Penny walked into the café and, for the first time ever, she reduced Spiro to tongue-tied astonishment. Behind him, Piotr's face was a picture. His eyes were wide and his tongue was hanging out of his mouth.

'So you've done it after all, Penny.' Jimmy, of course, was never at a loss for words.

'Done what, Jimmy?'

'Followed my advice and gone on the game.'

'I have not gone on the game.' She blushed and looked around. 'And keep your voice down, will you?'

'Don't be shy. We're all friends here. What is it I've been telling you for months? You'll make far more money on your back than you will serving food here.'

'Jimmy!' By now, Penny's cheeks were burning. 'I am not and I never will be a hooker. Have you got that?' She felt herself blushing even more. 'Can't a girl get herself a new hairstyle without being accused of prostitution?'

'Holy Mother!' Spiro had found his voice at last. 'You look… devastating. You're gorgeous, Penny, gorgeous.'

'You sure you not on the game?' Piotr sounded equally astonished, and unusually complimentary. 'You look very good, Penny. Bloody goodness, yes.'

Penny was beginning to feel better about herself now. She had spent much of the three hours between returning home and coming to work staring at herself in the mirror. She even took a couple of selfies to immortalise what had happened to her. Even this hadn't been a simple matter. First she had had to master the skills necessary to press the button, now that her fingernails were half an inch longer. However, hearing her friends' response, she felt an overwhelming sense of relief. So she really did look good.

'Definitely, Penny, just gorgeous.' Even Jimmy couldn't find fault with her appearance. 'But this must have cost a fortune. How did you manage it?'

Penny and Caroline had already discussed this possible line of questioning and Penny had come up with a cover story; good old imaginary Auntie Flo. 'My aunt won ten thou on the lottery and she gave me and my sister a makeover each. To be honest, I would have preferred the money. The only bills I get these days are final demands, but Auntie Flo booked the whole thing up and paid for it in advance, so I couldn't say no.'

'Well, good on your auntie, that's what I say.' Jimmy couldn't resist running his fingers through her hair, patting and twirling the ends. 'Whoever it was did a really good job. And that's a new top as well. Are you really sure you aren't doing something you shouldn't be doing?'

Penny shook her head, mentally reminding herself she should ensure she didn't let the boys see her in any more of the new clothes. Jimmy, in particular, would blow a gasket if he saw some of the really expensive stuff, the designer names no doubt far more familiar to him than they were to her. She was wearing this rather nice new cornflower blue top, with a lower neckline than she was used to, and one of the new bras, as all her old stuff was still hanging up to dry in her room. There was a washing line outside in the back garden, but she no longer used that after items of her clothing had started disappearing from it. She and Vicky from the top floor had their suspicions that it was the Strange Man in Number 3, but they couldn't prove it and they certainly had no intention of going into his room to look. She caught Jimmy's eye and subjected him to what she hoped was a withering stare.

'I am not, repeat not, doing anything naughty. Are we clear, Jimmy?' As she spoke she was reminded of the lawyer using these exact same words to her earlier that day and she wondered her deception would qualify as naughty.

'If you say so, darling. But I can't help noticing that you've started putting the goods on display.' Predictably, the withering stare had had no effect on Jimmy whatso-ever. 'And very nice they look too.'

'Jimmy, will you take you eyes off my boobs, please? It's bad enough having Spiro and Piotr looking at me like

I was a page three girl, without you doing it as well. It's not as if I was obscene, after all.'

'No, of course not. I was just making a purely aesthetic observation. As an artist you should be able to appreciate that.' He changed the subject before she could retort. 'By the way, I've been meaning to tell you, I've got some extra work, very well-paid work, for a firm who do catering for big events. For all I know, that might include art galleries and the like. If you're looking for some extra money, just let me know and I'll put in a word for you.' He grinned at her. 'Useful extra money.'

Penny gave him a smile and shook her head. Only a few days ago she would have leapt at the offer, but now, with the money she was going to get from Olivia, she had no need.

That night she managed to get to sleep without thinking too deeply about Rick and she dreamt of Venice again. This time she was wearing a frighteningly short skirt and the highest heels imaginable. She was making her way along the waterfront to a chorus of catcalls and whistles, but she ignored them all. All her attention was on a man with dark hair walking ahead of her. Frustratingly, although she hurried as best she could in the high heels, she was unable to catch him up.

Chapter 4

When Penny got home that evening, her mind was buzzing. So much had changed in her life in the past few days. Three days ago she had been just Penny Lane, the aspiring artist who worked at the Apocalypse Café, struggled to make ends meet and whose boyfriend was in Australia. Now she wasn't quite sure who she was. She put the kettle on to make herself a mug of tea. As she walked past the mirror on the wall, she caught sight of herself and felt the same surreal sense of disquiet she had been feeling all day. What had she let herself in for?

People react to emotional stress in different ways. Some turn to alcohol, some to chocolates, some to religion. With Penny, it was always a paintbrush. When she felt upset or troubled, she always started a new painting. Today was no exception. Paintings lined the walls of her room and her latest work in progress, an impressionistic nightscape of the Embankment, occupied the centre of the room on the massive easel her parents had given her for her twenty-first birthday. She removed the Embankment and leant it against a wall before locating the last of a pack of five canvases she had bought back in the summer. She stuck it on the easel and stood there for a few moments, staring at the clean white surface, lost in thought, until she was distracted by a tap at the door. It was Vicky from upstairs.

'Hi, Vicky. Come in.' Just at that moment she heard the kettle come to a boil. 'I'm just making tea. Want a cup?'

Vicky and she had moved in at round about the same time. In spite of the Spartan conditions, the house suited both of them for different reasons. For Penny it was because the large room, while almost impossible to heat properly, was the only place she had found that was big enough to serve as bedroom and studio. For Vicky, it was because she was within walking distance of the university where she was doing a degree in physio-therapy. She came in and shut the door behind her.

'Hi, Pen... Penny? What's happened? The hair? And those amazing nails?' She looked as bamboozled as Spiro and Jimmy had been. 'You look totally different.'

Penny fed her the same story about good old Aunt Flo, finding it improving with repetition. By the time she had finished, the tea was ready. She passed a mug across to Vicky and took a seat on the bed, pointing to the only unencumbered chair in the room.

'Come and sit down. Anyway, enough about me, Vick. How're you getting on?

'I'm fine.' Vicky sat down as instructed. As ever, she was wearing a tracksuit and trainers. She was very fit and, apart from the exercise she got from manipulating patients as part of her course, she went jogging most evenings. 'I came to see my heroic housemate. You're all over the news, you know. There's even an article about you in the paper. They're trying to start a petition to get you a knighthood or some such.'

Penny grinned. 'That's what the boys at work said, but there's no chance of me getting a trip to Buckingham Palace.' Although, as she said it, Penny found herself reflecting that in her new role as a make-believe multi-millionaire, there was every chance that she might get to rub shoulders with a few celebrities.

Vicky shook her head as she sipped her tea. 'I don't know. There aren't so many heroes going round these days. What does Rick think about having a hero as a girlfriend?'

Penny's smile slipped. 'What Rick thinks is neither here nor there.' She looked up, caught Vicky's eye and explained. 'He and I broke up last night.'

'You broke up? Why, what happened?'

'Another girl is what happened.'

'Oh, Penny, I'm so sorry. How awful for you.' Vicky gave her an encouraging smile. 'So, is that what the new look's all about? Is there some other man on the horizon? Now that you've suddenly had a makeover and you're looking so amazing, is there somebody else?'

Penny shook her head and replied with total honesty. 'No, Vic, no other man. I'm off men for a while. Besides, I haven't got time for a man anyway. I'm working my butt off at the café and any spare time I've got is taken up with painting.'

Vicky transferred her attention to the blank canvas. 'So, is there a name for this style of painting? Invisible, maybe?'

Penny grinned. 'I'm trying to work out what to paint. I've been doing London scenes for a while now, albeit in my own fairly loose way, but I'm wondering if

I mightn't just try my hand at a different genre. Maybe a change might be good.'

'Why don't you paint a dramatic reconstruction of your life-saving exploit at the station? Sort of an action picture.' Penny could see she was joking, but the idea wasn't as silly as it sounded.

'To be completely honest, Vick, I was thinking along those lines.' She saw the surprise on her friend's face. 'Not train lines. I was wondering about something abstract, trying to dig into what I felt at the time or, more probably, in the aftermath, when it all sank in.' As she spoke, an idea began to form and she was only too glad when Vicky went off a few minutes later and left her alone.

Selecting a broad brush from the pot by the basin she went over to the canvas. There was still a splodge of yellow oil paint left on the palette from the previous day. She added a few drops of turpentine and mixed it until it was a very weak solution. With this, she started sketching a series of swirls and shapes, doing her best to search her subconscious and reproduce the images that emerged. As she worked, she found herself deciding upon the best colours for the various parts of the painting. She squeezed out some red and some blue and as the minutes passed she produced a template from which she could envisage the painting developing. It was gone midnight by the time she decided to stop for the night. She cleaned the brush and stood back to study what she had done. It would need a lot of hard work, but she felt fairly satisfied that it had the makings of an impressive painting.

She went out to the bathroom, relieved to find it unoccupied for a change. It was cold in there and she didn't hang about any longer than she had to. Coming back into her room, the smell of turps was still very pungent so, in spite of the cold night air, she flung the window open to get some ventilation. She flicked off the light and started taking off her clothes. Since Rick had gone off to Australia she had reverted to wearing the stripy pyjamas her mother had given her for Christmas. While far from sexy, they were just what she needed in this cold, damp environment. The pyjamas were in the wardrobe, submerged beneath the heap of bags of designer clothes, and she had to pull some of the bags out of the way in order to get to them. As she did so, she happened upon a box containing very expensive evening shoes with very high heels, as favoured by Olivia and her mother. Feeling more than a little decadent, but secure in the knowledge that nobody could see her in the darkness, she slipped the shoes on and attempted to walk around the room in them.

With hindsight, it would probably have been prudent to make her first attempt at walking in such high heels with the curtains closed and the light on. Clothes might also have been a good idea. As she did her best to negotiate her way around the easel in the centre of the room, one of the shoes caught on something, later revealed as a tear in the carpet, and she tripped, falling flat on her face. Alas, as she fell, her outstretched arm caught the brand new painting, dragging it against her body and bringing it crashing to the floor alongside her. Her funny bone made contact with something hard and she found herself sprawled on the floor, nursing her elbow and cursing.

As the worst of the pain diminished, she sat upright. The first thing she did was to pull those wretched shoes off and throw them across the room onto her bed. She stood up, closed the window and drew the curtains together. Then she felt her way over to the light switch, turned it on and inspected the damage. The good news was that the painting didn't appear to have been damaged as it hit the floor and, even better, it had landed face up. The bad news was that as it fell, it must have rubbed against her body, smudging the paint, changing the composition out of all recognition. She glanced down at her left hand and saw her fingers covered in orange paint. Four distinct lines running diagonally across the canvas indicated quite clearly where they had made contact. More unsettling was a sticky sensation on her left arm. She went over to the mirror to find a blue smear across her upper arm that had even reached onto the side of her left breast. This contact, too, had radically altered the painting that now had a wide stripe across it from top to bottom, mercifully unrecognisable as the imprint of any particular part of the human anatomy.

'Bugger.'

It took half a bottle of cleaner and a torn up old T-shirt to get the worst of the oil paint off her body until she was able to pull her dressing gown on and make a run for the shower. As she scrubbed herself with soap to remove the smell of the paint and cleaner, she found she was still swearing under her breath. Finally, not far short of one o'clock, she returned to her room and locked the door behind her. She turned on the light and went over to retrieve the painting from the floor. She set it back on the easel and slipped out of her dressing gown into her pyjamas, sniffing her skin suspiciously in case the smell of the paint might still be lingering. After cleaning her teeth at the cluttered basin, she turned and took a long hard look at the embryonic painting. It took her a few minutes to confirm her initial reaction, but there was no getting away from it. To her amazement, she now found that she liked it even more. The accident had turned an interesting picture into a great picture.

She turned away at last and retrieved the shoes from the bed. As she packed them away in their box, she promised herself that she would make sure that future experiments at walking in such high heels would be carried out in a strictly controlled environment, and most definitely with the light on. She climbed into bed and pulled the duvet up over her shoulders. From here she could see the painting very clearly and her opinion of it didn't change. In fact, the more she looked at it, the more she liked it. She smiled to herself at the thought of the artist, Yves Klein, and what he had termed Performance Art, back in the sixties. This had involved naked, paint-covered girls and huge expanses of canvas laid out on the floor. Penny reflected that she had unwittingly just been continuing that tradition. Somehow, however, she didn't think she would be telling too many people the truth about exactly how the composition had been formed.

She flicked off the light. As she drifted off to sleep, she had the Venice dream again. This time she was standing, posing naked in the middle of an artist's studio. In front of her, working away at the easel, was the artist. He was a tall man, with dark hair and although she caught occasional glimpses of his bushy beard, try as she may, the canvas always blocked her view of his face.

Chapter 5

On Friday, armed with her pay packet from the café, Penny went into the shop in north London where she always went to buy her paints. It was while she was there that she ran into a familiar face. As she walked in past the long old-fashioned counter, she heard somebody calling out her name. She turned towards the sound of the voice and smiled as she saw who it was. His name was Owen, he was also an artist and he was rather dishy. She occasionally bumped into him, but they had rarely exchanged more than a few sentences. Of course, in those days, she had had Rick.

'Penny. Hi, you're looking amazing.'

'Compared to my usual scruffy state, is what you mean, I suppose, Owen?' She gave him a smile, secretly very pleased at his comment.

'No, not at all, but you've changed your hair, haven't you?'

'Very observant. I see yours is still the same; a cross between Hugh Grant and the absent-minded professor.'

He smiled back at her. 'Penny, just a suggestion, are you doing anything this evening?' She did a double-take. Was he asking her out? And if he was, did she want to go out with him? She had told Vicky she wasn't interested in another man and she had meant it. At least up to now.

'Are you asking me out, Owen?'

'Er, yes, sort of, if you'd like to.' He gave her an encouraging smile. 'How about taking in an exhibition?'

An exhibition didn't sound too compromising, so she decided to hear him out. 'Well, Friday's my night off. What sort of exhibition did you have in mind?'

'Your night off what?'

'I'm working as a waitress, in a desperate attempt to keep body and soul together.'

'Oh, right, I didn't know. Anyway, I'm not sure if you might be interested, but there's a new Turner exhibition just opened at the Royal Academy. It'll be open till nine tonight because today's a Friday. How about going to that and then I'll buy you a pie and a pint afterwards?'

'You old romantic, you. Whatever happened to champagne and caviar?' With a start, she reflected that she had already drunk champagne twice this week. It would probably be wise not to let that develop into a habit. 'And yes, that sounds lovely, but we can each pay for our own. Shall I meet you at the RA at, say, seven?'

'It's a date.'

As he went off, a smile on his face, Penny reflected on what they had just decided. On the one hand, she had been meaning to go to the Turner exhibition and it would be nice to have some company. On the other, she really wasn't interested in men for now, or was she? Her telling Owen they would split the bill had been a positive step if she did intend keeping him at arm's length. Mind you, she thought to herself, the idea of going out with a good-looking man who shared her interests definitely wasn't to be sniffed at. In fact, she thought to herself, he really was a *very* good-looking man.

The lady behind the counter was an old friend; she also commented on Penny's new appearance. She was particularly fascinated by Penny's fingers, or at least her new nails, asking her if they made holding the brushes more difficult. Penny shook her head, although she was nursing a little cut alongside her eye this morning, the result of an injudicious attempt to scratch an itch earlier on without due care and attention. At least, she reflected, she had avoided putting her eye out, but she knew she had to be careful. She also reflected, rather naughtily, that it was probably just as well if things with the delectable Owen didn't develop into anything more intimate, as she might end up scarring him for life.

The date, if that was what it was, went very well. The Turner exhibition was delightful and they were in there for well over an hour. From there, they went to a pub round the back of Piccadilly near Shepherd Market and drank beer and chatted. This was the first time she had been out with a man for quite a few months now and she enjoyed Owen's company and even found herself doing a little mild flirting with him. She had deliberately not dressed up specially, and had made a point of avoiding any of her new Olivia wardrobe. She felt relaxed and it looked as if he was having a good time too. She definitely had a very pleasant evening and she was happy to give him a hug and a goodnight kiss on the cheek before taking the tube home again, rather sorry that he had informed her he was going to France for the next week.

As she emerged from the station at the other end she saw she had a text from him saying how much he had enjoyed himself and saying he hoped they could do it again soon. She replied immediately.

Lovely evening. Definitely repeat when you get back. XX.

And she meant it. She really did like him a lot. She had been so busy finishing off her portfolio of paintings to present to the different galleries, she had had little time or money for socialising. Also, having to work full time to support herself had meant precious little free time for going out and having fun, even if she had had the money. And, of course, there had been the small matter of her having a boyfriend already, albeit on the other side of the world. Now, with Rick out of the equation and as the Olivia job reduced the need to work all hours, and with her latest collection of paintings effectively finished, she could at last start thinking about fun again. She smiled to herself as she walked along the quiet streets to the house. One thing was for sure: she was definitely getting Rick out of her system.

When she got back home, she found an email waiting for her from Caroline, apologising for the short notice and asking her if she could present herself at the Brookes-Webster's house in Notting Hill the following night, dressed for cocktails. Caroline explained in the email that this was the brainchild of Olivia's mother, who wanted to inspect and test the results of the makeover. Caroline said she would be there as well to offer moral support and assured Penny that she would be paid for her time on the basis of a hundred pounds an hour.

Much as the idea of a cocktail party, not to mention the company of the loathsome Mrs Brookes-Webster, didn't appeal in the slightest to Penny, a couple of hundred pounds would be very welcome to settle her outstanding account with the electricity company. This particularly scary bill, printed in red ink, had been sitting on her bedside table for some days now. She sent a short reply to Caroline saying she would be there at six thirty the next day as instructed and then sent a text message to Jimmy asking if he could cover for her at the café that evening. He phoned her back immediately.

'Anything for you, sweetheart. What's the big event?'

Penny hadn't banked on being asked that, so she took refuge in a little white lie.

'I'm going to the new Turner exhibition at the RA.'

'On your own?' He really was terminally nosey.

'Um, no, I mean yes.'

'No, I mean yes, eh? So it's like that, is it? So what's his name? You didn't waste much time, did you?'

She did her best to affect an exasperated tone as she replied, but, as usual, his hunch was bang on the money. 'Um, he's a friend, an artist I've known for years.'

'Eighty years old and decrepit?' Jimmy was mocking her.

'Um, no. I don't know how old he is. Older than me, anyway.'

'Like ten, twenty years older or maybe a little bit less? Maybe pretty much your age and handsome with it? Or am I wrong?'

'All right, Jimmy.' She gave a sigh. 'You've got me bang to rights. He's a man, and a good-looking one at that, but it isn't a date.' She realised as she said it that she was trying to convince herself of the truth of what she was saying every bit as much as trying to convince him. She might be making progress towards convincing herself, but Jimmy wasn't falling for it.

'Well, good for you, that's what I say. I told you you're gorgeous. See, no sooner has that scumbag Rick disappeared off the radar than the vultures have already started circling?'

'It's not a date.'

'Of course it isn't.' His tone was highly sceptical. 'Anything you say.'

'Oh, Jimmy…' Penny wasn't really sure if she was exasperated with him or herself or maybe just at life in general. 'Anyway, thanks for covering my shift.'

'Anything for you, gorgeous. Besides, I could do with the extra cash.'

Penny put the phone down, reflecting that she would make almost as much in two hours with Olivia's mother as she made in a whole week at the café.

Chapter 6

Among the new clothes hanging in her wardrobe were a couple of so-called evening dresses and Penny chose the less revealing one for Saturday night's cocktail party. She also located a heavy necklace that further protected her modesty. As she checked herself in the mirror, she had to admit that she really did look pretty good. She was getting used to her appearance by now and gradually finding that it was no longer a stranger looking back at her in the mirror. This hairstyle, these clothes, even the killer heels were gradually beginning to feel familiar and even comfortable. She had made a point of wearing the high-heeled shoes around her room as much as possible so as to familiarise herself with them. She was very careful, however, to make sure she avoided the hole in the carpet, and always kept the light on. She was getting progressively more confident in heels and had no doubt at all that the disguise would be good enough to fool pretty much anybody.

She rang the doorbell of the Notting Hill house at exactly six thirty as instructed, determined not to give Mrs Brookes-Webster any excuse to be any nastier than normal to her. The door was opened by Caroline who surveyed her with a big smile of approval. Alongside her was Gilbert the dog. This time his greeting was warmer.

Presumably by now he had got over the fact that his mistress had suddenly acquired a twin sister, and he came to meet Penny with his tail wagging. She reached out her hand to scratch his ears and would have bent down further to stroke him, but for the very real fear that a wardrobe malfunction might ensue if she did so.

As Caroline closed the door behind them, she whispered in her ear. 'Mrs B-W's invited a couple of distant relatives along. Aunt Peggy's the one with the white hair and Aunt Gloria's the fat one. Got that? Peggy white, Gloria fat. If you can fool them, you'll be doing well. Just try to say as little as possible and remember that Olivia's generally a bit quiet and reserved these days.'

'Why these days?'

'She's been like it ever since her dad died. She spends all her time with Gilbert and hardly says a word to anybody.' They were approaching the lounge door now. 'I'll tell you all about it some other time. Anyway, good luck. You certainly look the part. I'll be waiting outside and we can go for a bite to eat afterwards if you like.'

Olivia's mother was standing by the fireplace, a glass of champagne in her manicured hand. Beside her, looking vaguely sinister, were two elderly ladies. A noticeable smell of mothballs filled the air, but it certainly wasn't coming from Mrs B-W. Her very expensive perfume was strong enough to compete with the mothballs and completely swamped the modest amount of perfume Penny had applied before leaving home. To her surprise, Mrs B-W gave her a big smile when she came into the room and it took a moment before Penny remembered that she was now in the presence of the woman who was supposed to be her mother. She went across to the fireplace and had another momentary crisis before deciding to kiss the old ladies on the cheeks. She started with the fatter of the two, Aunt Gloria, and in so doing, she realised that the mothballs were most definitely from her wardrobe. She could feel her eyes watering as she stepped back.

'Hello, auntie.' She repeated the process with the other aunt before accepting a glass of champagne from a silver tray brought in by the housekeeper. The dog had accompanied her and he now sat down beside her, his nose pointing up at the tray hopefully.

'Olivia, darling, you look fabulous.' Aunt Gloria's voice was as strong as her mothballs. By the sound of it she had considerable experience shouting at hounds, horses, hockey matches or, more probably, housemaids. Beside her, Aunt Peggy smiled nervously, but said nothing. Olivia's mother bestowed another smile upon Penny that was almost welcoming, before turning to the two old ladies.

'Of course, you haven't seen Olivia since Roger's funeral, have you?'

'Poor Roger.' So Aunt Peggy had got a voice after all. Remembering her role, Penny dropped her eyes at the mention of Olivia's father and sought solace in the champagne glass. The wine and the glass containing it were exquisite. *Yes*, she thought to herself, *I could really develop a habit for this stuff.*

'Such a shame. The dear, dear man,' Aunt Gloria bellowed affably, before clapping Mrs B–W on the back with her free hand in much the same way as she no doubt greeted her favourite mare. 'So, how've you been holding up, Angela, and you, Olivia?'

Seeing Olivia's mother juggle with her glass as she regained her balance after the assault, Penny was thankful she had been out of range. A momentary look of annoyance was swiftly replaced by one of sorrow. For the first time, Penny thought she maybe glimpsed real human feeling beneath the impeccable make-up. 'Much better, thank you, Gloria. It's been a tough few months.' If it had been tough, it certainly hadn't left any lasting trace on Mrs B-W's face. Her skin was so smooth and wrinkle-free that even Penny, who had never knowingly come across any recipient of cosmetic surgery in her life, began to feel suspicious. Deciding it was best not to reply, Penny dropped her eyes in true Olivia style and mumbled something opaque, concentrating her attention on the Labrador, who slowly subsided onto his back on the floor beside her, emitting a series of contented canine grunts.

Over the next hour and a half, she managed to stay on the periphery of the conversation, only responding when absolutely necessary. She learnt quite a bit about the family, mainly that Olivia's father, Roger, had been much-loved and sorely missed by everybody. One question, however, came as a surprise to her.

'So are you terribly busy, Olivia, now that you're in charge of the Foundation?' Penny had been discreetly studying the Hieronymus Bosch triptych and Aunt Gloria's powerful voice made her jump, as a result of which she spilled a few drops of champagne. She turned towards the voice, wondering how to respond, but Mrs B-W got there first.

'I've been helping Olivia out, Gloria. The poor dear's not really been herself these past few months.'

'Is that so, Olivia? You were so very close to your father, weren't you?' Penny nodded and added a sniff for good measure as the stout lady launched into a few words of encouragement, accompanied by a clap on the back that further depleted Penny's glass. Out of the corner of her eye, Penny saw Gilbert the dog stretch out and lick up the fallen champagne. She found herself wondering idly whether this would be bad for him, or whether, as the pet of millionaires, he might already have developed a taste for such luxuries. 'But you've really got to buck up now, dear. Get back on the horse again and all that. Your father's gone, but you've got to carry on his good work.' Aunt Gloria's voice, while still loud, now softened in tone. 'It's what he would have wanted, you know. He always said you were the right one to take over from him.'

So that's the way it is, Penny thought to herself, realising now what Caroline had been hinting at. *The husband handed over control of things to the daughter, rather than the wife.* She glanced again at the ostentatious, conceited exterior of Olivia's mother and reflected that she couldn't fault his judgement. However, from what Penny had seen so far of the taciturn daughter, Olivia wasn't likely to do much better. She took a deep breath and murmured a soft thank you to Aunt Gloria, then turned away and surreptitiously licked the spilt champagne from her fingers.

The little gathering broke up just after eight and that produced Penny's trickiest moment of the evening. Just as the two old ladies were heading for the door, Aunt Peggy, who had said little more than Penny herself in the course of the evening, suddenly threw a spanner in the works. As she came over to kiss Penny goodbye, she caught her softly by the shoulders and looked deep into her eyes. 'You'll get over it, my dear. And if you'd like to come down to Edgecombe any time, you know you're very welcome. Sammy misses you a lot, you know.'

Who the hell was Sammy? A relative, friend, servant, dog, cat, horse? And what sex? The options were endless. Penny had to choose her words carefully.

'Oh, how sweet. Thank you so much, auntie. Sammy's lovely.' Penny's fingers were crossed behind her back as she spoke.

'He often asks about you, you know.' Penny registered that Sammy would appear to be human and male, unless Aunt Peggy had a talking horse. 'I was trying to remember the last time you came down to see us. Your brain's younger than mine, surely you can remember?'

From what Caroline had said, Olivia hadn't been out of the house since her father's death, so it was unlikely she had visited her aunt this year. Penny swallowed hard. 'Last year, was it? Or maybe even longer?' Penny decided to throw this out to the room. She turned towards Mrs B-W and smiled sweetly. 'Mummy, can you remember the last time I went to Edgecombe?' She was delighted to see Mrs B-W momentarily nonplussed.

'Easter of last year, I think it was. We came down for Uncle Sammy's eightieth. That was last year, wasn't it, Peggy?'

'Of course, that's right. Silly me.' The old lady shook her head. 'I'm getting so forgetful.'

Penny took another chance. 'Well do give Uncle Sammy a big hug from me, won't you?'

'Of course, dear. He'll be so pleased when I tell him how well you look and how lovely you are. Your hair's

62

'even silkier than I remember.' Aunt Peggy gave Penny's hair a little stroke as she kissed her goodbye. For her part, Penny tried hard not to look too relieved that the ordeal was over.

No sooner were the two aunties out of the room than Mrs B–W turned to Penny. For a few seconds she appeared to be lost for words, but finally she found her voice. 'I suppose you'll do.' With that, she swept out of the side door, leaving Penny unsurprised, but still annoyed, at her lack of common courtesy.

'Cow!' Penny kept her voice down, although the door had closed behind Mrs B–W. She grabbed the champagne bottle from the silver bucket and refilled her glass. She looked down at the dog, who was still at her side.

'Well, at least you like me, Gilbert.'

The dog nuzzled her leg with his nose and Penny stroked his head before going across to examine the painting on the wall at close range. She wiped her index finger on the back of a sofa to dry it before running it very gently across the surface of the wood. She felt a wonderful shiver of delight at direct contact with a work of art that had almost certainly been produced half a millennium ago. And if it really was a Bosch original, she knew she was touching one of the most valuable objects in the world. Her mood changed in an instant from grumpy to thrilled. As an artist, being offered the opportunity to study at close quarters and even touch something so rare and so valuable was an almost religious experience. The dog slid slowly back down until he was lying on the floor at her feet, all four paws in the air, grunting happily to himself. Penny rubbed him with her toe as she sipped her champagne and let her eyes roam across the three oak boards upon which the painting had been created. She was so engrossed in her inspection of it that she didn't hear the door open or the footsteps behind her.

'Penny?' Her glass was almost empty by this time so she didn't spill any wine as she jumped at the sound of the voice. Beside her, the dog sprang to his feet, tail wagging. She turned to find Olivia standing at her shoulder, a shy smile on her face. 'Caroline told me your studies have been on Renaissance Art. I see you've found our Bosch.'

Penny's eyes widened. 'So it really is by him?'

Olivia nodded as she stroked the dog who had positioned himself strategically between the two of them. 'He's hard to confuse with any other artist, isn't he?'

Penny nodded in return. The sylph-like pale naked figures in the paintings and the surreal monstrous shapes in the background really were unmistakable. She smiled at Olivia, still feeling greatly cheered by the sight of the triptych. 'I thought all his work was in galleries and museums.'

'My father bought this at auction in New York about ten years ago. It was found in a Dutch church, hidden in a hollow wall.'

Memory stirred in Penny's head. 'Of course, now I remember. It's thought to have been painted pretty much at the same time as his *Garden of Earthly Delights,* maybe even some sort of preliminary study.' She caught Olivia's eye. 'Thank you. I feel very privileged to have seen it up close like this.'

'You're very welcome.' Penny couldn't help noticing that Olivia, while more animated and less taciturn than the previous time they had met, was continually glancing nervously at the door in the wall through which her mother had disappeared. 'Anyway, Penny, I just wanted to thank you for doing this for the Foundation. It's a very worthwhile cause and my father put his whole heart and soul into setting it up.' As she mentioned him, her eyes misted over and Penny could see that she was close to tears.

'I promise I'll do my very best.' And she meant it. She was beginning to think that maybe Olivia wasn't as bad as she had first thought. From what Caroline had said, her morose demeanour was presumably the result of grief, rather than surliness. Olivia looked up and caught Penny's eye.

'Thank you.' There was an awkward pause and then she glanced down at the dog and changed the subject. 'I'm delighted Gilbert's taken to you. I suppose he must have been as surprised as I was when he first saw you. Tell me, do you find it a bit weird when you look at me? I have to confess that I find it so very strange... Just talking to you like this, I feel as if I'm talking to a mirror.'

Penny nodded. 'You and me both. I keep seeing my reflection in windows and thinking it's you following me.' Both girls laughed, but their amusement didn't last long. The door at the end of the room opened and Caroline appeared, an apologetic look on her face. She came across the room towards them.

'Olivia, Mrs Brookes-Webster would like to see you as soon as possible, please.'

Olivia's face fell back into its normal blank state and she excused herself, leaving the room immediately. Gilbert trotted along behind her and Penny was sorry to see him leave. Caroline caught Penny's eye. 'So, how did it go?'

'I think it went fine. Mrs B-W even managed to concede that she thought I might do.' She shook her head. 'Anyway, I've been admiring this painting and Olivia's just told me it really is a Bosch original. It's like finding myself in a room with Einstein or Elvis. It's mind-blowing.'

'Real Elvis or an Elvis impersonator? I suppose you don't get a lot of Hieronymus Bosch impersonators though, do you?' Caroline was smiling.

'You'd be surprised. Every now and then a painting surfaces that purports to be by the great man, but nine times out of ten, it's a scam. Whereas this... this is just incredible.' She gave the painting a final look and swallowed the last of her champagne, then suddenly had a much more practical thought. 'Erm, Caroline, I was wondering. I don't suppose there's any chance of being paid this evening, is there? The electricity company's going to cut me off any day now if I don't pay up.'

Caroline nodded immediately. 'Yes, of course. In fact, I'll tell you what. Next week you've got two engagements as Olivia. The first's just a drinks thing in London and then the weekend's the Brighton conference. Why don't I draw a thousand out and let you have it tonight so you can settle that and any other bills? Would that be enough for now? I'll let you have the balance outstanding when we're in Brighton.'

Penny was delighted and greatly relieved. 'Caroline, that's amazing. Thank you so much.'

'No, thank *you*. I was chatting to the two old ladies on their way out and they had no idea you weren't the genuine article. And they're blood relatives. I know Olivia very well myself by now and I'm finding it almost impossible to tell you apart. You've even got the accent dead right. Gilbert's worked out who's who, but he seems to have taken a real liking to you as well as Olivia. I'm sure you'll be a great success as her double.'

That night, Penny dreamt about Venice once again. This time, she was hurrying through darkened streets, accompanied by a big black dog. The strange thing was that every time she passed a shop window and caught sight of her reflection, she saw not one, but two figures. Her identical twin was right behind her, even if she couldn't see her.

Chapter 7

As Owen was away, Penny went alone to a Botticelli exhibition at the National Gallery. Several of the paintings were on display for the first time in many years and she spent a long time studying them in minute detail. It was while she was up on the first floor, standing in front of his *Primavera*, a painting she had originally seen at the Uffizi in Florence, that something strange happened. She happened to glance to her right and caught sight of a man in the next room, standing in front of a painting, his attention riveted on it, although the painting itself was hidden from her eyes by the wall.

He was a tall man. His mass of unruly dark hair hung down to his collar and he had a bushy and rather unkempt beard. He was wearing jeans and a leather jacket and she couldn't help noticing his broad shoulders and strong thighs. He looked fit and very handsome, almost like a film star in disguise. It was difficult to judge his age because of the beard, but she reckoned he must be a few years older than her, but not much, maybe early thirties at most. All of this in itself wasn't strange. What was strange was the effect he had upon her. As she gazed at him, her knees turned to jelly and her head began to spin. She had to slump down on the leather bench in the middle of the room for fear of falling over.

She dropped her head into her hands for quite some time before raising her eyes and glancing back into the other room, but the man had disappeared from sight. She sat there for some minutes more, breathing deeply, wondering what on earth was going on. Her eyes focused on Botticelli's painting once more, where Zephyr was reaching down towards the body of Flora, the woman clothed only in a diaphanous robe. His eyes were staring into hers and she was staring back at him in eager anticipation of his touch. For a moment Penny found herself identifying with the woman in the painting. Something weird had just happened; something that had never happened to her before.

For a moment she wondered if it might be some sort of epileptic episode or a minor stroke, but the truth gradually began to dawn on her. What she had felt was powerful attraction; not just physical attraction, but something stronger than that, altogether more cerebral, more emotional. Could it be, she asked herself, that she had just had her first encounter with the phenomenon known as love at first sight? This was something totally new to her, but the more she thought about it, the more she wondered whether she, just like Flora in the picture, been struck by the lightning bolt of love?

The problem Penny now faced was that not only did she have no idea of the identity of the mystery man, but he had disappeared. Getting to her feet somewhat unsteadily she went over to the opening that separated the two rooms, but when she peered inside, he had indeed gone. She hurried down the length of the room, totally ignoring the priceless masterpieces on the walls either side of her, until she reached the door at the end. Beyond that, there was just the wide landing. She looked around in all directions but there was no sign of him. Leaning over the edge, she scrutinised the heads of the people down below in the atrium, but couldn't see him anywhere. Making a quick decision she turned left, heading for the Impressionists. There, too, she found no sign of him, but she was prevented from broadening her search by a familiar voice.

'Penny! I bet you've been checking out the Botticelli collection, haven't you?'

It was Jimmy. Today, away from work, he was wearing a lime green suit that looked about two sizes too tight for him, the trousers finishing halfway up his calves, and the soles of his shoes about an inch thick. He looked like something out of *Grease*. Penny had no doubt that this represented the height of fashion, at least in some circles, although they weren't circles with which she was familiar. He caught her eye, a look of concern on his face. 'What's the matter, gorgeous? Somebody nicked your handbag?'

Penny shook her head, as much to clear it as anything. 'No, Jimmy, I'm fine. I was just looking for a friend.'

He reached over and took her arm. 'Well, you've found one. Why don't I buy you a cup of tea?' He smiled encouragingly. 'And a cake as well if you like. I'm in the money. I was at a very exclusive wedding yesterday, serving champagne to the great and the good, and they paid me handsomely.'

Penny took one last good look round and shrugged her shoulders. Her mystery man had disappeared and that was that. She looked back at Jimmy and laid her hand on his. 'That's a good idea, Jimmy, but you keep your money. We'll split the bill.'

They found a free table downstairs and ordered a pot of tea. Penny refused his offer of cake and suggested he try one, but he declined, telling her he had to be careful of his figure. From the tightness of his trousers, she believed him.

'So who was this friend you've been looking for?' He had his quizzical expression on.

Penny hesitated. Had she dreamt the man with the black beard? After a pause, she decided to come clean and tell Jimmy. It would be good to have his take on what had happened back there. At least he would be able to tell her if she was going bonkers. 'He wasn't really a friend. In fact, I've no idea who he was, if he existed at all.' She saw the interest in his eyes. 'You see, Jimmy, it's like this…'

He listened intently to her account of what had transpired, nodding sagely from time to time but, unusually for him, making no comment until she had finished. Only then did he deliver his verdict.

'Well, I don't think you need to worry about going bonkers. I'm sure he's real and I think it was just a simple case of animal attraction. If you'd both been dogs, you'd have gone up to him and stuck your nose up his butt.'

'Jimmy!' Even so, she had to smile at the image he evoked.

'From what you've said, he sounds like a real hunk.' He sighed melodramatically. 'Of course, I suppose there's still a chance he might be gay. You get a lot of them in here.' Daylight dawned in Penny's head. She had been wondering what Jimmy was doing in here.

Although he was a bright and a remarkably well-read boy, he had never demonstrated any particular interest in the visual arts for all the time she had known him.

'So that's what you were doing here; cruising?'

He gave her a look that was supposed to be stern. 'I came to view the artworks, if you want to know. If, in the course of my visit, I were to come across a young man who was looking for a friend with whom he could discuss the finer points of painting, then so be it. I do like culture in a man.' He took a sip of his tea. Although he drank regular builders' tea with milk at the Apocalypse, he had chosen to take his tea this afternoon with a slice of lemon in it and was holding his cup very daintily as he drank. 'No, there's no doubt about it, if you want my opinion. You saw him, you fancied him rotten, and you came over all unnecessary as a result. Never mind, you'll get over it. It happens to me all the time and I recover.'

'Well, that's a blessing.' She was feeling better now, but she knew it would take a good long while before she got over what had happened to her back there.

'So, are you telling me nothing like this has ever happened to you before? What about your ex down under?' He gave her a cheeky grin. 'That's his geographical whereabouts I'm referring to, not what you're thinking.'

'Rick? I was very fond of him, if the truth be told; in fact, I'm pretty sure I loved him, but I never had that sort of instant shock when I first saw him.'

Jimmy shook his head wearily. 'You're *pretty sure* you loved him? That doesn't exactly sound too convincing. I can't imagine that line coming up in a Shakespeare play. They don't call them Cupid's arrows for nothing, you know. Twang, and they head straight for the heart. You don't have to stop, bend down and pick the damn things up off the floor.'

Now it was Penny's turn to shake her head. 'I don't believe all that love at first sight crap, Jimmy. Surely it's impossible. I mean, the man could be a mass murderer or, even worse, an estate agent or something. And, in here, he could quite possibly be gay. How on earth somebody can claim to feel something as complex as love in the blink of an eye is inconceivable.'

'And yet it's been happening all the way through history. Anyway, for my money, that's what's just happened here.'

Penny drank her tea slowly and thought back to the effect seeing the man had had upon her. She still didn't think she believed the whole love at first sight thing, at least as far as she was concerned, but finding a credible explanation for what had happened wasn't easy. Finally, in her usual pragmatic way, she came to the only logical conclusion: she didn't know, but it didn't matter. 'The thing is, Jimmy, he's gone. I don't know who he was, in fact I'm not totally sure he was ever there at all. Maybe I was just so caught up by all those amazing paintings that my imagination got the better of me. But, anyway, real or imaginary, he's gone, I'm never going to see him again, so there's no point agonising over what did or didn't happen. As long as you're fairly sure I'm not bonkers, that's the end of it.' Yet even as she said the words she knew, deep down, that if he really did exist, she would dearly love to see him again.

The Venice dream came back again that night. This time she was at the top of a high building, maybe a tower, and she was looking down hundreds of feet to the square below. As she watched, a tall man with an unruly mass of dark hair and a black beard emerged from one of the buildings and walked diagonally across the square away from her. She screamed and shouted, but he didn't turn round and look back.

Chapter 8

Penny's first official engagement was the following week and it very nearly went disastrously wrong. She had been told that it was a lunchtime drinks party for wealthy patrons of a number of charities, due to take place at the Southbank Centre. She was given instructions to come to the Brookes-Webster's Notting Hill house at noon, dressed very smartly. Caroline spelled out in the email to her that this meant one of the more expensive designer dresses and high heels. Penny chose the very nice cream-coloured Chanel dress with a low, unsettlingly revealing neckline. Again on Caroline's instructions, Penny took a cab all the way from her home to Olivia's house, but she made sure she remembered to ask the driver for a receipt. Although Caroline had indicated that she would reimburse all expenses from petty cash, Penny didn't want there to be any question of her claiming too much.

As she had feared, when she entered the lounge, she found only Mrs Brookes-Webster waiting for her. From what Penny had learned of her so far, this sort of showy, ostentatious event was likely to be right up her street. Olivia's mother was positively dripping with jewellery and sporting yet another different hairstyle. Her finger-nails today were dark red for a change, and her dress was very elegant and matched the nails, although Penny couldn't help noticing that it was a little tight around the hips. She drew comfort from this as she endured another unsettling inspection. There was no sign of Caroline or Olivia, or even the dog, so Penny just had to grit her teeth and make the best of things. After subjecting her to close scrutiny, Mrs B-W reached for a box on the mantelpiece and took out a pair of earrings. She handed them to Penny.

'Here, put these on. You need to be at your best today.' Penny took them from her and looked down at them as they lay in the palm of her hand. They were surprisingly heavy. As she studied them, she had a terrifying feeling that the two sparkling stones she was holding were probably worth a fortune. They were.

'In case you didn't realise, these are real and very rare diamonds. They've been in the family for a long time, so make sure you don't do anything silly with them. And I'll need them back afterwards.'

Penny fitted them very carefully, making sure they were firmly attached. She wondered just how much single pendant diamonds like these, each the size of a very big pea, might be worth. Mrs B-W had evidently anticipated the question. There was just a hint of a smile on her face as she broke the news to Penny that the earrings were worth about the same as the Bentley outside the door. Penny had to clench her fists to stop her hands from trembling. What if she lost one?

The drive down to the Southbank Centre in the massive, luxurious car with its double-glazed windows was completed in near total silence. Only as they swept across Westminster Bridge did Mrs B-W deign to speak to Penny. 'Now, listen carefully. The people you're going to meet today are some of the most famous in the country. There will be faces you recognise from the television and the newspapers and I don't want you to come over all tongue-tied in their presence. We are Brookes-Websters. Just remember that. We could buy the whole Southbank Centre if it was ever for sale, so you don't need to kowtow to anybody. Got it?'

Penny nodded, not sure whether to be excited or daunted by the prospect ahead. But Olivia's mother hadn't finished.

'At the same time, I don't want you getting too familiar and flirting with the people you meet. Olivia's normally a shy sort of girl, so I don't want to see you launching yourself at some film star. Is that clear?'

Penny nodded. 'Totally. If Colin Firth or Jude Law come to me on bended knee, asking for my hand, I'll send them away with a flea in their ear.'

'And another thing. Don't try to be funny.'

Penny reflected that there was little likelihood of Mrs Brookes-Webster making that mistake.

The reception was in a private room on the third floor of the building, looking out over the grey waters of the Thames. A hefty man with a shaved head, wearing a dinner jacket, quite possibly a close relative of the doorman at the JC café, checked their names on his list and ushered them in. There were well in excess of a hundred people in the room, sipping champagne and talking. Penny immediately recognised a number of well-known faces, from the mayor of London to famous film and television stars.

'Come along, Olivia. Let's go and see Frances.' Olivia's mother took Penny by the arm and walked her down the room towards a group of people by the window. As they did so, she leant towards Penny's ear and whispered. 'You've met Frances before, but you don't know her very well. All right?'

Penny nodded and braced herself. This was a wise precaution. To her amazement, it turned out that Frances was none other than Dame Frances Waterhouse, the doyenne of the British film industry, who was commonly referred to as a National Treasure. In the group alongside her, Penny counted no fewer than three other very famous faces and gulped.

'Frances, darling, how lovely to see you again.'

The National Treasure raised her eyes at the sound of Mrs B-W's voice and bestowed a charming smile upon the two of them. 'Angela, darling, how simply super to see you. And of course this is your lovely daughter...'

'...Olivia.' Mrs B-W turned towards Penny and smiled sweetly. 'Olivia, darling, you remember Dame Frances, don't you?'

Penny took a deep breath and gave a half bow. 'Of course. It's lovely to see you again.' Remembering to stay in character, she hastily dropped her eyes again, but not before she had noticed the eyes of the man beside Dame Frances staring right down the front of her dress. She felt herself blush, partly because of the direction of his gaze, but mainly because she could hardly believe her own eyes. He was the actor described at Britain's answer to Brad Pitt. Penny, in common with several million other girls in Britain, had had an enormous crush on him for years.

'Olivia, of course. Come here, darling.' Dame Frances caught hold of Penny's outstretched hand and pulled her towards her. Penny was amazed to see that she had the skin of a twenty-year-old, although she was alleged to be in her eighties. Clearly, no expense had been spared in trying to maintain her appearance. It was only the wrinkled skin around her throat that gave her away. The great lady then took both of Penny's hands in hers and air-kissed her noisily on or around the cheeks with loud *mwah* noises before repeating the process with Mrs B-W.

Penny stepped back and raised her eyes. The Brad Pitt look-alike, whose name was Rafe Kingsholme, was still staring at her and she felt her cheeks flush yet again. Mercifully, his eyes had moved up to her face now, but the wink he gave her did little to cool her down. She took a deep breath and did her best to regain some self-control. That lasted just about as long as it took for the Brad clone to reach out his hand towards her.

'Olivia, is it? What a charming name and what a beautiful girl.' He sounded as if he meant it, but then of course, Penny reflected, he was a very good actor after all. She saw his eyes drop once more to her bust and had a sudden memory of what Jimmy had said about displaying the goods, but this actually helped to bolster her confidence. She shook the outstretched hand and realised that, close-up, he was fair bit older than she had imagined. His breath smelt strongly of nicotine and something a whole lot more alcoholic than champagne. She gave him a suitably shy smile.

'I'm very pleased to meet you, Mr Kingsholme.'

'Call me Rafe, please. And I'm absolutely delighted to meet you too, Olivia.' He held onto her hand for quite a lot longer than necessary and she distinctly felt him squeeze her fingers before releasing her. She took another deep breath, but was saved from any greater intimacy by the arrival of Olivia's mother at her shoulder. Eschewing the handshake, Mrs B-W caught hold of the actor and kissed him enthusiastically. He stepped back and greeted her a little less enthusiastically.

'Are you the mother or the big sister of this delightful young lady?' Penny repressed a grin. His thespian talents were truly impressive. 'I can see the family resemblance. So beautiful.'

Mrs B-W beamed at him, although Penny had yet to see any physical resemblance between Olivia and her mother. 'Why, thank you, kind sir. I'm Angela Brookes-Webster and, alas, I'm not Olivia's sister.' She smiled self-deprecatingly. 'Do, please, call me Angela.'

'So pleased to meet you, Angela.' He gave her a winning smile before transferring his attention back to Penny. 'And to meet you, Olivia. Charming, quite charming.'

'And what are you working on at the moment, Rafe?' Clearly, Mrs B-W had no intention of being upstaged by her daughter.

'A rather naughty series for the Beeb about a rakishly handsome university lecturer who falls for one of his students. All frighteningly politically incorrect.' His eyes were still trained on Penny, in spite of Mrs B-W's best efforts. Penny could feel herself beginning to blush so she hastily helped herself to two glasses of champagne from a passing tray and handed one to Mrs B-W. 'Champagne, mummy?'

'Thank you, darling.' The smile almost managed to look sincere. 'Now, I fear we must abandon Mr Kingsholme and do a bit of mingling.'

A look of regret crossed the film star's face, but his eyes were on Penny, rather than Mrs B-W. 'If you ever feel like doing any mingling over here, I'll be waiting, Olivia.' Penny could feel his eyes on her bottom as she let Mrs B-W steer her away.

'Remember what I said about flirting.' Mrs B-W's mouth was so close to Penny's ear, she had to wipe it afterwards.

'Hi, Olivia, I haven't seen you for ages.' Penny swung round towards the sound of the voice. She found herself confronted by a girl about her age, with platinum blond hair and gold earrings the size of saucers hanging from her ears. Penny summoned a broad smile of greeting and did her best to reply appropriately.

'Well, well, well, it's a small world.' Now would have been the moment to insert the girl's name, but Penny knew that wasn't going to happen. 'What're you doing here?'

'I'm here with Daniel.' The girl pointed vaguely across the room, before turning her attention to Mrs B-W, whose face was showing no signs of recognition. 'And this must be your mum. Are you going to introduce me?'

Oh, shit, Penny thought to herself, *now what do I do?* She turned towards Mrs B-W, desperately searching for a way out of her predicament. It came to her at the very last moment, just as the silence was becoming a little awkward. 'Mummy, you'll never guess who this is…' But, before she could say more, she turned back to the blonde girl, palming her glittery little bag expertly behind her back as she did so, and excused herself. 'Hang on a sec, I'll be right back. I've just realised I left my bag in the Ladies.' Before any more words could be exchanged, she scooted across the room and out the door, making sure she kept the bag firmly clutched to her front, out of sight of the pair she'd just left. Stopping just outside the door, she scrabbled in the bag and found the ten pound note she had stuck in there in case of emergencies. This definitely qualified as an emergency. She pushed the door slightly ajar and beckoned to the bouncer with one finger. The big man came across and looked out at her.

'Yes, miss. Can I help?'

Penny did her best to assume a clueless look. 'I'm in a bit of a spot. There's a girl over there who knows me and I just can't remember her name for the life of me. I don't suppose you know, do you? After all, you've got the list, haven't you?' She batted her eyelids and gave him her most alluring smile. 'Do you remember by any chance?' She pointed discreetly across towards the blonde girl who was still standing by Mrs B-W, side on to the door. To her great relief, the doorman produced a knowing smile.

'That would be Tiffany Lyons-Churchill. She's a regular at these events.' He leant towards Penny and lowered his voice. 'Everybody calls her Tiff.'

'You're such a star. Thanks awfully.' Penny beamed at him and slipped the ten pound note into his unresisting palm. 'You've saved my life.' Holding her bag out in front of her, she pushed the door open, hastened back into the room and across to the blonde girl.

'I'm so sorry, Tiff, I just couldn't bear it if somebody took my bag. My phone's in here with all my contacts. I'd be simply lost without it.' She wondered if she might be laying the clueless airhead act on a bit thick, but the girl nodded. Penny saw her immediately understand the enormity of the calamity that had just been averted. Turning towards Mrs B-W, she continued. 'Mummy, this is Tiffany Lyons-Churchill. We've known each other for ages.' She read relief and maybe even a momentary look of approval on Mrs B-W's face.

'Tiffany, of course. Your mother and I are such good friends. She's told me so much about you, but it must be ten years since I last saw you. Tell me, is your mother here today?'

'Yes, she's over there with Daniel. He's been telling her all about his trip to Antarctica. Why don't you come over and say hello?' Tiffany flicked a swift glance down to Penny's ring finger. Seeing it bare, she raised her left hand in triumph and gave a little wave in the air. The engagement ring sparkling on her finger had no doubt cost as much as her fiancé's trip to Antarctica and, just for a second, Penny found herself thinking of Rick. She had often wondered if he and she would end up engaged. *Well*, she thought to herself, *I know the answer to that now, don't I*? Swallowing her chagrin, she smiled broadly.

'Oh, I say, congrats. How super for you.'

They spent well over an hour and a half at the reception, with Penny making it up as she went along. She hadn't really spoken to Olivia for long enough to know her figures of speech, so a lot of it was trial and error. It was hard work and she started to develop a headache as the afternoon progressed. At one point, the mayor said a few words, followed by various important people from the world of show business, ending up with Dame Frances herself. Penny restricted herself to two glasses of champagne as she knew it would be suicide for her to get hammered at an event of this magnitude although, she noticed, a number of the other guests didn't appear to have similar reservations. In fact, as time went by and more drinks were dispensed, the noise level rose and the behaviour level dropped. She had her bottom felt up on three separate occasions; once, she was pretty sure, by a well-known television personality. She finally took refuge in a corner, with her back to the wall. She could just see Mrs B-W's unmistakable hair on the other side of the room so she could relax. Or so she thought. She jumped as a hand landed on her arm and squeezed.

'Olivia, I've been wondering if I would get a chance to talk to you alone.' She glanced up. It was Rafe Kingsholme. He had a half empty glass of what looked like whisky in his hand and from his glazed eyes, it wasn't the first he had had that day. 'Has anybody ever told you just how totally stunning you are? Of course they must have. So, Olivia, how would you feel about coming out on the town with me one evening?'

By now his eyes had given up any pretence at looking at her face and were firmly locked on her cleavage. Penny had never felt comfortable wearing revealing clothes in public and she realised too late that she should have considered making the transition to full Olivia exposure in small steps, rather than going for the Full Monty so soon. She saw the sweat beading on his forehead and did her best to remember to keep her shoulders back and her spine upright as she searched for a suitable put-down for the great man. Just as she was about to decline his kind invitation with as much grace as she could muster, she spotted a waiter approaching with a tray of drinks. She was on the point of breaking her rule and reaching for another glass of champagne when she caught sight of the waiter's face. Luckily, he was distracted by a group of very loud and very camp TV actors for the moment, so he hadn't noticed her yet. There was no doubt about it, though. It was unmistakably Jimmy from the Apocalypse café.

'Oh, shit.' It was under her breath, but Rafe still heard her.

'Now that's no way to treat a chap who's just asked you out.' Rafe looked and sounded positively miffed. Penny glanced round the room desperately. She had to get away, but Jimmy was so close, she felt sure he would recognise her if she tried. Instead, she opted for the only remaining course of action. She reached up her arms, grasped Rafe by the shoulders and buried her face in his chest. She felt his arms encircle her waist, his free hand dropping shamelessly to her bottom. This was no time to be prudish, so she just wrapped herself even tighter to him and made sure her face was towards the window. She was able to see a faint reflection back into the room that allowed her to watch Jimmy pause with his tray, glance briefly in their direction, and then continue on his rounds.

She hung onto Rafe for another half minute until Jimmy had disappeared completely. Finally, reassured, she tried to draw back from the actor's clutches and the ever more intrusive burrowing of his hand, but he held her ever more tightly. She felt a toxic cloud of nicotine and alcohol waft over her face as he pulled her towards him, reaching for her with his lips. She decided to let him kiss her in the hope that he would then release her, but was unprepared for the octopus-like groping that followed. After a brief struggle she decided that enough was enough and deliberately trod on his foot with her new high heels. He yelped and stepped back, bumping into a passing couple and dropping his whisky glass as he did so.

Taking advantage of this momentary respite, she summoned her most charming smile. 'I'm so sorry about that, Rafe. I'm afraid I sometimes get these giddy spells. I think I'd better go and powder my nose.'

Powder my nose? Where the hell had that come from? Penny didn't stop for introspection. She extricated herself from him and headed across the room towards Mrs B-W, carefully scanning the room for any sign of Jimmy as she did so. She decided that she couldn't stand on ceremony, so she grasped Mrs B-W by the arm with both of her hands and butted into the conversation she was having with three men in suits.

'I'm sorry, mummy, but I'm feeling a bit faint. Do you think we could go now?'

Mrs B-W looked surprised, momentarily annoyed, but then managed to produce a look of compassion. 'Olivia, darling, of course.' She turned to the suits. 'I'm so sorry, gentlemen, but Olivia's been a bit under the weather of late.'

They headed for the door and out into the corridor beyond. As they walked back down the stairs, Penny hastily explained what had happened back there. Mrs B-W, while clearly annoyed at having to leave the party early, grudgingly approved of Penny's course of action. Somehow, without Penny realising how she had called it, the Bentley whispered up to the kerb as they emerged onto the road behind the Southbank Centre. They climbed in and Penny sank back into the soft leather seat, finally able to relax.

'I'm very sorry about that, Mrs Brookes-Webster. Jimmy, the waiter, knows me very well and I know he would have twigged who I was.'

Mrs B-W glanced across at her. 'I suppose even nobodies have people who know them. Oh yes, and I'd better have those earrings back now.'

Penny managed to resist the temptation to slap her. There was a trip to Venice riding on this, after all.

Chapter 9

Penny and Caroline travelled down to Brighton at the weekend in a luxury limousine. Penny had raised her eyebrows at the expense, but Caroline told her this was what members of the Brookes–Webster family always did, so Penny had to do the same to stay in character. As for Olivia's mother, she would be coming along later in the chauffeur-driven Bentley. Clearly, her concern for the environment didn't extend as far as her own carbon footprint. As there was a glass screen between them and the driver, Penny and Caroline chatted about the goings-on at the Southbank Centre. Penny had phoned her as soon as she got home to recount what had happened and Caroline had been supportive. Now she wanted more details.

'So, Rafe Kingsholme, was he as hunky as he looks on TV?'

'Rafe Kingsholme smelled like the lean-to outside the Dog and Partridge, just round the corner from where I live, where all the drunks congregate for a smoke. His breath would kill at twenty paces.'

Caroline looked at her askance. 'Really? I've been dreaming about him for years now. How terribly disappointing.'

Penny nodded. 'Me too. I read somewhere they were trying to invent 4D cinema where you get smell as well as sound and vision. If that ever happens, his reputation will crumble overnight.' She grinned at Caroline and went on to tell her how she had been touched up by some other surprising people. Caroline was amazed.

'Really? You see her on TV and you'd never imagine for a moment... Anyway, from the sound of it, nobody questioned your identity and, apart from a few old friends pitching up and the incident with your friend Jimmy, it all went well. Mrs B–W's not one for giving credit to anybody, but she had no complaints, which is just about as good as it gets with her.'

Penny thought it was about time she did a bit of digging for information, but she lowered her voice just to be on the safe side.

'Tell me about the Foundation, Caroline. What does it do?'

'Olivia's father set it up thirty years ago. At first they provided scholarships for children from poor backgrounds to go to good schools but then, as the environment climbed the world agenda, the Foundation turned more and more towards saving the planet. There are universities all around the country benefiting from BWF grants to do research into the extent of global warming and ways to slow it.'

'So there's no question that global warming's a thing, then?'

Caroline grinned at her. 'Don't let anybody in Brighton hear you asking that. You can be quite sure that every single person at the conference this weekend believes in global warming with every brain cell they've got.'

Penny smiled back at her. 'Right, duly noted. So, the Foundation's pretty important to the climate change lobby, then?'

'Very definitely. You'll see for yourself. However stroppy Olivia's mum may choose to be, nobody'll dare say a word against her for fear that she'll take offence and suspend their funding.' She turned towards Penny. 'It's pretty distasteful, to be honest. It was never like that in her dad's day.'

'That sounds pretty uninviting.' Penny reflected that the conference wasn't likely to be too much fun if this was the way things were. 'Ah well, so be it. Now, who runs the Foundation?'

'It's run by a man called Nick, Doctor Nick Greaves. He's a specialist in climate research. You'll meet him tonight.'

'And what's he like? Is he likely to realise that I'm not the real deal?'

Caroline snorted. 'No way. He and Mrs B-W don't get on, so I'm sure he'll keep as far away from us as possible.' There was a wistful edge to Caroline's voice that Penny couldn't miss.

'Would you like to be nearer to him?'

Even in the limited light provided by the street lights, Penny was able to see that Caroline was blushing as she answered. 'Um, maybe. I think he's rather nice.'

'I'll look forward to meeting him then. And am I right in understanding that it's Olivia, not her mum, who's taken over from her father since his death?'

Penny saw Caroline glance at the driver's head once more. Clearly these were dangerous waters into which they were now sailing. 'That's right, but it hasn't quite worked out as he wanted so far. Olivia was very attached to him, and when he died she had a sort of breakdown. She's spent most of the past six months in her room, she's hardly been out of the house and, even then, it's only under protest. Mrs B–W's been representing the family on the board in her place.'

'And she hasn't been making too many friends?'

They heard a faint ringing sound and then the driver answered the telephone. They could see his lips moving, reflected in the rear view mirror, but couldn't hear a word he was saying. Encouraged by this proof of the efficiency of the glass barrier, Caroline answered the question. 'Mrs B–W isn't Olivia's real mother, you know.'

This was news to Penny.

'Olivia's birth mother died when Olivia was quite young and she's been brought up by a series of nannies. The present Mrs B–W came along about ten years ago and it can't have been easy for Olivia.' She paused for a moment. 'Mind you, she and her stepmum used to get on really quite well before Mr B–W died. Since then, for whatever reason, Mrs B–W's been getting very bitter and twisted.'

'What's she got to get bitter and twisted about?' Penny suddenly remembered what she had learnt from Olivia's old aunties. 'Is it because her husband left control of the Foundation to his daughter, not her?'

Caroline shook her head. 'I suppose that might be part of it, although the truth of the matter is that she's not the least bit interested in the goings on of the Foundation. Never has been. I think she's probably just miffed that it's been taking up her time. But there's got to be more to it than that. Whatever it is, she's become increasingly grumpy and bad-tempered.'

'Poor kid. So Mrs B-W's a stepmum. That explains why I couldn't see any kind of family resemblance. It must have been really tough losing her mum like that. What was that about money buying happiness?'

They got to their hotel at six o'clock and were escorted to their rooms. These were side by side and overlooked the sea. They were large and comfortable but, if Penny had felt like being picky, she would have said the furniture and fittings were just a bit tired. Mind you, she thought to herself with a smile as she lay in the huge bath, with bubbles threatening to engulf her, it beat the crap out of her current dwelling with its leaky roof, its resident rat, and one bathroom shared between seven occupants. Here, at least, she had a bathroom to herself and the water was hot.

She dried herself with a huge fluffy towel and changed into the other evening dress as instructed by Caroline. This was as low cut as the top she had chosen for the Southbank Centre party and although she was gradually getting more used to Olivia's dress taste, she had already relegated one or two of the newly-purchased outfits to the *only with a T-shirt underneath* category. All delegates had been issued with name badges on blue ribbons and she found that by tying a knot to shorten the ribbon, she managed to position her badge at a perfect strategic height to further protect her modesty. Even so, she felt very conspicuous as she and Caroline exited the lift at ballroom level and went through the double doors into the welcome party. She whispered across to Caroline as they entered the room.

'I'm not obscene, am I? I feel like I'm about to fall out of this dress.'

Caroline grinned and shook her head. 'Olivia's said the self-same thing to me on many occasions. Her stepmum has a big say in choosing Olivia's wardrobe and she likes that sort of thing. You should be okay, but if you drop a canapé on the carpet, whatever you do, just don't try and bend down to pick it up.'

Penny nodded. 'You bet your life. And, Caroline, you will help me out if somebody comes along and I don't know what to say, won't you?'

Caroline gave her a wry smile. 'Don't worry. Everybody's scared stiff of Mrs B-W, so they'll avoid us like the plague. It'll be fine. You'll see.'

The place was already full of people and there was a hubbub of background noise that made conversation difficult. For Penny in her role as Olivia, it couldn't have been better. Everybody had a name badge so identification was simplified, and there was so much noise it wouldn't really matter what she said. Her heart sank as she spotted Olivia's stepmother, surrounded by a number of delegates. In fact, Mrs Brookes-Webster was hard to miss. She was wearing so many diamonds that the light sparkled and danced about her as she moved, not unlike one of those old disco balls that used to hang in dance halls back in the mists of time. As Mrs B-W spotted her in her turn, she produced a charming smile. Penny used her hitherto undiscovered acting talent and smiled back as Caroline led her across to join her group.

'You all know Olivia, don't you?' Penny was pleased by the civility of the introduction, but was immediately dismayed by the reaction of the people around her. Some managed to muster weak smiles, others nodded formally, while a couple just looked away. Only one man, wearing a smart dark blue suit, held out his hand. He was quite good-looking, maybe in his late thirties, and he looked apprehensive. Penny reached out and shook his hand. She saw from his name badge that this was the CEO of the Foundation, Dr Nick Greaves. She could see from his face that although he was doing his best to be cordial, he was far from comfortable in her company or that of Mrs B-W.

'Good evening, Olivia. I hope you're feeling better.'

Penny could sense Mrs B-W's eyes on her as she replied. Although she had been told to stay fairly taciturn, she saw no reason to shun common courtesy, so she smiled at him as she answered. 'Yes, thank you.' He looked surprised at her cordial response, while Mrs B-W looked disapproving. Clearly, exchanging pleasantries with inferiors was not on her agenda. Penny turned towards Mrs B-W and, ignoring her expression, asked sweetly, 'Is there anybody you want me to meet or anything you want me to do?'

Olivia's stepmother shook her head. 'No, it's all such a bore, but we'll just have to make the best of it. Caroline, do you think you could find us a glass of something palatable?'

Caroline immediately headed off in search of drinks and Penny noticed that Nick Greaves went with her.

It was an excruciating evening and Penny couldn't help but feel the hostility of most of the other delegates towards Mrs B-W and, by extension, to Penny herself in the role of Olivia. Nevertheless, nobody had an impolite word to say to either of them, treating them both with fawning respect. It looked and felt completely phoney and by the end of the event, Penny had a pretty unpleasant taste in her mouth. She did her best to be friendly and to counteract Mrs B-W's negative attitude, but it was clear that the other woman's surliness had soured relations badly.

It was only half past nine when Penny and Caroline got back to their rooms, but Penny felt close to exhaustion after the stress of the deception she had been performing. Mrs B-W had disappeared some time earlier for dinner with a couple of benefactors from other charitable foundations. Penny had been nibbling canapés all evening and she didn't really feel like any more serious food. They found a box of peanuts and a bag of crisps in the minibar, along with a half bottle of champagne that they opened. As they drank it, Penny queried Caroline about Nick.

'So, do you think you and Nick are going to get it together? He's a good-looking guy.'

Caroline blushed. 'I do like him a lot, I have done since the very first time I met him, but I can't risk hooking up with him for fear of Mrs B-W finding out. The mood she's in these days, I'm afraid she might object out of spite, and she might even sack me as a result. I really do enjoy this job, not least because Mrs B-W's away on holiday more often than she's in London. And I get on fine with Olivia. She's really nice underneath the flashy clothes, or at least she used to be until her dad's death.' She gave Penny a weary smile. 'He was a lovely man, you know. Everybody liked him, and his daughter idolised him. His death was a crushing blow to her and she's only just starting to come out of it now.'

'So, just what is your job, Caroline?'

'Good question.' Caroline took a sip of wine. 'My official title is Personal Assistant to the Chairman of the Board of Trustees of the Foundation. That was Olivia's dad and now, theoretically, it's Olivia. But, because of her depression, she's been out of it, so it's been down to me and her stepmother to keep on top of things. To be honest, since Olivia's father's death, I've spent a lot of time acting more like a nursemaid than a PA, but I don't mind, just so long as Mrs B-W keeps out of my hair.'

'So, once Olivia's up and running again, you'll be able to take things to the next level with Nick?'

Caroline blushed. 'I sincerely hope so, but for now, I can't take the risk. I get a really good salary and I can't jeopardise that. Not with mortgage payments to make.'

'You've bought a house in London?' Penny was impressed.

Caroline nodded. 'In Crouch End; you know, poor man's Highgate. It's not huge, but it's very nice. You'll have to come round and see it.'

'I'd like that.' Penny reflected that she really would like that. She was rapidly coming to think of Caroline as a friend, and a good one at that. 'And so, what's my job? I mean, the real job. Whose idea was it to employ me like this?'

Caroline reflected before answering. 'To be totally honest, Penny, it was my idea. You saw what it was like here tonight. The atmosphere's putrid. In Olivia's dad's day, everybody got on, everybody was happy, and

96

happy people do the best work. You must have felt the animosity; it's all down to Mrs B-W. She's always been a bit snobby and a bit stuffy, but ever since her husband died, she's been getting worse and worse. It's almost as if she enjoys making people unhappy.'

'You can say that again.'

'I'm no psychologist, but I wonder if it's because she's unhappy, and subconsciously she wants everybody else to suffer as well.'

'What's a multi-millionaire got to be unhappy about, apart from the Foundation thing?'

'She really loved her husband, you know. I'm sure of that, and she's bound to be grieving, but the problem is she's not the kind of person to show it. I think the grief's burning her up inside. If she were able to communicate her feelings a bit better, things would be a lot different, I'm sure.'

'So, where do I come in?'

'When I saw your photo on social media, I couldn't believe my eyes. I've been doing my best to get Olivia back on her feet and back on the job before her stepmum sours things completely, but she's still a sick girl.' She looked across at Penny. 'Don't get me wrong. Olivia's getting better. In fact, I'm seeing improvement almost on a daily basis now, but I know it's a long haul. When I saw you, I realised that you might be a way of letting us give the illusion that Olivia was back on the case, and so we could begin to redress the balance and start cheering people up again.'

'Aha… and does Mrs B-W know that's why I've been hired? That would explain why she's been so rude to me.'

'I doubt it. As far as the rudeness is concerned, it's not just you. Let's face it, Penny, over the past few months she's been rude to pretty much everybody. I imagine she must suspect something, but when all's said and done, her heart's not in the job, so she's probably not sorry that your arrival frees her up to do other things.' She caught Penny's eye. 'Mostly with a coffee cup or a glass in her hand.'

'Thanks. Now that I know the background, I think I should be better able to do something to help.'

'Well, just take it slowly. You don't want to piss her off any more than necessary, otherwise you might find yourself out of a job.' She hesitated. 'As might I.' Then she changed the subject. 'Anyway, what about you and men, Penny? Is there a special someone in your life?'

Penny shook her head. 'Not now.' She went on to tell Caroline all about Rick, and she read sympathy in Caroline's eyes. She thought about mentioning the man with the pirate beard at the National Gallery, but she was coming round to convincing herself that he might, after all, have just been a figment of her imagination.

'And before Rick? Have you had lots of boyfriends? I mean, you're very pretty, you know.'

'A few. I was seeing this boy, Sam, on and off for the best part of a couple of years, but it fizzled out. But, come to think of it, I did go to an exhibition with a very nice guy just last week.' She was quick to explain. Maybe too quick. 'He's another artist and I bump into him from time to time. I'm supposed to be seeing him again this coming week.' She paused, wondering once more if that relationship was actually going to lead anywhere. 'And what about Olivia? Any men on the horizon there?' She grinned at Caroline. 'I suppose I shouldn't say it, but she is rather good-looking, you know.'

Caroline smiled, but shook her head. 'There've been a few, but Olivia's bright enough to realise that a lot of men are going to be attracted by her wealth, rather than by her for herself. As a result, she's been very resistant to any kind of serious involvement, although I think there was one boy that she liked but, of course, since her dad died, she's hardly left the house.'

'Girlfriends?'

'Nobody really close. I've met a few, but they're mostly out of the same mould as her stepmother. You know the type.'

Penny remembered Tiffany from the Southbank Centre. There was no need to say more. She nodded. 'Being an heiress isn't as great as it's cracked up to be, is it? Well, I'll do my best. Here's hoping I can make a difference.'

'Just remember what I said about taking it slow, Penny, and for God's sake don't start rocking the boat too much.' She glanced at Penny. 'I mean, from what you've said, it sounds like this extra cash is coming in very handy.'

'You aren't joking. I've already spent almost all the money you gave me the other day. I had so many outstanding bills, even without student loans, of course, which I haven't even started to pay back. But now at least I can breathe again. Next month, if all goes well, I should be able to afford to go to the dentist. I haven't had my teeth looked at for years.'

'Oh, Lord, I'd forgotten about that.' Caroline pulled out her phone and started writing. 'I'll get that fixed up for next week. A full check up and a bit of tooth whitening.   And that'll go on the Brookes-Webster account as well.' She looked across at Penny and smiled. 'See what I mean about not being able to take the risk of losing our jobs?'

Chapter 10

When Penny got back home, as ever, the first thing that attracted her attention was her new painting. Over the previous week she had been filling in the colour and defining the shapes and she was beginning to feel really excited about this new more abstract direction in her work. With the remains of the money she had been given by Caroline she had bought more canvasses and had already started to sketch out another. She did not, however, intend to rub this one across her naked body.

She glanced at her watch. It was still only eight o'clock so she would have a few hours to herself now to carry on painting. She shrugged off her smart coat and reached for the zip of her dress. Her phone whistled and she saw that she had a text from Caroline.

> What shift are you on tomorrow? How would you like to come round for a drink and a takeaway tomorrow evening?

Penny replied that she was on the early shift and would be finished by four, so they arranged that she would go round to Caroline's house at Crouch End at six. She found she was looking forward to spending more time with Caroline who, despite her posh accent, was turning out to be a good friend. Apart from Jimmy at the café and Vicky from upstairs, Penny didn't have many close friends of either sex and it was refreshing to spend time with somebody new.

She dropped the phone and looked round her room. In comparison to the hotel in Brighton or the Brookes-Webster's house, it was scruffy in the extreme. Her bed was tucked into one corner and the wash basin was almost hidden from sight by brushes, pots and rags. She slipped out of her smart "Olivia" clothes and changed into her old jeans and an even older jumper that didn't mind being smeared with oil paint. Then she went across to the easel and spent five minutes reviewing the last changes she had made and planning where to go from here.

After a bit, she left her room and went out to the bathroom. It was free for once and unusually clean for a change. As she washed her hands at the basin, she found herself studying her reflection in the mirror. It still felt a little strange to see herself with short, immaculately styled hair, but she was getting more and more used to it as the days went by, and she really rather liked the new Penny. After years of scrimping and saving, desperately trying to find somebody interested in her work, she was hoping against hope that one of the big galleries might offer her space. If that happened, she knew it would represent a major step forward. It seemed fitting, somehow, that new career and new look should go together and she prayed that this whole Olivia business might be a sign of greater things to come. She swilled out her mouth and turned for the door, but stopped dead in horror. She stifled a scream, but only just.

Her way out was blocked. Sitting between her and the door, apparently unworried by her presence, was a large grey rat. Presumably this was the same rat she had already spotted out in the corridor before, but there was no way of being sure. Maybe, she thought to herself, as she studied the repulsive beast with its bald, reptilian tail, this was a different rat, and the house was infested with a whole tribe of them. It wouldn't surprise her. She took a deep breath and made a shooing motion with her hand. No effect. She stamped her foot on the floor, but apart from hurting her heel, this did little good. By now, the rat's expression had changed to one of open confrontation, or so it seemed to Penny. His eyes met hers as much as to say, "Make my day". She shivered and looked around wildly for a weapon.

Her eyes alighted upon the only item in the room that wasn't bolted down; the waste bin. This unappealing metal container had lived under the basin ever since she had first taken a room in the house. To her knowledge, she was the only person who ever emptied it and now, as usual, it was jammed with rubbish. She reached down for it and raised it above her head. It was surprisingly heavy.

'All right, rat, you've asked for it.' She took a step towards the door and slammed the bin down with a crash that resounded through the whole house. A fraction of a second before the bin hit the floor, the rat leapt in the air, performed a *paso doble* worthy of a matador and disappeared, unharmed, underneath the bathtub. Penny hastily stuffed the rubbish back in the bin and made her exit. As she came out into the corridor, the door of number 3 opened and she was confronted by the Strange Man. Tonight, he was wearing a pair of pyjama trousers, dark blue socks and nothing else. She glanced back into the bathroom, very tempted to go back in and take her chances with the rat.

'Trouble?' He wasn't given to long speeches.

'There's a rat in the bathroom. A big, dirty, horrid rat.'

'Yes.'

'You've seen it?'

'Frequently.'

'And you haven't told anybody?'

He leant against the door frame and scratched his belly reflectively. Penny edged a little further down the corridor towards the sanctuary of her room. Finally he replied. 'I didn't want to frighten people.'

'Well, it just frightened the crap out of me.'

'Did you hit it?'

'No, I missed.'

'Oh… Well, all right then. Good night.'

Penny turned and fled, vowing to start looking for somewhere else to live as soon as possible.

A few minutes later, back in her room, just as she was beginning to calm down and thinking about picking up a paintbrush, her phone rang. She checked the caller ID and felt a little surge of pleasure to see that it was Owen.

'Hi, Owen, how's it going?'

'Hi, Penny, all good, but you sound a bit flustered. Is everything okay?'

Penny told him about the rat and her encounter with the Strange Man. He expressed disgust and sympathy. 'If I were you, I'd find somewhere else to live.'

With the extra money she was earning from Olivia, Penny knew she could now afford somewhere better and she agreed with him. 'That's the next thing on my agenda. Anyway, how was your week?'

'I've been in Aquitaine all week leading a residential painting course and eating too much *confit de canard*. I just got back this evening. How was Brighton?'

So as not to have too many different cover stories going round, Penny had told him she was going to visit her aunt and uncle in Brighton over the weekend. 'Fine, thanks. I've been eating too much as well, but not lovely French food, I'm afraid.'

'How about going out some time this week like we discussed?'

'Definitely, I'd love that.' As she said it, she realised how much she really did like the sound of another evening with him. 'Where and when?'

They arranged to meet for dinner three days later and, as she put the phone down, Penny found she was humming to herself. Apart from the rat, things were looking good.

–

She went into work next morning and found herself on the receiving end of the usual banter from the boys after injudiciously admitting that she had gone to Brighton for the weekend. Jimmy approved.

'Very sensible, sweetheart. Far better you go and do your dirty work away from your local turf. You wouldn't want to find yourself with one of your neighbours as a client, now would you?'

For a horrible moment Penny had a vision of the clothes-stealer from Number 3 appearing at her door in his pyjama bottoms with a handful of used banknotes. She took a deep breath before replying. 'Jimmy, you and I are going to fall out if you suggest anything like that again. We've been through it all before. I was in Brighton to see my auntie. I am not, repeat not, involved in sex for money. Now, are we totally clear on that?'

'Of course, darling.' Jimmy's response would have carried more conviction if he hadn't winked at her, and if Piotr from the kitchen hadn't chimed in as well.

'Your secret safe with us. We keep mouths closed. Maybe if you keep mouth and legs closed is better, too.' And then he dissolved into hoots of laughter.

To make matters worse, by this time a few of the regular customers had got wind of the accusations that Penny had turned to prostitution and the jibes continued throughout the day, some of them not so much humorous as creepy, and loaded with rather uncomfortable innuendo. As Penny sat on the tube en route to Caroline's house that evening she found herself wondering whether the time had come for her to seek not only accommodation, but employment elsewhere. She was still thinking about it when she got to Caroline's house. This was on a pleasant, tidy road with real trees, and the house itself was a charming 1930s terrace house that had managed to survive the Blitz and, clearly, had been on the receiving end of a lot of restoration work very recently. She rang the bell and Caroline opened the door almost immediately.

'Hi, Penny, come in.' Caroline led her through to a lovely open plan kitchen diner, looking out onto a well-kept garden to the rear of the house. This pretty clearly faced west, as the rays of the setting sun reached into the room, turning the floor pink. The floor was wood, probably maple, and the kitchen units were bright and modern with a gorgeous granite worktop and a battery of stainless steel cooking equipment.

'Caroline, this place is amazing.' Penny slipped off her jacket and took a seat by the window.

'Tea, coffee, champagne?'

'Oh, God, no. I'd better avoid the champagne. I like it too much and there's no point developing a habit I can't ever possibly afford. A cup of tea would be great.'

As Caroline made the tea, Penny told her about the rat, the Strange Man and the rather awkward atmosphere at work. Caroline had a suggestion for her as far as work was concerned. 'You know the coffee shop in Piccadilly where we met? The JC? Well, I was in there the other day and I saw a notice saying they were looking for staff. With your smile, your accent and your three-hundred-pound hairstyle, you shouldn't have any trouble getting a position there. And I bet it pays a lot better than the place you're in at the moment.'

'Three hundred pounds? Blimey.' Penny was appalled. 'At least tell me that included the nails and the facial. Please.'

Caroline shook her head and smiled. 'Nope. Just the hair. It's probably best I don't tell you what the rest cost.'

'Oh, God...' Penny was horrified and took a deep breath before continuing. 'Still, the JC idea sounds brilliant.' She remembered how daunting her first experience of the café had been and rather liked the idea of finding herself actually working there. Hang on, though. Isn't there the chance I might run into Olivia there? That would stuff everything up.'

Caroline shook her head. 'She still hardly leaves the house and, anyway, as far as I know, she doesn't know the place exists. It'll be fine. Mind you, it might be worth concocting some sort of cover story just in case you run into any of her friends or acquaintances.'

Penny nodded approvingly. A job there really did sound like an excellent solution, and she resolved to check out what they were looking for and what they were offering as soon as she got back to her laptop.

After making the tea, Caroline sat down with Penny and they chatted as the sun disappeared below the horizon. A bit later on, Caroline took her on a tour of the house, which was immaculate, consisting of three good bedrooms and two bathrooms. It was when they reached the big bedroom at the front that Caroline made Penny an offer. 'I'll be quite honest. I had an ulterior motive for inviting you here this evening. The idea came to me over the weekend. How would you feel about renting this room off me? From what you were saying about the place you're in at the moment, you probably need to make a change. You'd have your own bathroom and of course you could use the kitchen, sitting room and garden as well. More to the point, there's that home office chalet thing in the garden that I never use. How would that be as a studio for your painting? There's an electric heater in there and good lighting. I'm paying a load of money each month for the mortgage so it would help me no end.'

She named a monthly rental figure that was quite a lot more than Penny's current bed-sit, but the difference in quality between the two places was immense. They went out into the garden and Penny inspected the lovely light, roomy annexe. She took a look round, did a bit of mental arithmetic, and made a decision.

'Caroline, I'd love to. This place is wonderful and, as long as this job with Olivia continues for a few months, I should be able to afford it. The only unknown is what happens to me and where I go after Olivia resumes her place in the Foundation.' She had already told Caroline about her hopes for a place for her paintings in one of the galleries. 'If only I can manage to start selling my stuff, I should be fine.' She held out her hand. 'If you're happy to take me on that basis, it's a deal.'

–

Penny got a call from Caroline next day telling her that Olivia had invited them both to go to Notting Hill at six o'clock that evening for a drink. Apparently this was wasn't a formal event, just social, and her stepmother wouldn't be there.

Penny felt just a tiny bit nervous as she walked up the steps to the great house at one minute to six that evening. She still hadn't quite come to terms with the gulf separating her normal life from this other world of boundless opulence. The door was opened before she could reach for the bell. Caroline had been waiting for her, the dog beside her. She gave Penny a smile while the dog stood up on his hind legs and stretched his paws towards her. Penny fended him off gently and then crouched down to stroke his smooth black coat.

Inside the lounge, Olivia was standing by the far wall, staring at the Hieronymus Bosch. Coincidentally, she had chosen the exact same salmon pink jumper as Penny. As the others came in she turned and walked towards them.

'Hi you two. Come and sit down.' Olivia went over to the pair of massive leather sofas and took a seat, waving for them to follow suit. 'Dump your coat on the armchair, Penny.' There was a bottle of champagne in an ice bucket on the coffee table, and beside it a plate of nibbles. The Labrador immediately took up position beside the table, his nose trained on the food. 'A glass of champagne, or would you prefer something else?'

'Champagne would be fantastic, thanks.' Penny reflected yet again that when weighing up the pros and cons of being very rich, champagne was definitely a major factor on the plus side. They went across and sat down while Olivia busied herself with the bottle, opening it efficiently and filling three glasses. She handed two across and raised hers in a toast.

'Here's to your continued success, Penny. Caroline's told me how well everything went in Brighton.' She took a sip of wine before continuing. 'I'm really grateful to you for being prepared to do this, you know. My father's death, coming as it did right out of the blue, hit me awfully hard and I haven't been myself for some months now.' She summoned a weak smile. 'I'm getting better, honestly. The Foundation was my father's life's work and it's his legacy. It meant everything to him and I know if he were here now he'd be very grateful to you.'

'I'm very happy to help out, any way I can.' Penny also tried the wine. As usual, it was excellent.

'Anyway, like I say, I'm getting better. I really feel it. So, listen, if you can carry on taking my place for just a few weeks or maybe a few months more, say until Christmas, I'd be so terribly grateful. As soon as I feel confident enough to begin mixing with people again I'll take over.' Olivia took another sip of wine and smiled across at Penny, no longer a timid, hesitant smile, but a more open, friendly smile. 'I must say you're looking good. Salmon pink suits us, doesn't it?' They exchanged smiles and the conversation continued much more spontaneously and easily. By the time they left, Penny had warmed considerably towards her employer.

That night Penny had the Venice dream again and, this time, she was sitting alone in a luxurious hotel, drinking champagne. As she looked out of the window onto a narrow canal, a big black rat came swimming towards her and climbed out onto the shore, still heading in her direction. But before she could chase it away, it disappeared somewhere beneath her feet.

Chapter 11

The following evening, Penny and Owen went out on their second date, although she was still avoiding referring to it as a date. She toyed with the idea of wearing one of her 'Olivia' tops, but decided against it. She was still far from completely comfortable wearing the plunging necklines favoured by Olivia's stepmother and didn't want to make things awkward because of her choice of clothing. Instead, she went for jeans and a tight, but not revealing, top.

This time they had arranged to meet in a central London pub, but it wasn't the best idea. The place was crowded, there was football on a huge screen, and the noise was deafening. After struggling for half an hour, they gave in and headed outside. It was a pleasant autumn night, dry for a change, and not too cold. Owen stopped outside the door of the pub, took a few deep breaths and looked across at her.

'That's better. How about a walk?'

'That sounds like a great idea.' Together they walked for well over an hour through the heart of the city, across Trafalgar Square and down to the Thames, onto the Millennium footbridge, heading towards the Tate Modern gallery. Fortunately the autumn gales that had been raging for a few days had subsided. The sky was clear, but the stars almost invisible in the glow projected by the big city. Apart from the lights of a never-ending stream of jets passing overhead, a lone bright spot, low down on the horizon, probably a planet, was strong enough to make its presence felt. When they reached the middle of the ultramodern pedestrian bridge, Penny caught Owen's arm and stopped him, leading him over to the railings at the side. She left her arm linked with his as they stood there, out of the way of the steady stream of people crossing the bridge behind them.

'I've walked across here so many times, but I'm always rushing to get somewhere. We're in no hurry tonight. Let's just stop for a while and take in the view. It's quite something.'

He leant on the rail beside her, one hand reaching across to rest on top of hers. 'I know what you mean.' Looking east, they could both make out the shape of London Bridge, with the twin towers of Tower Bridge just visible in the distance. Owen pointed with his free hand. 'Well, you can't miss the Shard, can you?'

The shape of the pointed skyscraper was unmistakable, its lights standing out clearly against the dark sky. Penny wasn't in the least bit cold now after their walk and she realised she was very happy to be here with him. So much so that she reached up and kissed him on the cheek. He glanced down towards her, a smile on his face.

'Enjoying London by night?'

'Yes, and the company.' This time he kissed her, and it wasn't just on the cheek.

–

In the course of the next few weeks, Penny and Owen saw a lot of each other and she knew she was getting very fond of him. He was living in south London, not far from Dulwich, and she and he normally met up in central London. There was no question by now that what they were doing was dating. They ate together, drank together, even went dancing together on one occasion at her suggestion, though she soon discovered that dancing was not his forte. They visited galleries and even the Imperial War Museum, but rarely managed anything more intimate. They walked arm in arm, kissed and canoodled in shadowy places, but hesitated to take things to the next level. She was far too ashamed of her scruffy accommodation to invite him back there, and he was sharing a crowded house with three other men, so their relationship remained unconsummated. As the days went by, Penny came to realise that she was now in no doubt that she would indeed like things to develop between them.

She went to the dentist and emerged with gleaming white teeth, very glad she hadn't had to pay the bill. Fortunately, it wasn't too long before she was able to move out of her old place and into the warmth and comfort of Caroline's house in Crouch End. This happened sooner than she had anticipated, after the rat she had seen was discovered not to have been acting alone. When a nest of little rat-babies was found under the sink, the landlord had no option but to let her move out straight away and, to her relief, he even arranged the prompt return of her deposit, no doubt fearful that she might go to the Environmental Health department at the local council. Vicky also found herself new accommodation, but they were both unsurprised to learn that the Strange Man had opted to stay on, in spite of the rodents. Or maybe because of them.

Penny also left the Apocalypse and got herself a new job. As Caroline had predicted, her recent makeover and her swanky clothes ensured that the JC coffee shop offered her a job on the spot. The pay was quite a bit better than she had been getting from Spiro and the tips were amazing. With the extra cash coming in from her Olivia role, she was soon a lot better off than she had ever been, and debt free as well, as long as she didn't think about her student loan. She bade farewell to the boys at the Apocalypse with mixed feelings. On the one hand she was relieved to get away from the constant taunts and sometimes downright obscene comments of some of the customers, but on the other, she knew she would miss the old place. Spiro's job had helped her through some hard times and she would always be grateful to him. She knew she would stay in touch with Jimmy, who, now that he had finally given up implying that her new-found affluence was as a result of dirty deeds, had reverted to being her fashion advisor and general confidant. Naturally, this confidence didn't extend as far as her telling him the real reason for her improved circumstances, a secret she had revealed to nobody, not even her mother or Owen, for fear of legal repercussions.

Meanwhile, Penny had several more "official" engagements and these went much better than the Brighton conference, though it was still hard work, both in trying to keep up the illusion that she was Olivia and in the more specific task of improving relations between the Brookes-Webster family and the scientific community.

She attended some evening events and a couple of one-day conferences and Mrs Brookes-Webster was absent on all of these occasions. The conferences were in London and in Cambridge, and Caroline accompanied her to both. Without the handicap of Mrs B-W's presence, things were a lot less stressful and Penny was delighted for Caroline as she saw her spending time with Nick. There was no doubt that Penny was by now totally accepted by everybody as being Olivia, and she hoped that the enthusiasm she genuinely felt for the whole subject of the environment would shine through, and that her polite and friendly attitude would start to rebuild bridges. In this way she gradually began to see relations between the scientific world and the Brookes-Webster family begin to improve.

Once she had moved into Caroline's house, Penny started pottering about in the kitchen. She had always enjoyed cooking, but the facilities where she had been living up till now had been primitive to say the least. Now, with state of the art ovens and hobs to play with, she started experimenting with all sorts, from sponge cake to a Sunday roast. One Sunday, as she and Caroline were clearing away the plates after lunch, Penny had an idea. 'Why don't we invite Olivia round for a meal? It would be good for her to get out for once.'

'She won't come.' Caroline was sure of that. 'She still hardly ever leaves the house these days.'

'Well, all she'd have to do would be to get in the car and get the driver to bring her here and then take her back. She sees you on a daily basis and she certainly knows my face, so it shouldn't be too scary for her. Why not give it a go? I'm working days next week, so any evening would be good for me.' She had a thought. 'You'd better check what sort of food she likes, though, and if she's allergic to anything. It wouldn't look too good if we poisoned our boss.'

–

To Caroline's surprise, Olivia accepted the invitation. After due consultation, Penny decided to make a fish pie, accompanied by roast fennel cooked with onions and celery. As a starter she opted for a mixed salad to be served with slices of grilled goat's cheese. As the big day approached, both she and Caroline began to feel unreasonably nervous and worked off their trepidation by subjecting the already tidy house to a total spring clean, although it was now November.

Their nerves proved to be unfounded.

Olivia and Gilbert the dog arrived in a chauffeur-driven car, mercifully not her stepmother's ostentatious Bentley, just after the agreed time of seven o'clock. The driver removed a case of champagne from the boot and carried it up to the house, handing it over to Caroline on the doorstep. To be on the safe side, Penny was hiding inside the house in case anybody should see her with her identical twin. The dog spotted her as he trotted in and was evidently delighted to see her. Once the door was safely closed behind the other two, Penny emerged and came forward to lead Olivia into the kitchen. She and Caroline had discussed at some length whether to use the lounge, but had decided to keep things as informal as possible.

Olivia was wearing a short blue skirt and a pale pink top, this time without a plunging neckline. Penny had opted for jeans and a lovely light grey jumper she had bought recently because it matched the colour of her eyes. Caroline had a bottle of prosecco already in the fridge so she opened that and sat with Olivia and chatted while Penny busied herself with the preparations. The dog, on the other hand, in true Labrador tradition, stationed himself close to where the food was, in hopeful expectation. After a while, Olivia got up and came round to watch what Penny was preparing.

Penny looked up. 'Do you do much cooking, Olivia?' As she spoke, she had the sudden realisation that this was in all likelihood a rhetorical question. She imagined that millionaires probably didn't do a lot of food preparation. She was right.

'It's something I've never learnt. When I was little I sometimes used to help the cook with things like biscuits and cakes, but I wouldn't know where to start now.' She leant against the granite and watched as Penny chopped spring onions and avocado for the salad. 'I could probably do this kind of preparation of cold stuff, but it's the cooking that would cause me headaches.'

'There's nothing to it, really.'

'Have you been cooking all your life?'

'My mum's a great cook and I suppose I learnt from her.' As she said it, Penny remembered that Olivia's real mother had died when she was a little girl. Never one to dodge a challenge, she looked across and caught Olivia's eye. 'I heard about your mum. It must have been really hard, losing your mother when you were so young.'

She saw Olivia's eyes cloud and, for a moment, Penny thought she had maybe gone too far. Then Olivia managed to give her a little smile. 'It's sweet of you to say that, Penny. Yes, it was really, really hard. Sometimes I think I still haven't got over it.' She took a mouthful of wine. 'But my father was wonderful.' The smile increased in intensity. 'He was father and mother to me after her death.'

Now that they were on this road, there was no point beating about the bush, so Penny carried on. 'So his death was more than just losing your father.'

Olivia nodded, her eyes on her wine glass. 'He was my whole world. That's why it hit me so hard. I've just been feeling so empty since he died. So empty and alone.' She reached down and scratched the dog behind the ears. 'Well, almost alone.'

Penny realised there was real risk of this descending into a *vin triste* so she leapt in. 'Well, you're not alone now. You've got us two, a case of champagne and good old Gilbert. What more could a girl ask for?' She mentally crossed her fingers, hoping that her jollity would do the trick. There was an agonising pause and then Olivia looked up. The smile, albeit a bit pasty, was back on her face. She cleared her throat.

'Thanks, Penny. You're right. I'm not alone and you two are so very kind to have invited me. Let's see that we have a really good evening.'

And it was. Penny's food was pronounced excellent, the fish pie getting a special mention. By the time they finished, all three were full, fairly tipsy and getting on really well. The dog, after a few handouts, was stretched out on the floor, snoring loudly, and Olivia had loosened up and sounded much more cheerful. At the end of the evening, she thanked them both.

'That's the best night I've had for months and months. There's just one problem now. I can't offer to cook for you because I don't know how, and I can't offer to take you out to a restaurant because you and I, Penny, can't be seen together. It's such a pity. I'd really like to return the favour.'

'Um… well, there might be a solution.' Penny had been thinking about this ever since Olivia's confession that she didn't know how to cook. 'If you like, I could try and give you a few cookery lessons. I'm no great shakes, but I'm fairly okay on the basics. Then, if you wanted to, you could cook us a meal. Besides, learning to cook could come in handy and, you know what they say about the way to a man's heart being through his stomach… I'd be very happy to do that here, or at your place, if you want to give it a go.'

'Penny, I'd really love that.' Olivia looked and sounded really pleased, and they arranged that Penny would go to the house in Notting Hill the following week on Wednesday morning, by which time she would be on the late shift at work and free until two o'clock every day. Olivia kissed them both on the cheeks as she left with the dog, thanking them again most warmly.

After the front door closed, Penny sprawled on one of the low wicker armchairs by the window. There was still a drop of wine in the bottom of a bottle so she divided it between their two glasses, ignoring Caroline's feeble protests that she'd had enough. Penny had been thinking about Owen and how nice it would be to have him here with her now. Having only just moved into Caroline's house, she felt awkward about inviting him round to stay the night, although as far as she was concerned, the idea had considerable appeal. She took a sip of wine as Caroline looked across at her.

'Have you ever considered giving up art and taking up counselling? I wouldn't mind betting you've been better for Olivia and her emotional problems tonight than all the shrinks and pills she's had since her father died.'

Penny took another sip of wine, relegating thoughts of Owen to the back of her mind for now. She let it go down, drop by drop, and reflected on the way the evening had gone. 'You know something, Caroline? I really like Olivia. It just goes to show that you should never go by first impressions. When I first met her I thought she was a surly, spoilt brat, but she's not at all. Well, at least, not when you consider her upbringing. I mean, she's never had to lift a finger. Can you imagine not being able to boil an egg?'

Caroline nodded, leaning back and stretching her legs, resting them on the coffee table. 'I've always liked her. Before her dad died, she was a normal friendly girl, give or take a few millions. Yes, her lifestyle was a bit unusual, with the limousines, the jewellery and those ridiculously expensive dresses her stepmother insists she wear. But underneath all that, she's a nice girl and she's always been good to me.'

'Well, let's just hope she continues to make progress now, getting herself back to normal.'

'Well, if anybody can get to Olivia, you can, Penny.' Penny raised her eyebrows but Caroline carried on. 'Maybe it's because the two of you look so similar, but I can tell she definitely likes you a lot and listens to you. You must have noticed how she spent most of the evening talking to you, not me.' She took another sip of wine. 'Maybe she feels you're like a real twin sister.'

Penny half-closed her eyes and mulled over what Caroline had said. Her sister Diane was five years older than her and, although they had always been close, their relationship had always been big sister and little sister, with Diane sort of a halfway house between her and her mother. There were things Penny had told Diane that she hadn't felt she could tell her mum, but there had been other things that she had told her best friend at school and not Diane. Now, with Olivia, she was beginning to feel a link that she hadn't had before. Maybe they could become close friends, although as long as what the lawyer had called their *charade* continued, it would have to be a friendship behind closed doors.

That night's Venice dream was a comedy of errors as she and Olivia followed each other around the city, getting lost and terribly confused, and confusing all those who saw them. What she knew she needed was a guide, preferably a tall dark-haired guide with a bushy beard, but there was no sign of anybody like that in this dream.

Chapter 12

Next morning, before she went off to work, Penny checked her emails and found the one she had been praying for. She took a deep breath before opening it, hoping against hope that the response was going to be positive, and she read it with bated breath. The email was signed by a man called Ernesto Lefevre, whose title was Principal and Proprietor of the best-known art gallery in Piccadilly, coincidentally only a few hundred yards along the road from the JC café. She had sent him photos of her work almost two months ago and all she had got back so far had been a one-line acknowledgement of receipt. Now, at last, she received the news she had dying to hear. He expressed *considerable interest* in her work and he invited her to bring a *representative selection* to his gallery for scrutiny at ten o'clock on Tuesday.

She spent most of her free time over the weekend reviewing her paintings, checking that all was in order with them. As always, as soon as she started doing this she found herself having to fight the urge to start changing things. She painted in oils and she knew the paintings had to be dry for Tuesday, so she resisted the temptation to interfere with them too much. After a lot of deliberation, she decided to include the first of her abstract paintings, even though it was very different from the others. Since completing that one, she had started two more abstracts and she found she was developing a definite affinity for the genre. She attached a label to the back of each with the title and then packed them in bubble wrap. When Tuesday came, she called a taxi to take her and her precious cargo to the gallery.

She was met by Ernesto Lefevre himself. She hadn't met him before and she hadn't been too sure what to expect. From his name, she wouldn't have been surprised to find herself confronted by a Salvador Dali look-alike, complete with waxed moustache. Instead, she found Mr Lefevre to be a jovial, rotund gentleman in a silk waistcoat, with the sort of Cockney accent that would have done justice to a barrow boy.

'Penelope, darling, welcome.' He stretched out his arms towards her and greeted her with a hug. Due to the shortness of his arms and the girth of his waist, his fingers barely reached her, but she hugged him warmly in return.

'I'm so very pleased to meet you, Mr Lefevre.'

'Nesto, please. Everybody calls me Nesto.'

'Well, then I'm Penny. I only use Penelope on formal occasions.'

'Excellent. Now, Penny, let me see your work. I absolutely loved the photos you sent me, but there's nothing like the real thing, seeing them in the flesh, so to speak.'

All in all, Penny was with him for well over an hour. Partway through, he telephoned a colleague, a woman called Eleanor, who joined them. Penny recognised her face from a few art gatherings she had attended and was relieved to find her very friendly. They were both very pleasant, and Ernesto managed to put a very nervous Penny at her ease quickly, after which the conversation flowed quite freely. He was very interested to hear of her background, particularly her MA, and the fact that she had taken a year out after university to work alongside a big name artist in Florence. She saw interest in their eyes as she spoke about the developments her work had undergone as a result, but she left out the fact that the old Florentine had spent most of his time trying, in vain, to inveigle her into bed with him.

Hesitantly, after showing them her landscapes, she unwrapped the abstract painting and held her breath. To her amazement, both Ernesto and Eleanor loved it. They loved the shapes, the bright colours, and they particularly loved the inspiration that had made her rub a broad stripe vertically down the middle of the canvas.

'Jackson Pollock meets Kandinsky, darling. I love it.' Ernesto looked and sounded animated. 'What a versatile artist you are. Don't you think so, Eleanor?'

'Terrific. Absolutely terrific.' She looked across at Penny. 'Have you got any more of these?'

Penny shook her head. 'It's the first of a new series of abstracts. I've been working on another couple, but it'll be a while before I've got a worthwhile selection to show you.'

'Well, you just keep working on them, I love this stuff.' Ernesto returned his attention to the painting for some minutes before going back to the others and resuming his study of her work.

A few minutes later, however, the strangest thing happened. Penny was sitting back with her fingers crossed, staring out of the window onto Piccadilly, while

Ernesto and Eleanor discussed her work between themselves. As she gazed blankly at the passers-by, her eyes focused on a man walking past on the crowded pavement in front of the gallery. She only saw him for a few seconds, but she couldn't mistake him. The unruly mass of black hair and the bushy beard were all too conspicuous. He was looking in, but his attention was directed at the paintings in the window as he went by and then disappeared from view. She snapped upright so abruptly she almost sent her cup of herbal tea flying, and received a quizzical look from Ernesto as a result.

'You all right, darling?'

She turned back towards him, shaking her head as much in befuddlement as anything. 'I'm fine, thanks. I just thought I saw someone I recognised.'

Ernesto and Eleanor returned to their deliberations and Penny did her best to pull herself together. She had been sitting down this time and it was just as well. Her knees felt like they belonged to somebody else. Under other circumstances – assuming, of course, that she could haul herself to her feet – she would have run out in pursuit. Given that she was in the middle of an interview that might just result in her making the breakthrough she had so long desired, she knew she didn't dare leave, so she remained seated and tried hard to dismiss the image. It wasn't easy. Had she seen what she thought she had seen? Was that really the same man or was this, once more, just a trick of her imagination?

Finally, she was sent off for half an hour while Nesto and Eleanor discussed her work. The first thing she did when she got out of the door of the gallery was to scour Piccadilly for any sign of the tall man but, needless to say, without success. He was long gone, assuming, of course, that he existed in the first place. Shaking her head ruefully, she went along the road to the JC.

'Morning, Penny. I didn't think you were on till this afternoon.' Freddie the doorman and she were best buddies by now, so she stopped to chat, telling him about her hopes for the gallery. He was impressed. 'That's awesome. You'll still remember me when you're rich and famous now, won't you?'

Penny gave him a grin, assured him that fame, if it ever came, wouldn't change her, and went inside. She sat down and ordered a coffee, her head still spinning, partly as her long-repressed hopes for the future bubbled to the surface and partly as a result of having seen the man her brain had taken to calling *the pirate* once more, if that was indeed what had happened. Could it be that her brain was generating these tantalising images of an ideal man to compensate for the shabby treatment she had received at Rick's hands? Anyway, she told herself, she had Owen now, so why should she need some fantasy man? At least the introspection this caused prevented her from obsessing too much about what Ernesto and Eleanor might be deciding about her paintings. She made her cappuccino last as long as possible, constantly glancing at her watch until the thirty minutes had elapsed.

When she returned to the gallery, her heart fluttering with anxiety, she was greeted by two smiling faces. 'Congratulations, Penny. Eleanor and I are both of the same mind. We love your work. How would you like to have a one woman show here in early January?'

'Really?' Penny could hardly believe her ears. 'An exhibition of just my work?'

Ernesto nodded. 'That's right. Can I take it that you accept?'

Penny had no hesitation at all. 'Of course, thank you, thank you so much.'

'We'll see how your landscapes go this time and if they do well, we might think about another show in the summer, maybe of your abstracts next time?'

Penny could hardly believe her ears. In a daze, she sat down with him and signed all manner of forms, including an agreement about prices and commission. He explained this to her. 'I'd like to set the prices myself. I know what sells and at what price. We'll split the proceeds fifty-fifty.'

Penny had already been warned that galleries took exorbitant commissions for sales of paintings, and fifty-fifty was actually better than she had been expecting. As he then went on to name the sort of figures he thought each painting was worth, her knees turned to jelly once again and she had to sit down. Up until now, she had only ever sold any of her paintings for a few hundred pounds each. He was now talking in thousands.

When Penny emerged, shell-shocked, she made her way back to the café and ordered a glass of prosecco. She sat there, stunned, unsure whether she was going to laugh or cry. As it turned out, she cried. She cried for a full minute, staring into her glass, tears of relief and joy streaming down her cheeks.

'Penny, what's the matter?'

She looked up, wiping her eyes. It was Caroline and she looked concerned. She took a seat opposite Penny who, by this time, had located a tissue and was wiping her eyes. Finally she blew her nose and then looked up.

'It's the gallery. They've said yes to my paintings and they're giving me a solo exhibition.'

'Penny, that's amazing!' Caroline reached over and squeezed her hands. 'I'm so pleased for you. I had a hunch I'd find you here, seeing as the gallery's just down the road.'

Penny ordered more prosecco and they chatted. She didn't mention the man with the black beard, preferring to keep him to herself until she had had time to figure things out, and just talked about her art. Caroline asked her what she was going to do next.

'Keep painting, I suppose. If by any chance I start selling some of my work, I'm going to need more.' Then she remembered the Venice conference, scheduled to take place in only a few weeks' time, and the weekend in Paris coming up before it. She looked up from her glass. 'But I'm in no rush for the moment. I think I'll take it easy until after Christmas.'

'That sounds like a great idea. You deserve a bit of a break after all this hard work.'

'But, first, we need to celebrate. How would you feel about coming out for a few drinks tonight? I'll ring round my friends and see if we can turn it into a real party.'

'Just try and stop me.'

–

In the end, there were over twenty people at the pub that night. Among them were a number of fellow artists, as well as a few old friends, mainly from her time at university, who lived in or near London, Jimmy from the café, Caroline and, of course, Owen. It was a pity she hadn't been able to invite Olivia but, of course, the two of them couldn't be seen together in public. Penny had warned Caroline to dress down for the occasion and she appeared in jeans, blending in well. To Penny's surprise and slight embarrassment, seeing as Owen was there, albeit a little distance away, talking to one of the other artists, they were joined partway through the evening by Sam, her former boyfriend prior to Rick. She had no idea how he had heard the news, but somehow he had got wind of her success. Penny, after her initial surprise at seeing him, almost laughed out loud at the expression on his face when he saw her. She had also chosen just jeans and a plain top, but there was no disguising her new hair, nails and gleaming white teeth. He almost choked on his drink.

'Penny, hi. Congratulations. I heard the news... Wow, you're looking... erm... great. Yes, great.'

Doing her best to conceal her mirth, she gave him a hug. They had had an on and off affair over a couple of years and, although it had gradually fizzled out, she still bumped into him from time to time and still liked him. But she had never seen him as bamboozled as this before, ever. She gave him a smile. 'Hi, Sam. How's it going?'

'I'm fine, thanks. Still selling houses to foreign investors, seeing as they're the only people who can afford to buy in London these days. But, how come you're looking so... gorgeous?'

Penny trotted out the same story of her Auntie Flo's lottery win and he appeared to accept it. He disappeared off to the bar, returning with a bottle of prosecco and a handful of glasses. He filled a large glass and gave it to her, before splashing wine into half a dozen other people's glasses, among them Caroline and Jimmy. These two had struck up an unlikely friendship and were deep in conversation about the latest fashion trends in London this autumn. From what Penny could hear, Jimmy was much more knowledgeable than Caroline. She and Sam chatted for a while and she rather got the impression her makeover had stirred some renewed interest on his part. She was rather flattered, but felt no urge to resurrect the relationship with him, now that she had Owen. Partway through their conversation, Owen himself reappeared and Sam, unusually perceptively, soon took the hint and departed.

Owen took her to one side towards the end of the evening. She gave him a smile and a big kiss. He was a very good-looking man, and she was feeling ever more attracted to him. If they hadn't been in a crowded place with a load of other people around them she would have done more than kiss him. From the look on his face, he felt the same way and, tonight, he had a positive suggestion.

'How would you feel about coming away with me for a weekend?'

'Owen, really!' She feigned outrage. 'Are you proposing we go on a dirty weekend together?'

He grinned and nodded. 'Well, it can be as dirty or clean as you want to make it.'

She kissed him again. 'Very dirty, please. Where were you thinking of going?'

'Anywhere with a nice big bed. How about Oxford?'

'The big bed sounds very good. Wherever you like. And when?'

'How about next weekend?'

'That sounds marvellous.' She reached up and kissed him again, surreptitiously running her fingers across his thigh as she did so. Then she suddenly remembered. 'Oh, bugger it, no.'

He drew back, an expression of surprise on his face. 'No?'

Penny shook her head in frustration. Of course, this coming weekend she had to be in Paris for the conference. The problem she now had was to come up with a convincing story for Owen, to explain why she couldn't join him for their long-awaited dirty weekend without breaking her oath of secrecy. So far she had easily explained away her occasional absences by inventing relatives and friends she had to visit. This time all she could think of was her parents. In fact, when she had phoned them at lunchtime to give them her good news, they had asked her to come down to Devon at the weekend to celebrate, but, of course, she had had to say no. Now, she used them as her alibi, secretly sorry she couldn't be open with Owen about her plans.

'Bugger it, Owen, I'd completely forgotten. I've promised to take the train down to Devon to see my mum and dad this weekend. Could we make it the weekend after?'

'Of course. Pencil me into your busy schedule.'

'It's a date. And, Owen?' She kissed him again. 'I can hardly wait.'

By the end of the evening, Penny was feeling quite weary and fairly drunk. Caroline was little better so they called a cab to get the two of them home. When they got there, Caroline made two mugs of tea and sat down with Penny at the kitchen table.

'Thanks, Caroline.' Penny had almost been nodding off.

'You're welcome. I've been dying for a cup of tea for an hour now. Well, you famous artist, you, how does it feel?'

Penny grinned at her. 'It feels pretty damn good. I'll tell Olivia when I next see her. I'm sure she'll be pleased for me.'

'I know she will. I must say your Owen's a hunk. I rather like the look of him. Why haven't you brought him round here before? Are you afraid I'll steal him off you?'

'I thought I'd wait until you're set up with Nick before I start bringing men home.' She waved away Caroline's protestations. 'To be honest, if I got him anywhere near my bedroom I think I'd probably jump on him and I wouldn't want you to feel embarrassed.'

'It's your room and half the house is yours. You do whatever you like with whoever you like.'

'Well, we've got a weekend away planned for the end of next week so I'll be fine to hold on until then.'

'As you wish. Anyway, I liked your other friends. Jimmy's the chap who almost outed you at the drinks party, isn't he?' Penny nodded. 'He's such a sweetie. He told me he's trying to get into women's fashion.'

Penny nodded again and grinned. 'Designing, rather than wearing, although come to think of it…' She sipped her tea. 'He's lovely, and he's a bright boy. You can talk to him about anything and he's always so supportive. Far more so than any boyfriend I've ever had.'

'Not Owen?'

Penny had to think about that one for a moment. 'I'm sure he'd be good. The problem is that I'm sort of living a double life at the moment because of the whole Olivia thing, and it feels odd having to keep secrets from him. As a result we haven't really talked about personal stuff very much.'

'And that tall boy with the broad shoulders, he was one of your exes?'

'Sam? Yes, we went out for a good long time, but it wasn't going anywhere.' She grinned again. 'He's very nice and he's really rather fun to be with in bed, but it wasn't much more than a physical thing really.'

'So, no *coup de foudre* yet? No love at first sight?'

Penny took a long time making up her mind how to reply. In the end, the alcohol she had consumed gave her the courage to contemplate owning up to Caroline about her pirate man with the dark hair and the beard. 'Um, I don't know. Maybe, possibly.'

'Maybe, possibly? I'm not totally sure that qualifies. Who was the lucky man? Your ex in Australia?'

Penny shook her head quickly. 'No, definitely not Rick.'

'Well who, then? The new man, Owen?'

Penny shook her head again. 'Nope, not him either, although I do find myself liking him more and more. Anyway, to be honest, I'm not so sure that love at first sight's really a thing. How can you see somebody once and fall in love with them without getting to know them? Do you believe in it? Is that how it was for you and Nick?'

She saw Caroline blush. 'I don't know how it was for him, but I'm pretty sure that's how it was for me. You just know, somehow.'

'What, literally the very first time you saw him, you knew he was the one? Just like that?

Caroline nodded more firmly. 'Yes, just like that. And everything I've learnt about him since then has just confirmed my first impression.'

'I envy you that, Caroline. A lot. Like I say, I love Owen to bits, but I can't really say that I had that kind of revelation with him from the first. Who knows? Maybe with me and him it's a slow burn thing and it'll last longer as a result. No, the only definite love at first sight I've had so far in my life was when dad brought a puppy home when I was little. I loved that dog instantly and for all his life.' She closed her eyes and remembered Tom the Labrador who had been her constant companion as she grew up, back home in Devon. 'Pure, simple, uncomplicated love, that's what I got from Tommy.'

'So who were you talking about before, when you said maybe, possibly?'

Penny took a deep breath and launched into an account of her two sightings of the man with the beard. Caroline listened, fascinated, right through to the end.

'And you say you saw him again just this morning?'

Penny nodded. 'Like I say, it was just a fleeting glance and then he was gone. I couldn't get up to chase after him, so I've lost him again – always assuming that I didn't just dream him twice.'

'Have you ever had that sort of experience before? You know, hallucinating?' Penny shook her head. 'Did you have an imaginary friend as a child?'

'No, not at all. I was a perfectly boring little girl and the only hallucinations I've had were at university when some boys got hold of some wacky mushrooms. I can remember hallucinating a bit before I spent the rest of the night in the toilet.'

'Well, in that case, Penny, I think you've got to accept the fact that this chap exists. He's real. You really did see him.'

Penny nodded, her eyes on the remains of the tea in her mug. 'Yes, I'd pretty much come round to that conclusion too.'

'And the effect he had upon you was the same on both occasions?'

'I've never been struck by lightning, but there's no disguising the fact that seeing him had a weird effect on me. I went quite weak at the knees.' She looked up from her mug and across at Caroline. 'Surely that sort of thing only happens in books and movies.'

'Don't you believe it. I reckon you've been stricken.' Caroline was grinning at her, but Penny was far from cheerful.

'All right then, assuming, just for a moment, that you're right and what I suffered was some sort of love at first sight thing, where does that leave me now? If that was the man of my dreams, that means I've loved and lost all in one go. I saw him, I fell in love, and now he's gone. I haven't a clue who he is or where he lives. In all probability I'll never see him again. Are you telling me that I've just fallen in love and straight out of it again in the space of a few seconds?'

'Twice.' Caroline was still grinning.

'Twice…' Penny shook her head in disbelief. 'And that's that. So, I've just got to accept that for the rest of my life I'm going to be looking back on what happened in the space of just a handful of seconds, knowing that this was the love of my life?' She caught Caroline's eye. 'It's going to drive me barmy.'

'I wouldn't worry about it, Penny. You saw him once. You thought that was that. Then, out of the blue this morning, you saw him again. If it can happen twice, it can happen three times. Just you wait. And next time you see him, no matter where you are or what you're doing, grab hold of him and never let him go.'

Penny dreamt about Venice again that night. No doubt fuelled by all the wine she had drunk, it turned into a pretty fiery erotic dream involving a big bed in a huge room overlooking the Grand Canal and a tall man with a mass of dark hair. Frustratingly, when she woke up in the morning, although she could remember a worrying amount of close detail of her enthusiastic partner's anatomy, the one thing that still escaped her was his face.

–

On Wednesday morning Penny went round to the house in Notting Hill for her first cookery session with Olivia. Caroline was already there and she let Penny in. As usual, the Labrador was on hand to give her an enthusiastic welcome.

They walked through to the kitchen together and as they reached the door, Caroline stepped to one side and ushered her in. It was a huge room, high-ceilinged like the rest of the house, and with a magnificent central island, capped with a marble slab. The hob, ovens and sink were all of the highest quality. Standing by the sink, wearing a freshly-ironed or quite probably brand new apron was a slightly nervous looking Olivia.

'Hi, Penny. We've bought all the ingredients you asked for.'

'We?' Penny was surprised, but pleasantly so.

Olivia nodded, an expression of pride on her face. 'I went with Janice yesterday. By the way, she's got the day off today, so we can use anything we want in the kitchen. Anyway, we went to a supermarket.' From her tone it was clear that supermarkets weren't normally on her list of shopping venues. 'I'd forgotten how much stuff they've got in there.' There was awe in her voice.

Penny gave her a smile and checked the ingredients on the worktop. 'Now, then, let's get cooking. Today, we're going to prepare something that everybody likes. Lasagne's an easy dish, but it's a full meal. Serve it just on its own and that's fine. If you like, you can prepare a salad as a starter, but that's optional.' She gave Olivia a grin. 'And men all love lasagne. Remember what I said about the way to a man's heart being through his stomach.' She saw Olivia smile back at her and added wickedly, remembering some of the more memorable moments from last night's dream. 'Although the trouser route is also very effective.'

As they prepared the meal, they chatted, Olivia doing all the hands-on work while Penny stood by and advised, smiling as she saw the dog's eyes trained unblinkingly on what was happening on the worktop. Since their dinner together, the atmosphere was much more natural and relaxed between the three of them. Apart from food, they talked about a lot of things, from the Foundation to men. After a while, Olivia asked Penny about her relationship status.

'So, have you got a boyfriend, Penny? I'm sure you must have. You're very pretty.' No sooner had she said it than she blushed. 'I'm so sorry, I shouldn't have said that. Seeing as we're supposed to look alike, it sounds as if I'm paying myself compliments.'

Caroline stepped in to supply a neutral opinion. 'You *are* both very pretty. It's true. And I know the answer to this one; it's yes. His name's Owen, and he's a hunk, and I met him last night for the first time. Penny's been too shy to bring him home in case she were to lose control and ravish the poor boy while I struggle to avert my eyes.'

'But I will be bringing him home sometime soon, I promise, after our weekend in Oxford.' Penny surveyed Olivia's handiwork. It looked and smelt good. She watched carefully as Olivia began the process of filling the dish with alternating layers of pasta and meat. 'And what about you, Olivia? No men on the horizon?'

Olivia was concentrating hard, clearly anxious to get everything right. She didn't look up. 'I went out with a few boys when I was at university, but nothing terribly serious.'

'And none since then?'

There was a pause before Olivia replied. 'I don't know. Maybe, possibly.' Penny recognised the language. It sounded very familiar, but she decided not to pry.

'Sounds a bit like me. Still, there's time.'

Olivia nodded. 'I should hope so. We're the same age, aren't we? I'm twenty-five. I'll be twenty-six in January.'

'That makes you six months younger than me. Either way, you've still got time, hasn't she, Caroline?'

'Bags of it.'

'It would've been nice to invite you along to my little party last night; it's annoying that we can't be in the same place at the same time. There were a few quite good-looking boys there as well. Never mind, as soon as you're back on the job, I'll change my hairstyle and we can start going out together.' As she spoke, Penny realised she really rather liked her new hairstyle and would be reluctant to give it up.

'I'd like that.' Olivia glanced up with a smile. 'I used to go to all the student parties when I was at uni.' She glanced across at Caroline. 'And what about you and men, Caroline? You never talk about them. Have you got a special somebody in your life?' Caroline blushed red.

'Erm, I'm not sure. Maybe, possibly.'

Penny smiled. She appeared to have started a linguistic trend. Seeing Caroline's embarrassment, she was quick to step in and help her out. 'Caroline's being very coy about this one. She says she'll tell us all about him when it happens.'

Olivia had also noticed Caroline's blushes and was kind enough not to insist. 'How exciting! I'll look forward to hearing all about him in due course. Now, Penny, what do I do? The dish is full.'

'Turn the oven on, we'll have to wait for it to warm up, and then you just bung it in. Nothing easier. And, while we're waiting, why don't I make tea for us all?'

The lasagne turned out to be a great success and Olivia insisted that they sit down and eat some, even though it was still only eleven o'clock when it came out of the oven. They all agreed that it was excellent and Olivia was clearly delighted. Everyone having decided it was too early for wine, she toasted Penny with tea.

'Thank you so much, Penny. How come you're so good at making lasagne? Have you been to Italy?'

'Yes, quite a few times. I spent a year living and working in Florence and that's where I learnt quite a bit about Italian cooking. The lady I stayed with was a super cook and she gave me all sorts of tips.'

'So, do you speak Italian?'

Penny nodded. 'Pretty well now. I did A-level Italian at school and I went over there for three months as an au pair before I went to university. I know Tuscany best, like I say. I've spent quite a lot of time in Florence. When I left there, I had a couple of weeks in Rome and then a week in Sicily.' She looked across and explained. 'I hooked up with an amazingly handsome Sicilian boy when I was in Florence and he took me home with him.' She smiled. 'I was supposed to stay there a month or two, but I legged it after a week. It turned out he was related to the whole town and everybody knew everything about everybody. All a bit too oppressive, somehow. There's just Venice on my bucket list still to go.'

'Well, at least you can remedy that very soon when you go to the big conference over there.'

Penny grinned at her. 'I can't wait.'

'But first there's Paris to come.' Caroline's expression showed how much she was looking forward to the weekend. Penny, on the other hand, had mixed feelings. Somehow, attractive as a couple of days in the city of light had originally sounded, she couldn't shake the feeling that a big bed in Oxford would have been even better.

Chapter 13

'So how was Paris?' Olivia opened the door to Penny, but made sure she stayed out of sight of anybody on the road outside. Gilbert came charging up, delighted to see her, jumping up on his hind legs, his whole rear half wagging along with his tail.

'It was lovely.' Penny had thoroughly enjoyed the weekend in Paris after all, in spite of her reservations. She grabbed the big dog's paws and gently returned him to the ground, stooping to give him a stroke.

'And the conference?' Olivia waited for her to straighten up again and then led her through to the kitchen.

'Fascinating. There were delegates from all over Europe and it was so interesting to hear the different problems that exist from country to country.' Penny sniffed the air. 'What's that I can smell, Olivia?'

Olivia gave her a slightly nervous smile. 'I bought myself a cookery book and I've been experimenting with biscuits. I remember helping our old cook to make biscuits when I was little, so I thought I'd give them a go. Would you like to taste one?'

'I most certainly would.' Penny was very impressed. And when she tried a biscuit, she was even more impressed. Not only were the ginger biscuits really rather tasty, it was Olivia herself who then made tea for the two of them. She really was becoming quite domesticated. And more cheerful. Penny thought she should point that out to her. 'It's really good to see you looking and sounding happier these days, Olivia. Are you beginning to feel a bit more optimistic about life?'

Olivia set the mugs of tea down on the worktop and perched on a stool opposite Penny, the dog, as usual, positioned between the two of them, his eyes on the biscuits. She nodded her head. 'Yes, definitely. I saw the doctor on Thursday and we've agreed that I stop taking the pills I've been on. So I haven't had an antidepressant for four whole days now and I certainly don't feel any worse; probably better if anything.'

'That's terrific.'

'By the way, Penny, there's something for you here.' Olivia reached for a little package, tied with a ribbon, and handed it to Penny. 'I was really pleased to hear about you getting your big break in the art world. This is just a little something to mark the occasion.' Hesitantly, Penny took it from her and opened it. Inside was a velvet box and inside that, a thin gold chain. Hanging from the chain was a finely sculpted tiny artist's palette, also in gold. It was simple, elegant and beautiful. Penny caught sight of the jewellers' name inside the lid and almost dropped the box.

'There was no need for this, Olivia, really. How terribly sweet of you. It's gorgeous, really gorgeous.' She took it out of the box. 'Is it all right if I put it on?'

'Here, turn round, I'll do it for you.' Olivia clipped the chain around Penny's neck and nodded approvingly.

'The man wanted me to buy white gold, but I told him with our hair colour, it had to be real gold.'

Penny gave her a hug. 'Thank you so much. I feel quite overcome. But you shouldn't have.'

'It's not just to celebrate your success, I wanted it to be a sign of friendship too. I'm very pleased to have met you, Penny, and you've helped me more than you know.'

They sat and chatted as they drank their tea before Penny looked up. 'So, have you worked out what we're going to be cooking today?'

'There's pastry and eggs and asparagus. Could it be a quiche, maybe?'

'Dead right.'

They spent a pleasant morning preparing the food, chatting all the time. Caroline, after a tiring weekend in Paris, had taken the day off and Olivia had told the housekeeper to take the day off again, so they had the house to themselves. Penny told Olivia lots about her childhood and background and learnt a lot about her in return. The quiche they prepared was a great success and, as they tasted it, Penny pointed out another advantage of the dish. 'And the great thing about a quiche is that you can eat it hot or cold, so when some handsome man comes knocking at your door, you'll have something to give him.' She grinned. 'And somehow I don't think it'll be long before a handsome man appears on your doorstep.'

Olivia blushed. 'I think I might have found him already.'

'Is this the one you meant when we were talking about love at first sight?'

Olivia nodded, hesitated and then clearly decided she wanted to tell Penny all about him. Penny listened, enthralled, as Olivia told her story. 'I went out with a few different boys when I was at university, but since then, there's only been one I really liked. I knew as soon as I met him that he was something special. The trouble was, I only just started going out with him a matter of days before my father died. I'm afraid, since my dad's death, we haven't been in contact very much.' She looked across at Penny. 'Well, to be totally honest, he's been sending me loads of emails, but I haven't felt up to going out anywhere with him.'

'And you knew he was the one as soon as you first saw him?' Penny was getting more and more interested in this phenomenon. So yet another person was telling her it existed. If it really was a thing, had it happened to her with the mysterious pirate man?

Olivia nodded again. 'I can tell you where it was, what he was wearing, what I was wearing and even the music playing at that moment.' She looked across at Penny with a smile. 'It was at a friend's birthday party and the theme was the 1960s. I was wearing a really short red mini skirt and the music playing was *When a Man Loves a Woman.*'

'Oh, I love that one. I should know who sang it, but I can't remember.'

Olivia shook her head. 'I've forgotten too. I did know. Anyway, like I say, apart from that, I can remember everything.'

Penny looked across at her. There hadn't been any music playing on either of the two occasions when she had seen her mystery man, but she knew she could describe him and his clothes right down to the smallest detail. So, she reflected, it was looking more and more likely that she, too, had fallen foul of this love at first sight phenomenon. But a fat lot of good it was going to do her, seeing as she knew nothing about him, and the chances of seeing him again in a city of eight million people were slim in the extreme. Anyway, she told herself firmly, she had Owen now and their weekend in Oxford was only a few days away now. She felt a wave of excitement.

'Percy Sledge!'

Olivia's voice interrupted her train of thought. For a moment she didn't follow.

'Percy who?'

'Percy Sledge. He sang *When a Man Loves a Woman*. I knew I knew it.' Olivia sounded pleased. Penny put all her internal considerations on the back burner for now and gave Olivia an encouraging smile.

'I'm not sure I'd have known that. Well, now that you're getting better, that's something to look forward to.'

Olivia smiled and changed the subject. 'So, Penny. And what about you? Have you always wanted to be an artist?'

Penny nodded. 'I've always liked drawing and painting, and I've never been much good at anything else.' She picked up a last bit of pastry from her plate and nibbled it, doing her best to avoid making eye contact with Gilbert, who was giving her his baleful *they don't feed me* expression. 'And I don't regret it one bit. I love what I do, even if I've yet to make any serious money out of it.' She relented and gave the final piece of pastry to the dog; it disappeared instantly and without a trace.

'Have you sold many of your paintings?'

'A few. There's a local gallery down in Devon where they sell one or two every now and then, but there's no way I can live on what I get from my painting. At least not yet. If, and it's a big if, this exhibition in Piccadilly results in sales, then maybe I'll be on the right track.'

'Well, if you invite me round to your house again, you must show me your work. I'd love to see what you do. By the way, did I hear you say that your special subject at university was Renaissance art?' Penny nodded. 'Well, I had an idea the other day. I don't know if it could appeal to you, but I thought it might.' Penny looked up with interest. 'Would you be interested in having access to our Bosch triptych? Maybe you could write a paper on it or something. The only thing I'd ask is that you don't reveal where it's hanging. The insurance company told Daddy it should be kept in a bank vault, but he loved it so much, he wanted it kept on display.'

Penny's eyes opened wide. 'Interested? Olivia, that would be awesome. And of course I won't mention where it is.' She thought quickly. 'I could do a study of it, take a few photos, and see if I could get a paper published in one of the journals. That would look really good on my CV.' She looked across and caught Olivia's eye. 'Let's face it, if the January exhibition bombs and I don't start selling my paintings soon, I'm going to have to find a real job. I don't think I could stick the prospect of spending the next forty years of my life waiting at table. So the more I can do to make me more employable in the art world, the better. I don't know how to thank you.'

'You're very welcome, Penny. Since I've got to know you, you've helped me a lot. I feel loads better these days and I know a lot of it's down to you.'

'That's really good to hear, but you're the one who's doing it. To be honest, I don't think you'll need me to take your place at conferences and meetings for much longer. You'll do just fine. You know you said you wanted me to hang on for another few weeks? Well, of course I will and you know how keen I am to go to Venice. But, after that, I reckon you'll be well able to step up to the plate.'

Olivia finished her slice of quiche and took a mouthful of tea. 'I think you're right. I really believe I'll be up for it. To be honest, if something happened to you now, I reckon I'd just about be able to handle all the people and the crowds once more. I'd be scared stiff, but I think I could do it.'

'That's very good news.' Penny really was pleased for her. This job had been a lot of fun and had pretty much saved her from financial disaster, but she realised it couldn't go on forever. The conference in Venice was less than two weeks away now and the exhibition in Piccadilly would be at the end of January. With the money she was making from replacing Olivia, she knew she had enough to pay the rent at Caroline's house and get by until February or March, by which time she would have a good idea as to whether she stood a chance of making it as a professional artist. If not, she would need to start looking round seriously for a better job than wait-ressing, and the chance to get her hands on the Bosch was a marvellous opportunity to make her a more marketable proposition in the art world. She looked across at Olivia and smiled. 'I'll tell you something, though. I enjoy spending time with you.'

'Me, too, and I hope we can stay friends, Penny.'

'Of course we'll stay friends. I'd like that. A lot. And I'm pretty sure Gilbert would agree.' She glanced down at the dog at their feet and then looked up again, as did Gilbert, both of them sniffing the air. 'There's just one thing, Olivia. After you cut the quiche, what did you do with it?'

Olivia looked surprised. 'I put it back in the oven to keep it warm.'

'I rather thought that was what you'd done.' Penny was grinning now. 'Tell me, do you normally have smoke coming out of the oven?' She saw Olivia follow the direction of her eyes and jump to her feet.

'Oh, Lord. I didn't turn it off, did I?'

Together they went over to the oven. Olivia turned it off and pulled the door open. A billowing cloud of smoke came wafting out and, as it did so, all the smoke alarms in the kitchen started sounding. To make matters worse, the dog decided he should join in and started barking furiously. By the time they had finally managed to climb up on chairs and poke the alarms with a mop handle to silence them, and then calm Gilbert down, both girls were half deaf. Penny glanced across at the carbonised remains of the quiche and smiled. She looked back at Olivia.

'You don't often see that on the cookery programmes.'

Chapter 14

Penny had tried to call Owen a few time since coming back from her weekend in Paris, but, unusually, his phone had been off, or maybe broken. She tried again before going to bed that night, but there still wasn't an answer. She began to feel worried that something might have happened to him. When she got home the next evening she had a cup of tea with Caroline and then went up to her room and tried phoning him again. She wanted to tell him she was looking forward more and more to the weekend ahead, but she was beginning to fear that something was wrong. As the phone rang and rang yet again without answer, it occurred to her that although she knew roughly where he lived in south London, she didn't know his exact address. If she continued to be unable to get through to him, her only other course of action would be to go to the art shop where they knew him pretty well; either that or try ringing round a few other artist friends. After a while the call went to voicemail so she just left the same message she had left previously. 'Hi, Owen. It's me. Is everything all right? Give me a call.'

About ten minutes later, she got an incoming call. She had a momentary feeling of disappointment as she saw that it wasn't Owen. Instead it was Olivia and she sounded cheerful.

'Hi, Penny, I was wondering. Would you have time to come shopping with me one of these days? Your clothes look so much more practical and comfortable than mine and I'd really like it if you could take me to the places you normally go.'

'Certainly, any time, but you do realise my stuff's a considerable step down from your usual clothes, don't you? In fact, I've just bought a couple of T-shirts from that very same supermarket where you bought the ingredients for the quiche. Are you sure you want to slum it?'

'That stuff looks great on you. Why not on me? We *are* almost the same person after all.'

'Okay, I'd love to go shopping with you.' Then Penny had a thought. 'But, hang on a minute. We can't be seen out together, can we?'

Olivia laughed. 'I think I've come up with the solution to that one.'

No sooner had the call ended when Penny's phone started ringing again. To her delight and relief, she saw that, finally, it was Owen on the line. Her delight changed to apprehension when she heard his tone.

'Hi, Penny. Look, I need to see you. We have to talk. Something's happened.'

'What's happened, Owen?' Penny was suddenly anything but delighted. 'Are you all right? Has there been an accident?'

'No, nothing like that. I've just got to see you. Could I come up to your place or could you manage to meet me somewhere central?'

Penny didn't like the sound of what he might have to say, so, rather than invite him round and have to explain things to Caroline at this stage, she arranged to meet him in a pub near Kings Cross station an hour later. She showered, changed, and went straight out, just telling Caroline she was going to meet Owen. Caroline gave her a cheery wave, but Penny felt anything but cheery as she left the house. There had been something in Owen's voice that worried her greatly. The eager, loving tone was sorely missing and she began to get a cold feeling in the pit of her stomach. Could it be that this relationship, that had been starting to feel so good and so right, might not be working out so well after all?

The place where they arranged to meet was a bar on the ground floor of a hotel. It was fairly clinical and characterless, but at least it was nearly empty and very quiet. She found Owen sitting at a table in the far corner, an untouched pint of bitter and a glass of prosecco in front of him. He waved her into a seat without kissing or even touching her. She shrugged off her coat and sat down, the sense of foreboding now stronger than ever. She glanced down at the Prosecco. 'For me?' He nodded so she picked it up and took a big mouthful. 'So what's this all about, Owen?'

He stared down at his beer, making no attempt to drink any of it. He was still as handsome as ever and now, with an expression of sorrow and something like remorse on his face, she felt she wanted to reach over and cuddle him. But she didn't. She just sat there, in that sanitised, sterile room, waiting for him to say what he had to say. He took so long in formulating a reply that she was on the point of prompting him when he finally found his voice.

'Penny, look, I don't know how to say this and I'm very, very sorry, but I don't think we can go out together any more.'

Penny really didn't know what to say for a moment. She sat there, stunned for a while, before making an attempt. 'But I only saw you a few days ago and we arranged to go away together next weekend. And now you tell me you're breaking up with me?' Her voice sounded as puzzled as she felt. She drank a bit more prosecco and waited for him to explain.

'Penny, it's like this. You know I told you I'd been in a long relationship that fell apart about six months ago?' Penny nodded mechanically. 'Well, I saw her again. I was invited for a curry with a group of friends on Saturday night and she was there.' Penny sat silently waiting for him to continue, the cold feeling in her stomach intensifying as he went on. 'I hadn't seen her since the break-up. She went off to Australia and she's been there all summer.' Penny shook her head as this made her think of Rick; Rick, the man who had dumped her in favour of another woman. And now this... She stifled a snort as she reflected that, once again, it appeared that the continent of Australia was conspiring against her. She did her best to concentrate as Owen went on. 'Her name's Sally and as soon as I saw her again I knew I was still in love with her. And she's told me she's still in love with me. It's as simple as that.' He finally summoned up the courage to raise his eyes and meet Penny's stare. 'I've been with her every day since then. I'm terribly, terribly sorry.'

Now it was Penny's turn to drop her eyes to the table. Her head was spinning and it had nothing to do with the prosecco. Of all the things she had been expecting him to say, this wasn't one of them. How could he just flit from what had appeared to be deep attraction for her to what he described as love for another woman in the space of a few days, hours even? She struggled to find adequate words.

'So you're telling me you're in love with this girl and that's that as far as we're concerned?' She watched the bubbles in her glass appear, rush to the surface and disappear into thin air. Just like her hopes for their relationship, she thought bitterly.

'I'm afraid I am. Look, Penny, I know it makes me sound like a terrible person, but I really thought it was all over between me and her. Honestly. It all came as just as much of a surprise to me, believe me.' Penny steeled herself to look up again. His beer was still untouched and he looked as bewildered as she felt as he carried on. 'I like you very much and I really thought we'd got something, a real spark between us. Everything was going so well and I really thought it was all over between me and Sally. And now this... You've got to believe me.'

'So, that's it. It's all over between us?'

He paused and then answered in a low voice. 'Yes, Penny, and I'm really, really sorry.' He looked it, but that didn't help. Penny picked up her glass and drained the last of the wine before standing up and reaching for her coat. She took a deep breath, determined not to show weakness.

'Well, thanks for letting me know, and I wish you all the best. And thanks for the wine. Goodbye Owen.'

'Goodbye, Penny.'

That night, she didn't dream of Venice. In fact, as far as she could recall in the cold light of dawn next morning, she hadn't dreamt about anything at all. Maybe it was because she hadn't managed to go to sleep.

Chapter 15

The shopping expedition took place just before the Venice conference. It made a welcome break for Penny in what had turned out to be a dismal few days since bidding farewell to Owen. She had done a lot of thinking in the immediate aftermath of his announcement, as she tried to make sense of what had happened. The euphoria of the news from the Piccadilly gallery had evaporated in the wake of his revelation. She had felt herself strongly attracted to him and had really got the impression he felt the same way about her, yet he had dumped her and gone back to his old girlfriend. Was it her fault? Caroline had been very supportive, but it took an hour with Jimmy, drinking cocktails in a very gay bar, coincidentally less than a hundred yards from the pub where she and Owen had last met, to provide her with some closure. Jimmy, as ever, had been upbeat.

'Well, it's a bloody sight better to find out now, rather than later on, once you've surrendered your honour to him.'

His choice of language brought a reluctant smile to her lips. 'You've been reading too many romance novels, Jimmy. Nobody surrenders their honour any more. Anyway, I'd rather not have found out at all. I mean, I'd rather it hadn't happened.'

'What hadn't happened?'

'Him getting back together with this bloody Sally woman, of course.'

'But it wasn't his fault, sweetheart. You can't fight love, you know. Remember, love is a many splendored thing, after all.'

She was still thinking about Owen days later as she waited for the shopping trip to start. In fact, she had only been waiting near Marble Arch for a few minutes when a Bentley purred to a stop right in front of her. As Penny looked on, an elegant woman with a mass of stunning long blonde hair stepped out, her face hidden under heavy dark glasses. She walked up to a surprised Penny and gave her a conspiratorial grin. 'Hi, Penny. Fancy a bit of shopping?'

'Olivia?' It was a great disguise and the hair looked totally convincing. She mentioned this to Olivia and got a grin in return.

'I should think so, too. It's real hair, just not mine.'

Penny was reminded of how close she had got to selling her own hair a few months earlier. She glanced over at the Bentley. 'What about the car?'

'I've told Arthur I'll text him when we've finished. Now, where's our first stop?'

They spent most of the morning working their way along Oxford Street, calling into shop after shop, some expensive, but most much closer to Penny's more afford-able end of the spectrum. By the time they stopped for a late morning cup of coffee, they had accumulated a hefty pile of bags. Olivia had insisted on paying for almost everything, and in most cases had bought two of each item, one for her and one for Penny. Finally they both slumped into comfortable seats in the café and relaxed after their efforts. They ordered a cappuccino each and Penny found it very pleasant to be on the receiving end of waitress service for a change. She looked round critically. It was much, much more salubrious than the Apocalypse, but it wasn't a patch on the JC.

Across the table from her, Olivia was struggling a little, clearly unused to having such long hair, and it wasn't long before disaster struck. As she leant forward to take a mouthful of coffee, her eyesight hampered by the dark glasses, a long lock of the thick, heavy hair slipped into the cup. Penny found herself giggling furiously as Olivia did her best to dry the coffee-stained hair with a handful of paper napkins. By the time she had removed the worst of it, Olivia was close to hysterics herself.

'If I laugh any harder, I'm going to spill this coffee all down myself.'

It was a minute or so before Penny was able to talk again. She looked across at Olivia. 'So, it's Venice on Sunday.'

'Are you looking forward to it?'

'You bet. I'm really, really looking forward to it. I could do with a break after the whole Owen business.'

'Oh, you poor thing.' Olivia had been one of the first people to whom Penny had turned for support the day after her conversation with Owen, and this had made her realise just how their friendship was developing. Olivia had been very sympathetic then. Penny shook her head as she once more thought of what might have been with Owen, the laughter now long gone. She took a deep breath and did her best to change to a happier subject.

'So, what about you and that boy you were telling me about?'

Olivia took a cautious mouthful of coffee, making sure her hair was well out of the way this time. 'I've got some news. I plucked up the courage to send my boy a long, newsy email at the weekend. I got a reply last night.' She looked across at Penny, her eyes shining. 'He still feels the same way.'

'So meet him.'

'I plan to. He's away somewhere until just before Christmas, but we've arranged to go out for dinner on the 23rd.' She was looking very pleased with herself, as she had every right to be. 'He can be my Christmas present.'

'Fantastic, Olivia, I'm so pleased for you. So, tell me more. What's he like?'

'His name's Jon, short for Jonathan, and I met him at that party last March.' She looked across at Penny. 'He's got red hair and he looks a bit like Prince Harry. Anyway, as soon as I saw him, I just knew. We only went out a few times and then he had to go abroad, because he's in the army. And then it was only a few days later that Daddy had his heart attack and, of course, after that, I dropped out of any social events.' She paused to take another sip of coffee. 'As you know, I sort of fell apart for a good long while.' She managed a little smile. 'Until you came along and helped me, Penny.'

Penny was really happy to see Olivia looking so much more cheerful and to hear that she had somebody in her life. After the depression caused by her father's death, she badly needed it. 'Well, you're all right again now, Olivia. Look at you. We've just spent the morning in amongst thousands of Christmas shoppers and you've been fine. I reckon you're mended.'

'I think I am, or at least well on the road to recovery.' She caught Penny's eye. 'So, what about you? How're you doing now? Have you got over the shock of Owen's announcement?' She sounded concerned.

'I've pretty much come to terms with it. When all's said and done, I'd only been out with him a few times and we hadn't really got serious, so I suppose it's just water under the bridge. Freezing cold, smelly bloody water, but just water.'

'I'm so sorry, Penny. But Venice'll cheer you up. You'll see.'

Penny nodded, doing her best to think happy thoughts. 'Caroline's been telling me about the fantastic hotel where we're going to be staying, and even the place where the conference is taking place. Apparently the conference centre's on an island. That's amazing.'

'You haven't been to Venice before, have you?' Penny shook her head. 'You're going to love it. The hotel's one of my favourites in the whole world. And specially for somebody interested in art, Venice is a wonderful place to visit.'

'I'm sure it is. By the way, thanks again for letting me take a good close look at the Bosch triptych. I've written a paper and I showed it to my supervisor from when I was doing my MA. She's very excited about it and she's promised to send it in to one of the good journals. If I can get that published, it'll help my cause no end if I have to find myself a proper job. As for Venice, I've been making a list of all the churches, galleries and museums with artworks I'd really like to see when I'm there. For a start, there are so many amazing paintings at the Galleria dell'Accademia. I can't wait.'

'Excellent. Venice really is an amazing place. I used to go every year with my father and I know it well now. By the way, I've been thinking about going to an art gallery here in London myself.'

'Exciting. Who with?'

'Just on my own. Not even with Gilbert.'

'Great.' Penny was really delighted. This was very good news. Apart from walking the dog and a few brief trips to the supermarket, this would probably be Olivia's first real outing unaccompanied for months and months. 'So what's the exhibition?'

'I thought I'd go to the Botticelli exhibition you were telling me about. It's still on at the National Gallery, isn't it?'

'That's right. And you'll love it. It's up on the first floor. Check out the Hieronymus Bosch paintings in the room next door as well. They're not as good as yours, but still quite amazing.'

'I'll make sure I do. I'll tell you all about it next time we talk. Anyway, while you're in Venice, you really have to visit the islands, and you should take the boat across to the little island of Burano and maybe the one next to it, Torcello. They're delightful.'

'Well, just think, next time there's an event over there, you know you'll be able to go to it yourself.'

'I really think you're right. Now promise me you'll call me every day from Venice to tell me what's been going on.'

Penny nodded, delighted to hear Olivia sounding so enthused. Yes, she was well on the road to recovery all right. 'It's a promise. And enjoy Botticelli.'

Shortly after lunch, as Penny was upstairs in her room, making a start at packing in readiness for Venice, her phone rang. She didn't recognise the number, but she swiped the green button anyway.

'Hello.'

'Is that Penny?' The voice sounded very familiar, but she couldn't put her finger on it immediately.

'Yes, who's that?'

'Angela Brookes-Webster.'

Penny almost dropped the handset and her heart sank. 'Oh, hello. I thought you were on holiday.' She did her best to sound pleased to hear from Olivia's stepmum.

'I'm off in a couple of days' time, but I wanted to talk to you before I go. Could you spare me a few minutes this afternoon or this evening?'

Penny was bewildered. It was unmistakably Olivia's stepmother, but her tone was polite, almost friendly. It was unusual, unexpected and very disconcerting. Penny glanced at her watch. It was almost half past two and she was working at the JC later on. 'Um, I'm afraid I'm working at the café from four to ten.' Maybe, she thought to herself, this might prevent her having to face a woman she cordially detested. Alas, it didn't work.

'That's the café in Piccadilly?'

'That's right. The JC café.'

'Well, how would it be if I get Arthur to bring me round to your house in half an hour or so, if you wouldn't mind? We could have a little chat and then he can give you a lift to work so you're there in time for four. Would that be all right?' She sounded positively charming and Penny had a sudden thought. Maybe this affability was to soften the blow when she broke the news that Penny was fired. Maybe, Penny thought with dismay, she wouldn't be going to Venice after all. She replied automatically, a feeling of dread descending upon her. It was like the call from Owen all over again. Her voice almost broke with emotion as she replied.

'Erm, yes, that's fine. Do you know where I live?'

'Olivia tells me you're sharing with Caroline. That's right, isn't it?'

Penny confirmed that this was the case and Mrs B-W rang off, leaving Penny staring blindly down at the open suitcase, her hopes crumbling beneath her. She stood there blankly for quite a while before realising that in little more than twenty minutes, Mrs B-W would be here. She turned and ran downstairs.

Caroline was at work and the lounge was fairly tidy. Penny grabbed the vacuum cleaner and ran it round the room, then straightened a few cushions and removed the bits and pieces left on the coffee table. She had a moment of panic when she wondered if there was milk and sugar in the house. She knew there was tea. She ran through to the kitchen and checked, discovering with relief that all was well. She located the nicest mugs and, although they had just come out of the dishwasher, she washed them again, all the while getting more and more worked up at thought of the interview coming up. What, she kept asking herself, had she done to annoy Mrs B-W? She had hardly seen her for weeks now.

She was still turning this over in her head when the front doorbell rang. She was so tense by this time, she almost dropped the mugs. Hastily setting them on a tray, she wiped her hands and headed out to face the music.

'Hello, Mrs Brookes-Webster. Would you like to come in?'

Unusually, Mrs B-W was smiling. Somehow, this was even more sinister than her usual look of barely-concealed animosity. To Penny's surprise, Mrs B-W hesitated politely.

'If you're sure, Penny. It occurred to me in the car that I should have offered to take you out somewhere rather than just descending upon you like this. Would you like to go somewhere for tea?'

'Um, no, it's fine, really.' If she was going to get fired, Penny knew she would prefer it not to be in a public place, just in case she burst into tears or, more probably, walloped Mrs B-W across the face. 'Come in, please.' She ushered Mrs B-W into the lounge and showed her to a seat, then she ran out to the kitchen and put the kettle on, before rushing back in again, feeling decidedly flustered. She sat down opposite Mrs B-W and made an attempt at a smile. Mrs B-W, on the other hand, managed a real smile.

'Penny, I've come to say thank you.'

Penny felt her jaw drop. 'Thank me?'

Olivia's stepmother was still smiling. 'That's right, for helping to lift a great weight from my mind.' Seeing Penny's bafflement, she explained. 'You know I'm not Olivia's real mother, don't you? Even so, we're very close and I've been worried sick about her ever since my husband died. It's only now, months later, that she's coming out of the deep depression into which she'd descended, and a lot of the credit for that is down to you, Penny.'

Mrs B-W wasn't the only one to have had a great weight lifted from her mind. Penny's mood of despondency disappeared like a flash and her heart sang at the knowledge that it definitely looked as though she wasn't about to be sacked. So she would, after all, be going to Venice! Feeling like Cinderella with her foot sitting snugly in the glass slipper, she produced a broad smile as she replied. 'I'm really pleased if I've been able to help in any way. I like Olivia a lot and I'm as delighted as you are to see her coming out of her shell once more.' She caught Mrs B-W's eye. 'I went shopping with her this morning and we were even talking about boys. And, more importantly, she reckons she's just about ready to take over from me again, going out, meeting people.'

'That's excellent news.' Mrs B-W's expression became more serious. 'You can't imagine just how good that makes me feel. I'm no fool, Penny, and I know I've been very grumpy of late. The fact is that last Easter I lost my husband and my daughter in one go. He died and she turned in on herself and I've been left all alone, trying to keep going, but it's been terribly hard. I knew next to nothing about my husband's Foundation and yet I found myself thrown into the thick of it and I've been terrified people would realise just how little I know. I suppose I've been putting up barriers to hide my insecurity. I've been feeling very vulnerable and so awfully lonely.' Penny could hear the catch in her voice and see the tears in the corners of her eyes. A wave of sympathy swept over her, and she jumped to her feet.

'What you need is a nice cup of tea. Just give me a moment.' She disappeared out to the kitchen and by the time she returned with the tea, Olivia's stepmum had had time to collect herself once more.

'Milk and sugar?'

'Just milk please, Penny.' Mrs B-W managed a weak smile. 'I'm sorry for burdening you with my troubles.'

'Not in the slightest. We all need to talk about stuff. You can't just keep things bottled up. I'm just so pleased that Olivia's doing so much better and, if you don't mind me saying so, I've never seen you so bright and happy. Here's hoping you both get back to living and enjoying life again.'

They spent almost half an hour chatting and Penny, once she had managed to dismiss her initial astonishment that this version of Olivia's stepmother was a really nice person, actually enjoyed the experience. To her surprise, partway through the afternoon, Mrs B-W made an unexpected request.

'Olivia's been telling me about your upcoming exhibition. I don't suppose I could see any of your work, could I?'

Penny led her out to the studio in the garden. 'Some of the canvases are already at the gallery in Piccadilly, but I can show you the others if you like.' She pulled out the remainder of her work and propped the paintings against the wall. Mrs B-W made her way around the room, inspecting each of them and making some very complimentary remarks, until she reached Penny's first abstract work, the one she had landed on with her naked body. Mrs B-W stopped dead and stared at it for a good long while, before turning to Penny, an expression of admiration on her face.

'This is magnificent. I just love it.' She caught Penny's eye. 'I don't suppose you'd be prepared to sell it, would you?'

'There's no need for that, really. If all goes well, the gallery will manage to sell some of my work and then my career will hopefully take off.' She was deeply touched at Mrs B-W's generosity, but she didn't want her to buy a painting just because she was trying to be make up for her earlier frostiness.

'Of course they will. What sort of prices are they going to be asking?'

Penny shook her head, still amazed and appalled at the valuation Ernesto had put on her work. 'A small fortune. I think the smaller ones are going to be about fifteen hundred pounds and he's even talking about three to four thousand for the bigger ones.'

'And what size is this?' Mrs B-W's eyes were still locked on the abstract canvas.

'One of the larger canvasses, I suppose.'

'So how about I write you a cheque for four thousand pounds? I just love it and I know it'll look phenomenal on the wall of the lounge.'

Penny swallowed hard. This one wasn't part of the winter exhibition so she was still free to sell it, but four thousand pounds...? 'I couldn't possibly accept that amount. The gallery takes fifty per cent so, if you really want to buy it, you could have it for two thousand, maybe?' Penny could feel her heart racing.

'That's very kind of you, but you mustn't just give your precious work away. Why don't we split the difference? I'll write you a cheque for three thousand. Have we got a deal?' Mrs B-W held out her hand and Penny shook it, her head spinning.

'Erm, yes, thank you. Thank you very much indeed.'

Chapter 16

Caroline and Penny flew to Venice in a private jet. Penny was appalled at the expense, but Caroline told her it was necessary so as to stay in character. 'If Olivia decides to make a few changes to her lifestyle in the future, that's up to her, but for the moment we'd better try to make it look as genuine as possible. Besides, you never know who you'll meet at the airport.'

Penny could barely contain her excitement as she settled into one of the luxurious leather armchairs inside the surprisingly roomy little aircraft. This was it. At long last her dream of visiting Venice was about to be realised. She glanced out of the porthole windows at the damp grey tarmac outside and for a moment, an image of a dark-haired gondolier sculling up the Grand Canal in brilliant sunshine filled her head. She had had a pretty tough few months, what with Rick's affair and then the body blow from Owen, so the surge of anticipation pulsing through her body brought a smile to her face even before they took off. She was going to Venice! She felt happier than she had been for ages.

The pilot was sitting only a few steps from them, and Penny could see all the dials and buttons in the cockpit. She had never experienced anything like this before and she was fascinated. The difference from any flight she had taken before was highlighted when the co-pilot offered them champagne or tea before takeoff. Both girls glanced at each other and then opted for champagne. Penny grinned across at Caroline as the cork popped and the wine was poured. 'I suppose we'd better not drink it all between the two of us. Pity we haven't brought Nick, he could have shared it with us and, besides, he could have saved a few pounds in airfare.'

Caroline shook her head ruefully and lowered her voice. 'That would've been good, but it would have been out of character. No, it's got to look right.' She grinned at Penny. 'But, somehow, it wouldn't surprise me if we do manage to finish the bottle.'

'So, talking of Nick, are you and he going to give in to your animal desires at long last here in Venice?' Caroline blushed bright red and Penny grinned. 'You can't keep the poor man waiting too long.'

'I sincerely hope so. It's not just the poor man who's been waiting.'

'Good for you, girl. After all, what use is love at first sight if it doesn't develop into something tangible? And when I say tangible, I mean touchy-feely, rumpy pumpy.' As she spoke, she thought back to the tryst in Oxford that had never happened and her mystery man who was now lost to her forever. She gave a little sigh for what might have been, but her moment of gloom only lasted until the aircraft started moving. As the roar of the engines increased, her heart sang. She was going to Venice!

Caroline turned back towards Penny, looking as happy at the prospect of visiting Venice as she was, although for different reasons. 'By the way, Penny, Olivia asked me to give you this.' Caroline passed over a white envelope from her bag. Penny opened it and found it stuffed with money. Caroline saw the expression on her face and explained. 'There's a thousand euros in there. She said you should have the money for any unexpected expenses.' She grinned. 'No need to account for it. Anything you don't spend is yours at the end of the week.'

'Blimey.' Penny didn't know what else to say. As it was, she was going to pick up a pay check of five thousand pounds at the end of the week. With that and the three thousand for the painting Mrs B-W had bought, her financial worries, at least in the short to medium term, would be sorted.

The flight took less than two hours and included an excellent cold meal with the offer of fine wine, although they both decided that the champagne they were drinking was enough. Nice as the wine would have been, Penny wanted to be in a fit state to appreciate the delights of Venice without a hangover. They flew across France and then over the already snow-covered Alps. As they cleared the mountains and started to descend, Penny got her first good look at the unique and wonderful city, *La Serenissima*. From high up she could see the wide plain leading off from the mountains towards the Mediterranean and there, in all its amazing beauty, lay Venice itself, a mass of red roofs and monuments, cleft in two by the Grand Canal. All around the city was the lagoon with a host of islands, far more than she had been expecting, set amongst reeds and mud banks. As they dropped lower, the boats crisscrossing the lagoon were clearly visible, their white wakes marking the shallow waters, like chalk marks on a blackboard.

'Did you know that there are more than a hundred islands in the Venice lagoon?' Penny was so caught up with the view, she hardly heard Caroline at first. She turned towards her, hearing from her voice that Caroline was enjoying being her guide.

'Wow. That many? I somehow thought there was just Venice itself and one or two more. I know there's Murano, the place they make the glass.'

'That's right, but there are loads of others islands, some uninhabited, a few big enough to have roads. You can see why the standard way of travelling round these parts is by boat.'

'Excuse me ladies, we're on our final approach now. Could you fasten your seatbelts, please?' The co-pilot was so close to them, all he had to do was turn his head to give the instruction.

Looking out of the window again, all Penny could see was water beneath them as she heard the sound of the wheels coming down. She glanced across at Caroline and whispered. 'He does know this isn't a seaplane, doesn't he?'

'Don't worry. He knows what he's doing.' As they came in to land, Penny was glued to the window. Venice Marco Polo airport is built so that it protrudes out into the lagoon and their final approach was entirely over water. They dropped lower and lower until finally, just as it looked as though Penny's prediction of a sea landing was to come true, tarmac appeared beneath them and almost immediately afterwards the aircraft touched down lightly. Penny looked across at Caroline and grinned.

'That's a relief. I didn't bring my water wings.'

'You could probably stand up in a lot of the lagoon. It's very shallow, you know.'

'Deep, shallow, I'm just grateful we didn't land in water. So, how do we get from here to the hotel? Do we get to see the view?' Penny checked her watch. It was almost three o'clock. At this time of year they probably only had another hour or two of daylight.

'We'll take a water taxi. We've got a bit of a walk down to the pier, but we'll get a porter to carry our bags.'

The formalities were dispensed with very quickly. Penny was travelling on her own passport so as to stay on the right side of the law and both of them were waved through the VIP entrance by the officer on duty, along with their bags. Caroline had insisted that Penny should bring two big suitcases, even though Penny had objected that there was no way she would be able to wear all those clothes in just six days. Caroline's answer had been predictable.

'This is how Olivia and her stepmum travel, so you've got to do the same. You never know when a dinner invitation's going to pop up and, of course, you can't be seen twice in the same clothes.' She grinned. 'That would bring shame upon the Brookes-Webster family name.'

Outside the airport it was very cold, close to freezing, although the sky was clear and a weak winter sun was shining. Both girls pulled their coats tight around themselves as they followed the porter and his trolley along a walkway down to the waterside. It only took a few minutes, but Penny was frozen by the time she got there.

Clearly, Venice was going to demand more layers and thicker clothing than London.

The water taxi was a beautiful, sleek, highly-varnished vessel with room inside for about ten people, although Caroline had taken this one for their sole use. The porter stowed their bags for them and Penny reached for some of the banknotes she had just been given, but Caroline shook her head. 'Leave it to me.' She gave the man a tip and Penny thanked him in Italian. As the man went off, Caroline frowned and lowered her voice. 'Olivia doesn't speak Italian so it's probably best if you don't either. Don't worry, English'll get you anywhere in Venice.'

Penny nodded in realisation. She would have enjoyed practising her Italian, but she had a job to do. English it would be from now on.

In spite of the racy appearance of the boat, it cruised along relatively slowly. The driver explained in quite fluent English that there were speed limits all over the lagoon, to avoid waves being created that could lead to the erosion of banks and foundations of buildings. In consequence, they had a very leisurely ride over to the city of Venice and Penny had ample time to savour the view. Every fifty metres or so, there were tripods marking the channel, made of hefty wooden timbers, thicker than telegraph poles. Seabirds perched on top of almost every one; mainly seagulls, but from time to time there were beautiful white ibis, cormorants with their wings extended like sinister vampires, and even a massive statuesque grey heron on one of them. Penny sat back and relaxed, breathing in deeply, the sense of gloom that had settled upon her since Owen's declaration definitely beginning to wane. She glanced across at Caroline, enjoying the feel of a smile on her face.

'It's a really, really great feeling when you're fulfilling a lifelong dream. I've dreamt about coming to Venice since I was a little girl. Did I ever tell you I have dreams about Venice?'

Caroline gave her a grin. 'Let me guess, with a handsome gondolier or two?'

Penny grinned back. 'How did you know? Anyway, like I say, it's been a thing for me for years. I've been fascinated by the idea of a town without cars, without congestion, with no noise.'

'Yes, to the first one, but definitely not the other two. You'll see for yourself. The waters of the Grand Canal are some of the busiest in the world and there's plenty of noise in Venice proper, you'll see. The boats chugging up and down the canals make quite a racket, but the worst offenders are the people. Millions and millions of tourists flock to Venice every year and sometimes it's like the tower of Babel. And as for congestion, in the really busy months, you can hardly walk anywhere without risking asphyxiation in the crowds. Mind you, they do say that this is just about the quietest period of the year for Venice.' She turned to the skipper. 'Is that so? Is this a quiet time?' He gave her a broad smile.

'The only time Venice is quiet is in the very early morning, just before dawn, when the night people have finally gone to bed and before the deliveries start and the road sweepers get to work. But, as far as numbers of tourists are concerned, yes, this is a quiet time. You should be able to see Venice at your ease, without being squeezed by the crowds.' He gave a lazy wave of the hand to another water taxi as it came past them, presumably on its way to return other visitors to the airport in a never-ending cycle. 'If you're here next week, Christmas week, you'll see the difference. For now, it's the calm before the storm. Next weekend it'll all go crazy once more.'

Penny had almost forgotten that Christmas was nearly upon them. She made a mental note to buy presents, not least as, for the first time in years, she now had some spare cash to use. As they approached the city of Venice itself, they passed close by the island of Murano, and Penny remembered what Olivia had told her. 'Olivia says I have to visit the islands if there's time.'

'Well, there's nothing scheduled for us for tonight. We could take a boat back here to Murano, have a walk around and then have dinner here. How does that sound?'

'That sounds perfect.'

The water taxi dropped them on the quay directly in front of their hotel, squeezing in alongside a line of glossy black gondolas, their intricate fretwork bow ornaments, like massive-toothed steel combs, glittering in the late afternoon sunshine. Seconds after they made landfall, a very elegantly-dressed porter came out of the hotel to collect their bags. The hotel itself was a magnificent Venetian palace that Penny recognised from a number of paintings she had seen over the years. She felt a tingle of excitement at the thought that she was going to stay in such an iconic place, where heads of state, princes, even kings and queens, had stayed over the centuries, not to mention Hollywood stars in more recent years. She paused outside the surprisingly small main door and looked up at the warm, earthy orange ochre colour of the walls, the ornate white tracery of gothic pillars and arches around the windows, and breathed out in admiration.

'Wow, Caroline, what a place!'

'If you think the outside's good, just wait until you check out the inside.' Caroline was smiling. Penny followed her through the rickety revolving wooden door that looked as if it was as old as the palace itself and into the amazing interior that was more like the inside of a sultan's harem than one of the greatest hotels in the world. A magnificent marble staircase at the far end led up to a mezzanine flanked with Byzantine arches, every horizontal surface tastefully adorned with Christmas decorations in gold and silver.

'*Signorine, buona sera.*' They were greeted by a tall man at the Concierge's desk. He was wearing an impeccable deep grey suit and he looked every bit as elegant as his surroundings. On his lapel was a glittering gold badge.

'Good evening, Filippo.' Caroline turned to Penny. 'You remember Filippo from last year, don't you, Olivia?'

By now, Penny was getting pretty good at reacting to this sort of hint. She walked across and held out her hand to the porter. 'How very good to see you again, Filippo.'

'And your father, *signorina*? I trust he is well.'

'I'm afraid my father died at Easter.' Penny saw his eyes drop. 'It was very sudden.'

'My condolences, *signorina*, he was a fine man. I remember him with affection.' Penny found herself feeling unexpectedly emotional and she felt her eyes stinging as she managed a reply.

'Thank you, Filippo, that's so very good to hear.'

They walked across to the small reception desk and Caroline did the checking in while Penny just stood and stared in silent awe at the spectacular surroundings. She knew that the main building, where she was now standing, dated back over six hundred years and had been the home of a noble Venetian family. It was sobering to think that this place had been standing long before Canaletto or Titian had even been born. A shiver went down her spine.

'We're on the second floor. Do you want to take the lift or shall we walk? The porter'll bring our bags.' Caroline had completed their registration and a friendly-looking girl in a stylish grey suit was waiting to accompany them to their rooms.

'The stairs, definitely.'

'You've got a room with a balcony overlooking the canal, and I'm in the room next door.'

Penny was under no illusions as to how much a room with a balcony in a place like this was likely to cost. She did her best to dismiss the thought from her mind and act as if spending thousands on a hotel was a matter of no concern. She spared a thought for what Jimmy would say if he saw her now. She suppressed a grin as it occurred to her that this would just be further proof that she had indeed gone over to the Dark Side.

As they climbed the ornate marble staircase, Penny found herself looking back down on the entrance hallway in all its magnificence, marvelling at the sheer beauty of the place. It was only when she was ushered into her room that she realised that the beauty inside the building was more than matched by the view from the window. High glazed doors opened onto a narrow balcony. She went over and opened the windows, stepping out into the cold. From there, she found herself staring in wonder at the view across the water towards other islands, the roofs a series of cupolas and towers, all now tinted pink by the dying rays of the winter sun. She turned back into the room to reach for a tip for the girl, but she had already left. Caroline was still standing by the door, watching her reaction and smiling.

'What do you think of it so far?'

'Unbelievable, just unbelievable. To think that I'm inside one of the most stunning buildings in probably the most amazing city in the world! I've seen this very same window, this same balcony, in countless pictures and now here I am.' Penny turned back and caught Caroline's eye. 'Thank you so much for giving me this opportunity to realise my dreams. I feel humbled.'

'Not too humble, remember you're a Brookes-Webster.' She gave Penny a wink and pointed to the left. 'My room's right next door. Just shout if you need anything.'

—

That evening, they took a water taxi to Murano. At Caroline's request, the driver travelled up the Grand Canal after leaving their hotel, taking them under the Rialto bridge, and then through the maze of side canals, some little wider than their boat, before emerging once more into the open waters of the lagoon. Although it was dark by now, there was more than enough light as they passed through the main part of the city for them to make out a never-ending succession of *palazzi* on either side of the waterway, each more magnificent than the other. Inside some of the high-ceilinged rooms, they could clearly see massive, stunningly beautiful old chandeliers hanging from sculpted and painted wooden ceilings. Once back in open water, it only took another fifteen minutes to get across to the island of Murano. The boat dropped them by an elegant hump-backed bridge that crossed the main canal bisecting the island. Penny climbed out in a daze, totally overwhelmed by the succession of amazing sights she had seen on the way there.

'The taxi man says there's a little restaurant in a square somewhere over to our right where the food's good and it's not too touristy.' Caroline was grinning at Penny. 'I'll believe that when I see it. Venice has always had a reputation for fleecing tourists.'

Penny smiled back. 'And the reputation goes back a long, long way. I seem to remember Venice got very rich indeed from ferrying crusaders to the Holy Land, way back in the twelfth and thirteenth centuries. Still, let's go and look for it.'

As the water taxi manoeuvred out into the canal again, heading back to Venice, they set off along the stone-flagged road that ran parallel to the water, past houses, shops and factories where the glass for which the island of Murano had been famous over the centuries was still produced and sold. When they reached the next bridge, they turned away from the water into a narrow side street as instructed. It was darker down here and eerily quiet, the only sound the echoing of their footsteps. From time to time they passed one or two other people, looming out of the shadows; a couple walking their dogs, a mother and two little children hand in hand, but it was remarkably empty and just a tiny bit spooky. Nevertheless, after all the warnings she had received about how crowded Venice could be, Penny was pleasantly surprised. At the end of the street, they found the boatman's square. It was surprisingly large and even boasted a massive tree in the middle of it as well as street lights. As they stood there, searching the darkness for anything that might resemble a restaurant, Caroline's phone rang. It was Nick.

Penny left her and wandered away towards the far end of the square to give her some privacy, and it was only when she reached the other side that she spotted the restaurant. It was small and looked very unprepossessing from the outside. She went across and checked for a menu, but there was nothing visible. Peering through the steamy windows, she saw that it was already quite full, so she gave Caroline a wave, indicating where the restaurant was, and then went in to bag a table. Inside it was warm, noisy and crowded, with a bare wooden floor and plastic tablecloths, the total antithesis of their luxury hotel. An elderly gentleman behind the counter gave her a welcoming nod and raised one finger. Penny shook her head and raised two. He pointed to a little table for two, set against the wall, and she went across to take possession of it.

All around her were people speaking Italian. The local accent was noticeably different from the way people talked in Tuscany and she had trouble understanding. From the way some of the men were dressed, in overalls and work clothes, it was clear that this was a place frequented by Venetians. She settled back and did her best to make out some of what the people around her were saying, but without any great degree of success. A rather good-looking waiter with a stubbly chin came along and deposited two laminated menus on the table, along with a basket of bread and a plate of what looked like butter beans in olive oil.

'*Due persone?*'

Penny hesitated. Although she had promised Caroline she wouldn't use her Italian, she deemed this sort of place sufficiently far removed from Olivia's usual surroundings for her to decide to reply in kind.

'*Si, siamo in due.*'

'*Da bere?*'

Penny did a bit of quick thinking and then made a decision. '*Due bicchieri di prosecco, per favore.*' The waiter nodded and went off.

The prosecco and Caroline arrived at the same time.

'So, what's Nick's news? Where was he phoning from?'

'Gatwick. He's just about to get on the plane. He won't be here in Venice until very late.' Caroline's voice was wistful. 'So I won't see him till tomorrow.'

Penny had been thinking about the two of them. She lifted her glass and clinked it against Caroline's. 'How about the three of us go out for dinner together tomorrow night?' She gave Caroline a big smile. 'Although somehow I have a feeling I'm going to find myself developing a headache partway through and having to leave you two lovebirds to it. What do you think? Sound like a good plan?'

'I've already told you what a wonderful schemer you are, haven't I? Sounds like an excellent plan.'

The meal was superb. The food was fresh, hot and tasty, served with no frills, but it didn't need any. Both of them were hungry and the fish they chose was perfect. They discovered that the restaurant served a gently sparkling form of prosecco by the carafe and by the time they reached the almond tart at the end of the meal, they were both feeling full, warm and very cheerful. Going back outside again was a shock to the system and they wrapped their jackets tighter round themselves as their breath formed clouds in the sub zero air.

They walked back towards the main canal, gradually acclimatising to the cold. They passed a number of glass factories, some still lit up, even though it was late at night. They also walked past several restaurants, all of which looked far more touristy than theirs. Some even had hardy touts outside, doing their best to lure passing strangers in for a meal. The two girls shook their heads and carried on down to where they could pick up a taxi. As they stood waiting, Penny phoned Olivia as promised.

'Hi, Penny, good to hear from you. How's Venice?' Olivia sounded very buoyant and Penny was pleased for her.

'Olivia, it's amazing. It's everything I'd been expecting and more. We've been chugging around in a water taxi and the views just get better and better.' She remembered her manners. 'Caroline gave me the envelope with all that money. That was so very kind of you, but you shouldn't have. I'm already being paid lots for this. For the chance to come to Venice, I should be paying you.'

'Don't be silly, Penny. By the way, your amazing abstract painting's now hanging in the lounge directly opposite the Hieronymus Bosch and it fits in beautifully.'

'Oh, good Lord, really?' The thought of one of her paintings even being in the same room as such a priceless work of art took Penny's breath away.

'Yes, it really looks great. And, another thing, Penny, my stepmother's looking and sounding a whole lot happier as well. Somehow, it feels as though we've both turned a corner.'

'That's the best possible news.' Penny went on to tell Olivia all about their day, up to and including their evening meal. Olivia took note.

'That sounds amazing. Next time I come to Venice, I'm going to have to go to that little restaurant on Murano. It sounds lovely. So, are you all ready for the conference out on the island? It's a delightful place.' She sounded quite nostalgic and Penny couldn't miss her upbeat tone.

'Yes, all ready, and remember, Olivia, next time it'll be you.'

'You're right, Penny. I know it will.' She hesitated. 'And I've definitely made my mind up. I'm going to the National Gallery tomorrow morning.'

'Excellent. I look forward to hearing all about it tomorrow night.'

After finishing the call, Penny put her phone away and looked across at the lighthouse just along the coast from them, its light flashing regularly to warn boats of the proximity of the island. It created a mesmerising, almost hypnotic effect. Thoughts of Owen and her mystery man filled her head. It would have been nice to have one of them with her in such a romantic place as this, but she knew that wasn't to be. She had to shake her head to clear it before returning her attention to Caroline. 'So, what's the plan for tomorrow morning?'

'The conference starts at ten. We'll ask the hotel to book us a water taxi for quarter to. Shall we meet up for breakfast at eight thirty? Or would you prefer to have breakfast in your room?'

'No, let's go to the restaurant. I've been reading about it. It's up on the top floor and the view's supposed to be amazing.'

That night, strangely, she didn't dream about Venice. But, of course, at long last, she was already there.

Chapter 17

The view from the hotel restaurant on the top floor was indeed amazing, as was the breakfast. They sat by the window and admired the view out over the lagoon, Penny doing her best to restrict herself to just some coffee and toast while watching a series of plates passing by heaped with exotic fruit salad, cakes, biscuits, croissants and buns. Others came past bearing hot bacon, sausage and eggs that bore no resemblance to the countless plates of bacon and eggs she had served to customers at the Apocalypse. She took a deep breath and stiffened her resolve to try not to eat too much. It was unfortunate that she chose the very moment that two hefty plates of aromatic hot food were carried past their table and the wonderful smells filled her nostrils. Her resolve wavered, but just held. Her new wardrobe of clothes contained some pretty tight items. If she gave in to temptation, the results could be catastrophic.

'If you squint far over to the left you can just see the island of San Servolo where the conference is taking place.' Caroline's voice shook her out of her food-induced reverie.

Penny did as instructed and made out the shape of a low island in the distance, the white buildings flushed pink by the early morning sunlight. The sky was once more clear and it looked set to be a stunning, if freezing cold, day.

'And what's the plan when we get there?'

'We go straight into a plenary session where there'll be speeches from a whole host of big name environmentalists from all over the world. Then there's the inevitable coffee break where we stand around and chat to all and sundry before breaking off into a whole heap of different lectures that'll be taking place throughout the rest of the day.' She grinned at Penny. 'Just like being back at university.'

The trip across to the island in the water taxi only took ten minutes and the views were as magnificent as Penny had been expecting. Penny was all for taking the water-bus, the *vaporetto*, but Caroline cautioned her that this might look out of character for a Brookes-Webster. The island itself, home to Venice International University, was situated part way between Venice and the Lido, and the conference took place in the complex of lovely old white buildings, relics of the days when the place had been a hospital. They stepped off the taxi and were immediately swallowed up by a mass of people, among them quite a few faces Penny recognised from the other conferences she had already attended. Waiting for them by the entrance was Nick, his face breaking into a broad smile when he spotted Caroline.

'Hi, Caroline! Hi, Olivia.' He looked delighted to see them, particularly Caroline. 'How's your hotel?'

Penny just managed to stop herself as she was on the point of gushing enthusiastically about the fabulous hotel, the enormous room with the balcony overlooking the lagoon, the amazing bed with a choice of different types of pillow, the giant antique mirrors framed with Murano glass flowers, the mind-boggling selection of complimentary toiletries, the biggest television screen she had ever seen in her life, the vast and varied breakfast buffet and the views to die for. Just in time she remembered that she was now in her role of multi-millionaire, so she stayed silent and let Caroline do the gushing for her.

Nick accompanied them into the auditorium and they sat down to listen to the welcome speeches. It was all very organised, with headsets available offering a translation service. In fact, as it turned out, almost all the speeches were in English, including the one from the Polish president. The aims for the conference were spelt out and then, as Caroline had said, the plenary session broke up and coffee was served. Penny, in her role as Olivia, was delighted to find that a number of the UK delegates she had first met in Brighton and who had been very hesitant to approach her were now looking and sounding much more relaxed with her. It looked as though her charm offensive was beginning to pay off. She redoubled her efforts.

There was a break for an hour during which lunch was served, but Penny had determined she was going to limit herself to only one big Italian meal a day. Instead, she bought a sandwich, left Caroline with Nick and went down to the pier. She found a water taxi waiting and decided to spend some of the thousand euros given to her by Olivia taking a trip past the beautiful tree-covered island of *San Lazzaro degli Armeni* with its monastery built on the site of a medieval leper colony. They travelled on across to the big, long, island breakwater of the

Lido, the main land barrier between Venice and the open sea. As the boat nosed in from the open waters of the lagoon into the canal that led towards the Lido casino, it felt strange to look up and see cars parked on either side of them. Clearly, the Lido was a much more modern development than Venice itself, with good links to the mainland. Penny didn't have a lot of time, so she told the boatman to wait while she went for a quick walk. As she did so, she discovered a rather good-looking restaurant for the meal with Caroline and Nick that evening. She went in and made a reservation before completing her hasty circular tour of that part of the island. Finally she looked at her watch and headed back to the water taxi. As she approached the waterfront, her phone rang. She slowed, checked the caller ID, and saw that it was Jimmy.

'Jimmy, hi, how are you?'

'Hello sweetheart, I'm fine. Where are you?'

She told him and he was sounded surprised. To make sure he didn't go off on one of his prostitution romps again, she hastened to specify that this was her treat to herself for having been accepted for the Piccadilly exhibition. He accepted the story without hesitation and then he asked a question that stopped her in her tracks.

'Penny, have you ever heard of bilocation?'

'Bi – what?'

Jimmy sounded smug. 'I looked it up in the dictionary. Bilocation, you know, sort of like time travel, being in two places at once.'

'I'm afraid you've lost me, Jimmy. What about time travel? Have you just been to see some sci-fi movie at the cinema?'

'No, I've just been to the National Gallery.'

'The National Gallery?' Penny hadn't got a clue what that could have to do with time travel. What he said next made that abundantly clear.

'Yes, and what I don't understand is how you could be at the National Gallery and in Venice at the same time. See what I mean about time travel?'

Olivia! The penny dropped. Today was the day she was going to the Botticelli exhibition. *Oh bugger*, Penny thought to herself, desperately searching for a convincing explanation. To buy herself some time she tried pleading ignorance. 'I don't follow. I'm here in Venice, not in London. Whoever it was you saw, it can't have been me.'

'That's what I found out, sweetheart, when I went over and spoke to you, and discovered that you weren't you after all.'

'Oh, bugger.'

'Oh, bugger, indeed. And before you try to fob me off by telling me it was just a massive coincidence, how come the person I spoke to started blushing like a traffic light when I mentioned your name?' He paused for dramatic effect before continuing. 'So I think it might be time you told Uncle Jimmy just what the hell's going on, don't you?'

'Oh, Lord… Jimmy…' Penny's mind was racing as a vision of Mr Jenson the lawyer flashed through her head. The bald man was standing behind his desk with a stern expression on his face, holding the formal legal undertaking in his hands and repeating 'Do I make myself clear?' over and over again. She took a deep breath. 'Jimmy, look, I promise I'll explain everything, but just not now.' To make matters worse, just at that moment a couple of people she recognised from the conference came walking towards her. She dropped her voice to little more than a whisper. 'Listen, I can't talk now. Are you working tonight? I'll call you?'

'Until midnight, but I'm sure I'll be able to take your call. Is it something naughty? You and your evil twin up to something?'

'No, not at all. Listen, I'll tell you about it tonight, but in the meantime promise me you won't mention it to a soul. I really mean that, Jimmy. I'd be in deep, deep trouble if it got out.'

'How fascinating.' His tone echoed his words. 'All right, I promise, Scouts' honour, lips sealed and all that. Now you go back to your spying or whatever it is you're doing. Talk to you later.'

Penny knew she had to speak to Olivia before calling Jimmy back that evening. Although she felt pretty confident he would keep his mouth shut, this was a complication she really hadn't expected. She swiped the red button and dropped the phone back in her pocket just as the couple from the conference came up to her. She recognised them as representatives of a well-known British charity and she gave them a little wave.

'Hello, you two. Have you been you bunking off as well?'

The two people, a man and a woman a few years older than her, grinned back at her and the woman answered first. 'Sort of. It's such a wonderful day and neither of us has been to Venice before, so we thought we'd skip lunch and take the *vaporetto* across here.'

The man was looking at his watch rather anxiously. 'It's just a bit complicated getting here. We had to take two different boats. Somehow, I think we're going to be late back.' Penny checked the time as well. It was almost two o'clock.

'Can I give you a lift in the water taxi? That should get us back pretty quickly.'

'That would be great, thanks.' He sounded relieved and Penny led them to the boat. On the way back, they chatted, and Penny remembered meeting them for the first time at Brighton. On that occasion they had been reticent to talk to her and had clearly treated her with mistrust. Now, it appeared that her attempts to repair the public relations damage done by Olivia's stepmother were beginning to pay off. By the time they arrived back at San Servolo, they were all smiles.

When she returned to the conference, she only just squeezed into the afternoon session as the speaker took the stage, so it was the mid-afternoon break before she could tell Caroline about the phone call from Jimmy. Caroline listened carefully, but wasn't too bothered.

'I wouldn't worry if I were you, Penny. First, you have no concerns on the legal front because it was Olivia who was unmasked, not you. Besides, now that you're over here and she's a thousand kilometres away, it isn't going to matter. The people that count as far as this deception's concerned are all here for the most part.' She looked across at Penny. 'It'll be fine as long as he doesn't go to the newspapers or anything.'

Penny shook her head. 'I'm sure he wouldn't do anything like that, besides, he doesn't have anything though, has he? The thing is he only knows who I am, not who Olivia is.' By this time she was beginning to recover from her shock. 'I'll talk to Olivia tonight and then I'll give him a call and make sure he stays schtum.' An idea occurred to her. 'I'll promise to bring him a present from Venice. That should do it.'

'What sort of present were you thinking of, a gondola?'

'More likely a gondolier, knowing Jimmy, but I'll think of something.'

-

That evening Penny, Caroline and Nick took the *vaporetto* from right outside their hotel across to the Lido. The icy wind had picked up and they were glad to find seats inside the water-bus where it was relatively warm. If Nick was surprised to see them using public transport, he didn't show it. Along with the wind had come waves, not big waves, but enough to cause both the boat and the pontoon moored to the quay to sway about uncomfortably. By the time they got across to the Lido, Penny, never a good sailor, was glad to get off. It occurred to her that one advantage of London over Venice was that you were unlikely to get seasick travelling from Hyde Park to Trafalgar Square. However the views from the Lido back over the dark water to the sparkling lights of Venice were breathtaking and it took her a few moments to realise what made it so special. It came to her in the end – street lights. All big cities nowadays are bathed in a nighttime glow of street lights, car headlights and the bright windows of high rise blocks but here, with ancient palazzi instead of skyscrapers, water for roads and only small, low-mounted street lamps everything was far darker than London and, as a result, much more atmospheric.

Penny stood on the quay with the other two for a few moments, admiring the scene, before heading inland and walking round to the restaurant she had found at lunchtime. The cars parked at the sides of the roads, the tarmac rather than flagstones, and the number of relatively modern apartment blocks and houses reinforced just how very special Venice itself really was. Any place in the twenty-first century without cars was a true rarity and to be cherished. Even so, as they walked along the road that ran parallel to the lagoon, the regular splashes as the waves were driven in on the wind made Penny realise just how precarious Venice's hold on life really was. Every wave represented a few grains of soil or foundations being eroded. Nick was thinking along the same lines.

'This is an unbelievable place, isn't it? You know, they're building a massive barrier to help protect Venice against the worst of the high tides, but it may be too little, too late.'

'It's a World Heritage Site. Doesn't that count for something?' Penny felt acutely concerned for the future of the city.

'Yes, but you can't fight the forces of nature indefinitely.' Nick was walking between the two of them and he looked across at Penny. 'It's no coincidence they picked Venice for this conference on the environment. Sea levels are rising all round the globe. Enjoy Venice while you can. Our grandchildren might not get to see it at all.'

The restaurant was very full, mostly with Italians. Unexpectedly, the house specialities included game, as well as fish, and Penny was reminded that Hemingway had come to Venice to shoot wildfowl. She chose a wonderful *fritto misto* of lightly fried little fish, prawns and octopus, while the other two opted for tuna steaks. They split a bottle of prosecco and then moved onto some excellent Bardolino Classico from the lands to the north of Venice. It was a glorious ruby red colour and Penny would happily have stayed and drunk more of it, but she knew she had to put Plan B into operation, or rather Plan N, as Nick was the target for tonight. After finishing her fish, she drained her glass and looked across the table apologetically.

'I'm sorry, guys, but I think I'm going to have to go back to the hotel. I've got a screaming headache that I can't seem to shift. You two enjoy the rest of the night.'

She stood up as Nick protested that they would accompany her back to the hotel, but she was having none of it. 'I'll be fine. A breath of fresh air, a short ride on the *vaporetto* and I'll be there. Now, you just enjoy yourselves.' Just for a second her eyes met Caroline's and the slightest hint of a smile passed between them.

It was barely half past nine when she got off the water-bus outside their hotel. She was wearing her warm winter coat with a scarf, and tights under her jeans, so she wasn't cold. She retrieved her gloves from her pockets and decided to take a walk around Venice in spite of the temperature that must have been very close to freezing. The squares, streets and alleys were virtually deserted at this time on a cold winter's night, with few people choosing to venture out in the December chill. She walked along the waterfront and turned into St Mark's Square. A huge Christmas tree had been erected at the far side of the front of the basilica and was covered with white lights. The arched galleries all round the square were festooned with more lights, giving it a Christmassy feel, although there were very few passers-by to admire the view. Penny took some photos and then headed off into the narrow side streets, following arrows indicating the way to the Rialto.

The narrow lane was lined with shops, many of them gift shops selling the carnival masks for which Venice was famous, as well as everything from wallets to T-shirts and, this time of year, woolly hats. Some were still open even at this late hour, but most were closed up, their heavy metal shutters pulled down and padlocked. Penny didn't hurry, enjoying the chance to loiter at her leisure without being pushed along by a crowd of other people. Although she was alone, she felt very safe here in Venice. After a while she turned off this main thoroughfare and began to make her way through the maze of little lanes and alleys, some barely wider than her shoulders, leading her deeper into the old town. From time to time she came upon narrow canals, crossed by ancient bridges that left just enough height for gondoliers and their boats to squeeze through underneath. Occasionally the alleys would emerge onto little squares, many boasting amazing baroque or even medieval churches. She lost track of time and direction, just loving being able to wander through the darkened streets, breathing in Venice in all its crumbling glory.

It was while she was walking alongside a silent, motionless canal, the wind unable to penetrate among the houses to even ripple the surface, that she got a surprise, a major surprise. In fact, she couldn't believe her eyes at first. On the other side of the canal, a man emerged from an archway and started walking in the same direction as her, probably only thirty or forty feet ahead, separated from her by the water. He was a tall man, wearing a leather jacket. He had a wild mass of dark hair down to his collar and, in the light of a wrought-iron street lamp, she saw that he had a beard. Because he was walking slightly ahead of her, she couldn't see his face clearly so she found herself speeding up, the sound of her shoes on the flagstones the only noise to be heard. Then, as he reached another light, he glanced across, not directly at her, but far enough for her to see his whole face illuminated by the light, and she stopped dead.

It was him.

She couldn't miss his piratical beard, now a bit shorter than she remembered, his broad shoulders and his handsome face. It really was him. And in case there might have been any doubt about his identity, her knees confirmed it without any possibility of mistake. She felt that now familiar surge of emotion that the sight of him aroused in her. She wobbled and almost fell over, catching hold of a railing to steady herself. This time, however, she had no intention of letting him out of her sight. She summoned all her strength and set off once more, hurrying to catch him up. Then, just as she started to draw level, the path she was following along the waterside abruptly finished, turning ninety degrees to the right into a narrow alley. This led away from the canal and disappeared down between two tall *palazzi*.

Cursing under her breath, she started to run down the alley, her footsteps echoing up the tall, blank sides of the buildings. At the end, the alley turned back left again and she hurried along it. Here, the street lighting wasn't nearly as good as elsewhere and she wasn't able to go very fast on the uneven stones, for fear of falling over. At last she spotted a gap between two buildings to her left and ran back in the direction of what she hoped would prove to be the canal. As she emerged at the end of the high walls on either side of her, she realised she was right. This path did indeed lead to the canal, but, alas, there was no bridge. The path just stopped dead at the water's edge. Less than fifty metres further on, away to her right, she saw a bridge, but it might as well have been five hundred metres away. There was no way of getting to it, short of jumping in and swimming. As she watched, she briefly spotted her man, just as he reached the bridge, turned away from the canal and disappeared into another little lane. As he disappeared from view, she found herself on the point of screaming with frustration. This was the third time she had seen him and, yet again, it looked like she had missed him.

By the time she had fought her way back into the alleys and along until she finally reached the bridge over the canal, he was long gone. She stopped on the little bridge and sat on the cold stone balustrade, growling to herself and shaking her head in annoyance. The thing she couldn't grasp was just how it was he could be here in Venice at the same time and in the exact same place as her. Surely home for him was London, seeing as she had glimpsed him there twice. The chances of him choosing to come on holiday to Venice at the precise time she was here was mind-boggling. For a moment she wondered if it might be more than a coincidence. She wondered whether he might be following her, maybe mistaking her for Olivia. Did he intend to kidnap her, or worse?

She glanced around into the shadows. Everywhere was dark apart from a little light filtering down from a top-floor apartment in one of the *palazzi* by the canal side and an antique street lamp just ahead of her. For a moment she felt a shiver of fear, but no sooner had it come than she dismissed it. He hadn't even seen her, he had been walking ahead of her, not behind her, and there was no way he could have known where she was going to be. In fact, even she had no idea where she was.

She went across and checked a sign on the wall by the street lamp. It read *Ponte de l'Acquavita*. The bridge itself was sandwiched between a group of faded pink houses, the lower parts of the walls badly scarred where the decrepit plaster had fallen off, now reduced to bare brick. Somebody with more time than sense had sprayed graffiti along the wall and across the grey metal shutters of a locked shop front. She pulled out the map she had got from the hotel and pored over it in the light, but without success. She couldn't see any more signs so she came down off the bridge and decided to follow the narrow lane her pirate man had taken. This led her away from the water into another maze of buildings. It was much darker here and she couldn't help feeling a sensation of anxiety, all alone in the shadows.

Fortunately, in less than a hundred yards, she found herself at a crossroads, illuminated by a street light. She was relieved to find there was a café here and it looked open, so she pushed the door and went inside, partly in case her pirate man might have been heading here and partly so as to get away from the freezing cold out in the echoing streets. It immediately became clear that her pirate wasn't here. In fact, there were no customers in the café at all. She glanced at her watch. It was almost eleven o'clock and the proprietor was pretty clearly in the process of closing up. He looked up as she came in and shook his head.

'Sorry, no coffee. Closed.' He spoke in English, having accurately guessed her nationality. Penny nodded and went across with her map. She asked him in Italian if he could show her where she was and he turned out to be very helpful. He not only showed her where on the map she had ended up, but also the best way back to St Mark's Square. He became more cordial as he realised he could speak to her in his own language.

'I'm afraid I'm just closing up, otherwise I would have made you something hot. You look frozen stiff. It's very cold outside, isn't it?'

Penny realised that her face was burning in the warmth in the bar, after the cold night air, so she nodded. 'Yes, very, but at least it's dry.'

'I know what you need. Here.' He reached behind the counter and, before she could object, he produced two shot glasses and filled them with transparent liquid from an anonymous bottle. She looked down, pretty sure she knew what she was being offered.

'Grappa?'

He nodded and pushed a glass over to her. He picked up his own and held it out to her. '*Cin cin*. With my compliments. You look as though you need it.' She picked up her glass gratefully and clinked it against his. He took a big mouthful and she followed suit, praying it wouldn't burn the roof of her mouth off. She was relieved to find it was really very good, remarkably smooth compared to some other types of grappa she had

201

sampled over the years. She returned his toast, swallowed and nodded appreciatively.

'Yes, that's a very good grappa.'

He smiled back at her. 'My father-in-law makes it, with his own grapes. Once upon a time it was forbidden to distil liquor and he had to make it on the sly. Now our lords and masters in Rome permit us to make a small amount for personal use and he always lets me have some.' He gave her another smile. 'I sometimes have a little drop when it's cold, but I don't like drinking alone.'

'Well, I feel specially privileged.'

'At least you're looking better now. When you came in, you looked as if you'd just seen a ghost.'

She looked at him over the rim of her glass. 'I rather think that might be what just happened.'

–

When she got back to the hotel she was intending to go straight to bed, but she was in for yet another surprise. As she walked in, a man sitting in the lounge bar area adjacent to the main lobby jumped to his feet and hurried across to greet her. 'Olivia, it *is* you.' He sounded very pleased indeed to see her. 'I checked the list of participants at the *Save the Planet* conference and I saw your name. How amazing you should be here. You didn't say you were coming to Venice.'

Penny mustered a broad smile and set about wondering what she should do. He was probably around her age, tall and rather good-looking. He was wearing a very formal suit and what could have been an old school or regimental tie. His shoes were immaculately polished and his red hair was short-cropped and very neat. As she spotted the hair, a memory came back to her. She found herself thinking back to the time Olivia had talked about the boy she really liked. She had said he had red hair. Now what was his name? Stalling for time, she took a gamble, reaching out her arms to him and giving him a big hug. As she did so, it suddenly came back to her; Jonathan, abbreviated to Jon. She uttered a silent prayer that she had got the right man and stepped back from the clinch, still smiling.

'Jon, how wonderful to see you.'

It worked. His smile broadened.

'You look absolutely lovely, Olivia. I'm so, so pleased to see you.' He looked and sounded it.

'And you, Jon.' She remembered now that Olivia had said he was in the army. 'So, are you over here on duty or is this a holiday?'

'I left the army in the summer. I wrote to you about it, but you probably don't remember.'

Penny affected a sudden surge of memory. 'Of course, silly me, I'd completely forgotten. And now what're you doing?'

'You know my father's in the art business.' Penny's ears pricked up immediately. 'He's setting up a new gallery over here and I've been sent over to represent the family at the grand opening.' Penny would dearly have liked to hear more, but he immediately changed the subject back to her, or rather to the girl he was convinced was Olivia. 'But how're you doing now? I was so sorry to hear about your father and even more sorry to hear you haven't been well.' He glanced over his shoulder. 'Can I get you a drink?'

Penny was still burping the grappa she had drunk earlier and she knew the last thing she needed was more alcohol, so she hesitated. She also knew full well that drinks here in the five star hotel wouldn't be cheap. Either he was seriously loaded or he was in for a shock. She could see he was very keen for her to join him, so she made a decision. 'Thanks, Jon, you know what I'd really like? A hot chocolate. I've been out walking and it's bitterly cold out there.'

He led her over to the table where he had been sitting and caught the eye of a hovering waiter. 'A hot chocolate and another scotch and soda please. No ice.' He was very attentive, relieving her of her coat and hanging it over the back of a spare chair, on top of his. Penny sat down and prepared for the performance of a lifetime. From what Olivia had said, she liked Jon a lot, but there hadn't been time for them to develop any great intimacy before the death of her father had interrupted relations. Penny hoped this was right, anyway. Although more than happy to attempt to impersonate her employer to the best of her ability, she knew that this definitely didn't extend to an exchange of saliva with some random man. She looked across the table and killed two birds with one stone, starting the conversation and finding out about this art thing he had mentioned at the same time.

'So, tell me all about what you're doing here, Jon. The new gallery sounds amazing.' She reflected that he had ordered the drinks in English. Did this mean he didn't speak Italian? Surely this would be a major handicap for somebody starting a new enterprise over here?

'Well, it's our Foundation, really. We've found amazing premises right beside the Grand Canal and we've got a whole series of big-name exhibitions planned, with paintings being borrowed from all over the place.' Penny would have dearly liked to know more about this Foundation. Presumably it was some kind of charitable trust, rather like Olivia's own BWF. If his family had so much money they could start giving it away, pretty evidently he was going to be able to afford a cup of hot chocolate even in this place. Just then the waiter reappeared with the drinks and Penny had time to give Jonathan a covert examination.

He was really quite handsome in a terribly well-groomed sort of way. He was extremely smart, polite and attentive and it certainly looked as though he liked Olivia a lot. His accent was a bit too public school for Penny's tastes and he was altogether far too well turned out for her, but even so... Maybe if he grew a beard he might look better, but that would make him look even more like Prince Harry. Olivia hadn't been joking. There was a distinct resemblance. Thought of beards reminded her, yet again, of her mystery man. This was really starting to trouble her now. Who was he? What was he doing here? Did he even exist? Could it be he was the product of her imagination; somebody her subconscious had dreamed up to satisfy some unfulfilled schoolgirl desire for a love at first sight experience? On her way back to the hotel after a pleasant chat with the barman at what she was referring to in her head as the grappa café, she had come close to screaming her frustration down the echoing, empty streets of Venice. Who the hell was he? Doing her best to shake his bearded image out of her head, she concentrated on Jonathan.

She didn't learn much more about his gallery as he kept turning the conversation back to her and how she was feeling. Penny did her best to reassure him that she was now well on the way to recovery after her sort of breakdown, confident that what she was saying was the truth. Certainly, the real Olivia had definitely started to come out of herself much more over the past few weeks. Thoughts of Olivia reminded Penny she still had to call her and then, of course, Jimmy. She took a surreptitious glance at her watch and saw that it was past midnight, even if back home that meant eleven o'clock. She knew she needed to get back to her room to make the calls pretty soon. She swallowed the last of the excellent, highly calorific, hot chocolate and looked across the table apologetically.

'Look, Jon, I'm going to have to go to bed as I've got an early start in the morning.' His answer was predictable.

'When can I see you again, Olivia? Could I take you out for dinner tomorrow?' He hesitated as Penny desperately searched for a convincing excuse. Luckily, she didn't need to, this time. He shook his head in annoyance. 'Oh, blast, I've just remembered, I'm in Milan tomorrow evening. I won't be back until Wednesday. How about Wednesday night?'

Penny decided she had better say yes. The last thing she wanted to do was to screw things up between Olivia and her love at first sight man. At least the forty-eight-hour delay gave her more time to discuss with Olivia just how she wanted to play it. 'That would be delightful, Jon. Shall we meet here at, say, eight?'

'Perfect. I do so look forward to it.' Yes, Penny thought to herself, just a bit too formal and polite for her taste. She stood up and he immediately jumped to his feet and retrieved her coat for her. 'Sleep well and I'll be counting the hours until Wednesday.'

Penny hesitated, unsure how to conclude the evening. In the end she decided to offer him a bit of encouragement. She stepped forward and deposited a light kiss on his lips. 'Goodnight, Jon. I'm so, so pleased to see you again.' She saw his eyes shine.

'Me, too, Olivia. Me, too.'

Penny went up in the lift and straight to her room. The housekeeping staff had made the bed, tidied everything, even folding the jumper she had left over the back of a chair and adding it to the collection of clothes now unpacked and stashed in the wardrobe. There were fresh flowers on the table and a little brown box of Gianduiotti chocolates at the bedside. It all looked lovely. Penny dropped her coat and reached into her bag for her phone. Her first call was to Olivia.

'Olivia, hi. I hope I'm not calling too late. I haven't woken you up or anything, have I?'

'No, not at all. I was just thinking about you. I made a cake this afternoon.'

'Wow, that's progress. What sort of cake?'

'Victoria sponge. It's a little bit burnt on top because I didn't take it out in time, but I've just had a slice now and it's really rather good. Gilbert's here at my feet and he's given it his seal of approval. I'll work on it and hope to be able to present you with a non-burnt one when I see you next. Anyway, what about you? How's it all going?'

'A couple of interesting developments. The first concerns your visit to the National Gallery.'

'Oh, dear, yes, I quite forgot. I think I met your friend from that café where you were working.'

'Jimmy, that's right. I got a phone call from him. Olivia, he's smelt a rat.' As she mentioned the rat, she was reminded of her previous place of residence. She shuddered and continued. 'I haven't said a word to him about what we're doing, you know, because of that legal thing I had to sign, but he doesn't miss much and I reckon he's twigged that you aren't me.'

'Oh dear, I rather thought that was the case. He came up to me and started stroking my hair and I was a bit sharp with him until I realised that he thought I was you. I can't imagine how difficult it must be for you, living a double life like you're having to do at the moment. So, do you think he's going to tell anybody?'

'No, I don't think so. He's a sweetie really and I've asked him not to say a word. I told him I'd phone him tonight, but I wanted to talk to you first.' Penny hesitated. 'I'd really rather like to tell him the truth, or at least a doctored version of it. He's a good friend and I'm sure he won't breathe a word to anybody, but after that meeting I had with the lawyer, I'm terrified of being chucked in prison.'

'Oh, don't worry about Miles. You go ahead and tell your friend whatever you want, Penny. Apart from any other considerations, I reckon I'm pretty well back on my feet now, so if it did all come to light, I think I'm just about ready to stand up and face the music.'

Penny felt a tremendous sense of relief. 'Excellent. Well, with your blessing, I'll tell him just enough to keep him quiet and I'll really impress upon him that he keeps it to himself.' She found herself grinning into the fabulous, gold-framed mirror on the wall of her room. 'That'll be good. Up to now he's been convinced that my new hairstyle and fingernails are because I've turned into a call girl.' She heard Olivia giggle on the other end of the line and changed the subject. 'Anyway, there's been a very interesting development here. And you're right about how tricky it is to pretend to be somebody else. I've just been having a drink with Jonathan.'

'Jonathan?' Olivia sounded amazed. 'You mean, Jon, Jonathan Carstairs?'

'I don't know his surname, but I remembered what you had said about him and took a guess. Yes, it's your rather good-looking Jonathan with the red hair.' She went on to tell Olivia all about the conversation they had had and the invitation to dinner on Wednesday. 'I suppose the best thing will be for me to invent some excuse and wriggle out of it, unless you feel like contacting him and explaining what's been happening. I'm afraid it's going to be almost impossible for me to keep up appearances if we do go out for dinner.' A thought came to her. 'Alternatively, here's a better suggestion. Why don't you consider coming over and taking my place?' She heard an intake of breath at the other end of the line, but she carried on. 'You know, you pretending to be me pretending to be you.' Now it was her turn to giggle. 'Bloody hell, but it's complicated.'

'Oh, Penny, I don't know…' Penny couldn't miss the note of longing in Olivia's voice so she did a bit of pressing.

'Seriously, why don't you fly across tomorrow or Wednesday? Apart from anything else it might get me out of a hole. I gave him a goodnight kiss tonight and who knows where that'll lead on Wednesday night.'

'You did?' Olivia sounded part excited, part worried. Also, Penny noted with a grin, she even sounded slightly jealous as she went on. 'What sort of kiss? On the cheeks? Lips? Passionate…?'

Penny took pity on her. 'No, no passion, just a gentle brush of lip against lip, but he definitely enjoyed it. So, like I say, give it some thought. I know for a fact that he would be really, really pleased to see you in the flesh.'

'I don't know, Penny…' Olivia was repeating herself, but Penny was delighted to hear that she still hadn't said no.

'Anyway, you think it over and let's talk tomorrow. You ring me or I'll ring you. I'll give Jimmy a call now and see that he keeps his mouth shut. And give my big hairy friend Gilbert a hug from me.'

When Penny rang Jimmy, she had to wait a while before he answered. He hastened to explain. 'Hi, Penny, give me a minute and then call me back, would you?' He was whispering. 'I'm serving champagne cocktails to a load of footballers and their WAGS. Just give me time to slip out to the loo. Bye.'

Talk of going to the loo reminded Penny this was something she had been wanting to do for quite a while now. She took her phone into the bathroom with her and then had the surreal experience of sitting on the loo, talking to Jimmy, knowing that he, too, was in the toilet on the other end of the line. She caught sight of her reflection in the mirror and started giggling to herself as she spoke to him.

'Jimmy, do you remember Caroline?'

'Yes, of course. The very elegant girl you're sharing a house with now.'

'That's her. Anyway, she works for a girl called Olivia and I've been employed to act as Olivia's double.'

'Her double?' Penny could hear the incredulity in his voice.

'You must have seen how similar we look.'

'Absolutely identical, even down to the shape of your ear lobes.' Penny found herself amazed that he should have noticed such fine detail in either of them. 'She had me totally fooled this morning. It was only when she started speaking to me that I began to realise there was something dodgy going on. That and the fact that I thought she was going to give me a slap at one point. So, why her double? Doing what?'

Penny explained, but without giving away Olivia's surname or telling him anything too specific about the Foundation. She finished by saying, 'She's been terribly upset since her dad's death and she's just coming out of it now. Please promise me you won't breathe a word of this to anybody. If it got out and the media started hounding her, I'd be terrified it might undo all our good work and send her right back into deep depression again, or worse.'

This time, Jimmy sounded much more sincere. 'I promise. Poor kid, I lost my dad when I was just a little nipper and I still remember getting the news. I cried for weeks, it was just so awful. Anyway, Penny, I promise, cross my heart and hope to die, I won't tell a soul.'

Relieved, Penny chatted to him for a while longer. In the end, as she knew she would all along, she came round to telling him about her new sighting of her pirate man. Jimmy was fascinated.

'That's amazing, Penny. How awfully romantic. So, do you think he's following you around? That would just be *the* most romantic thing anybody could do.'

'No I don't and I'm not sure I see it as particularly romantic if it really turns out that's what he's doing. It's more like creepy. That's stalking, you know.' She paused for reflection for a moment. 'But he can't be tailing me. He just can't. There's no way he could have known where I was going.' She was about to tell him that she had flown across to Venice in a private plane so that would have prevented her mystery man from knowing her destination, but then decided against mentioning it as being too overwhelmingly flashy. 'And this evening, I was hopelessly lost. There's no way he could have followed me and, even if he had done, how come he popped up in front of me and on the other side of the canal?'

'But at least you now know he's real. He's not just a figment of your imagination like you were thinking before.'

Penny hesitated. Was he real? Did she believe he was real? She had followed him for some time tonight, but she hadn't ever had any form of physical contact. In fact, there had been no eye contact on any of the three occasions she had seen him. What did that mean? Was he just like one of her dreams?

'You still there, sweetheart?' Jimmy sounded worried.

'Yes, sorry, Jimmy. Look, I don't know what to think anymore. With all this Olivia business, I'm not even quite sure who I am half the time. Maybe I do keep making him up. I mean, how on earth could he just materialise here like that?'

'Well, I suppose it's possible, but it's one hell of a coincidence. That's three times now, isn't it?' He lowered his voice. 'It's almost as if it's meant to be. Anyway, sweetheart, I've got to go. Somebody's knocking on the door. Their need's probably greater than mine. See you.'

'Bye, Jimmy, and remember, mum's the word.'

'All right, mum.'

Chapter 18

Next morning at breakfast, Caroline had a broad smile on her face. Penny was already there, tucking into a plate of the best fruit salad she had ever eaten and she looked up with a grin as Caroline came in. 'All go to plan last night?'

'Oh, yes.' Caroline gave a contented sigh and took a seat opposite Penny, both of them by the window where they were able to look out over the empty terrace and onwards across the lagoon. The wind appeared to have dropped, although it still looked bitterly cold out there. Four or five brazen seagulls huddled together on one of the windowsills, eyeing the breakfast plates on the other side of the glass covetously, presumably enjoying whatever warmth radiated outwards to them. It was another fine day, and early morning sunshine was reflecting on the cupola of the basilica on the island directly opposite where they were sitting, turning it to burnished gold. Penny put her spoon down and looked back at Caroline.

'You'll have to give me all the gory details, but first, let me tell you what happened to me last night.' She went on to recount the events of the evening, including her phone call to Olivia. Caroline was goggle-eyed at Penny's story about seeing the pirate again, but her expression turned to concern when Penny told her about her conversations with Jimmy.

'Do you think he'll keep his word? I imagine he realises this story could make him quite a bit of money if he sold it to the tabloids.'

'He won't talk. I know him. He's a little monkey when he wants to be and he likes nothing more than a bit of salacious gossip, but I also know he's a really good friend. He told me his lips are sealed and I trust him.' She caught Caroline's eye. 'Besides, I didn't tell him who Olivia is.'

Caroline nodded. 'That's good. And you think Olivia might really come over to Venice to see Jonathan?'

Now it was Penny's turn to nod. 'I'm not sure, but I think she might. She certainly sounded very interested when I told her I'd met him and that I, or rather, she, was invited out for dinner tomorrow. I wouldn't be surprised if she did come over.'

Caroline ordered a cappuccino from the waiter and waited until he had left before continuing. 'But what happens then? You're already here. She can hardly pitch up and share your room with you. Besides, let's face it, with two identical girls wandering round, people are going to notice.'

'I've been thinking about that. It's not a problem. If she does come over, I'll just disappear. There are hundreds of hotels in Venice and it's the low season for another few days. We're only staying until Saturday, aren't we? I shouldn't have any trouble finding myself a room and I've got all that money she gave me. I'll just check into another hotel, somewhere in the side streets or even at Mestre or somewhere else on the mainland,

and keep a low profile. Let's face it, with this cold weather, I can easily disguise myself with a hat and a scarf and nobody'll be any the wiser.'

Caroline still looked concerned. 'Are you sure? Venice isn't really that big and, remember, there must be a couple of hundred people from the conference who would recognise your face by now.'

'Yes, but as long as Olivia and I aren't out and about together, there should be no problem. Besides, Olivia said I really have to visit the far flung islands, so that would get me even further out of the way. No, if she decides to come over, we'll make it work.'

'So what about you and your pirate man? What on earth's going on there? The last time you talked about him, you were beginning to wonder whether you'd imagined the whole thing.'

'I still am, Caroline. I really don't know what to think.'

The waiter arrived with Caroline's coffee. Noticing that Penny had finished her fruit salad he removed the plate and glided away. Caroline glanced round at the nearby tables, but most of the other guests that morning appeared to be a group of Chinese tourists and nobody was close enough to overhear anyway. 'But, assuming he's a real person, do you think he might be stalking you?' Caroline sounded concerned.

'That's what Jimmy said, or at least he wondered if the pirate was following me on purpose because he was in love with me.'

'He's a real romantic, isn't he, your Jimmy? But, seriously, Olivia's a very wealthy girl. If you have the slightest concern that he might be up to no good, we should go to the police.'

Penny shook her head. 'No, there's no need for that, not least as it would be terribly complicated. First, he hasn't done anything at all yet. And second, we would have to explain that I'm not really who I'm supposed to be. I flew over on my own passport, but you booked me in here at the hotel using Olivia's passport, didn't you?'

Caroline shook her head. 'Her driving licence, actually. We thought it best to leave Olivia her passport in case she needed to go somewhere. By the sound of it, if she's considering coming over, that was probably just as well. But, yes, I take your point. Theoretically she wasn't recorded coming into the country, but she has popped up here in your shoes, so I suppose we could get into trouble for breaking Italian immigration laws.' She caught Penny's eye. 'But you're sure he's not a threat?'

'I'm sure he's nothing sinister. Besides, there's no way he could have known I was here.' She gave Caroline a smile. 'The main thing at the moment is for me just to convince myself that he's real. I'm beginning to wonder if I'm going potty.'

—

The conference was particularly interesting that Tuesday as a number of scientists were presenting hitherto unpublished data about the shrinking polar ice cap and rising water levels in the Indian Ocean. By the end of the day, any doubts Penny might have had about global warming had been swept away. As she travelled back from the island, she found herself looking at the water level alongside the quays with real concern. There was probably less than half a metre between the surface of the lagoon and the pavement in some places. Indeed, all along the waterfront between the hotel and St Mark's Square, trestles were stacked up, ready to be put down as walkways the next time the phenomenon known as the *acqua alta* took place and all that area flooded. Yes, she thought to herself, Venice, in common with so many low-lying parts of the world, was living on borrowed time.

Back at the hotel she dumped her briefcase and headed straight out to visit the Galleria dell'Accademia, just a little bit further up the Grand Canal. A few stripy-shirted gondoliers looked up hopefully as she emerged, but the waves splashing against the hulls of the sleek black gondolas, coupled with the near freezing conditions, firmly decided her against that as an idea. Gondolas and gondoliers were all very well in her dreams, but the reality was not quite so appealing, at least not in winter. Instead, she jumped onto a *vaporetto* and let the boat take her up to the gallery, even though it probably wouldn't have been a long walk. The Accademia was only a few stops along the canal and the *vaporetto* was just like a regular bus, but the views it afforded were better than any bus she had ever taken. It was about half past four when she got there and she knew she had almost three hours before the place would close. As an artist, what she really loved was to study not only the subject, but the way the painting had been created, feeling a sense of connection, a shared heritage, with artists who had been working here in Venice five hundred years earlier.

The Accademia itself was a magnificent cream-coloured stone building, situated on a little square, right on the side of the Grand Canal, with stunning views out across the water. But Penny hadn't come for the views today. She had come for the paintings. She went up the three steps and into the reception area to buy her ticket. There was nobody queuing and she hoped that would mean there wouldn't be too many other visitors to disturb her as she worked her way through the rooms. She took her time, moving slowly and methodically, admiring and studying the most magnificent collection of paintings from the Middle Ages to the late Renaissance. She saw works by such giants as Bellini, Mantegna, Tintoretto and Titian and she lost all sense of time. Outside, night fell, but she hardly noticed.

Finally, she stopped in front of one of her all time favourites, seeing it now for the very first time in the flesh. It was Giorgione's *Tempest*, a simple-looking landscape with a woman holding a baby on the right, a man standing on the left, a storm brewing in the background. It had been painted right at the beginning of the sixteenth century, over five hundred years ago, and it was exquisite. Clearly, it was also massively valuable as it was securely housed behind a glass screen. She stood in awe in front of it, doing her best to follow the brush strokes of the master with her eyes.

She had been there for a considerable time when she became vaguely aware of footsteps behind her and then heard a voice at her shoulder. It was a man's voice and he was speaking Italian.

'The most wonderful painting in the world.'

Penny smiled. Without turning her head, she allowed herself a comment in Italian. 'Try telling that to Botticelli.'

'Giorgione eats Botticelli for breakfast. Look at this, the mastery of the artist, the enigma of the subject, the expressions on the faces, the raw sexuality of both the man and the woman. Quite stunning.'

Penny liked the man's confidence. It was a masterful painting, but there were too many other contenders in the world for the *most wonderful* appellation. She turned towards him, ready to tell him that she would place it in her top ten, but couldn't afford it the ultimate accolade.

She didn't even manage to get a single word out. She found herself confronted by a tall man with a mop of dark hair and a piratical beard. She stopped dead in amazement, the old familiar feeling in her knees causing her to reach out and grab a pillar for support. It was him, and he was real.

'Are you feeling all right?' His hand caught her forearm and he steadied her. 'Here, come and sit down.' He led her two or three paces to an upholstered bench. She sat down gratefully and he sat down beside her. 'You looked as if you just saw a ghost.'

Penny shook her head, more to try to shake some sense into her brain that had suddenly gone numb, than to deny seeing a ghost. Here he was, her mystery man, alive and in the flesh. And he was Italian. She blinked a few times, took a couple of deep breaths and did her best to regain some sort of composure. She cleared her throat, speaking to him in Italian. 'Thank you, I'm fine. I think I must just have been standing in front of the *Tempest* for too long. My legs must have gone to sleep.' In fact there was absolutely no doubt in her mind as to what had happened. It had been him, his appearance, that had made her knees turn to jelly. So did this mean it had really happened at long last? Was this the bolt of lightning? Was this the famous love at first sight that only happened to other people?

'I'm not surprised. I saw you standing there a quarter of an hour ago when I came in, and you were still in the same position when I came past again now.' He held out his hand. 'My name's Federico. My friends call me Rico.'

Penny had a momentary panic as her befuddled brain refused to decide who she was. In the end, to be on the safe side, she opted for being Olivia, even though she was speaking Italian. 'Olivia. I'm pleased to meet you. Thanks for your help.' She shook his hand, but that did nothing to calm her whirling mind. She felt his touch all the way up her arm and across her body. She released him and turned away, taking a few more surreptitious breaths.

'Are you on holiday?'

She turned back towards him to answer. 'Um, yes, sort of. And you?'

'No, I live here.'

'What a lovely place to live.' Well, she thought to herself, that explained why she had seen him here, but it didn't explain why he had been in London. She decided to do a bit of digging. 'I live in London. Do you know London?'

He nodded, his eyes still trained on the Giorgione on the wall in front of them. 'I pop over every couple of months, when there's an exhibition I specially want to see.'

This sounded interesting. 'Did you go to the Botticelli exhibition at the National Gallery by any chance?'

'You like Botticelli, don't you?' He turned towards her and for the first time she noticed his eyes. They were emerald green and they appeared to sparkle as he spoke. 'And yes, I did. It was amazing to see so many of his works together, side by side. I love comparing different paintings, seeing how his style changed over the years. Do you paint?'

Penny now was seriously regretting having chosen to be Olivia. If she had just told him her real name, she would be able to tell him the truth about her work and her upcoming exhibition. He was still wearing the same fairly battered looking leather jacket and he probably didn't have the money for a haircut, so she knew it wasn't as if he would be able to buy any of her work, but he was obviously very knowledgeable, or at least opinionated, about art and it would have been nice to talk to him about it as equals. As she was in the Olivia role all she could do was to play it down.

'I do a bit. But I know what I like and I really, really love the *Tempest*, whether it really is the greatest painting ever painted or not.' She caught his eye and smiled. 'What about you?' He smiled back.

'I do a lot more than a bit of painting. I'm afraid I'm a junkie. I spend more time painting than I do sleeping.'

'What sort of thing?' This really was infuriating. She loved talking to fellow artists about their work and now she was only able to talk as an interested outsider, rather than a hands-on, oil-paint-under-the-fingernails, artist. 'Abstract, photographic, or what?'

He snorted, presumably at the idea of art that tried to represent scenes with the accuracy of a photograph. 'Difficult to describe. I suppose I'm going through a fairly abstract period at the moment, but there's no getting away from the inspiration. I'm a Venetian and my paintings are always inspired by this place, one way or another.' He glanced at his watch. 'Well, if you've finished your study of the painting, maybe I could buy you a drink?' Then, before she could answer, he made an alternative suggestion. 'Or, if you haven't already got plans for this evening, how would you like to join me and some friends for a few drinks and something to eat a bit later on?' He hastened to explain. 'It's a bunch of local artists and we meet up once a month or so in a restaurant not that far from here. You'd be very welcome to join us.' He smiled. 'We don't bite.'

Penny didn't hesitate. She owed it to herself to find out more about this man and she knew that she craved his company. There was no doubt about it, what she had seen of him and learnt about him so far was fascinating. She decided to say yes. 'That sounds really good, thanks. Where and when?'

'How well do you know Venice?'

She shook her head. 'Not very well, I'm afraid.'

'Where are you staying? I could call by and pick you up.'

Penny took another look at him and decided she couldn't confess to staying at what was just about the best hotel in Venice, if not the whole of Italy. Almost certainly, as an impoverished artist, he wouldn't have approved. Once again she found herself forced into a little white lie. 'A little place just near St Mark's Square. But I can meet you anywhere.'

He hesitated. 'Well, how about here? Let's say we'll meet in the middle of the bridge just outside here, the

Ponte dell'Accademia, at half past eight. All right with you?'

Penny took the water-bus back to the hotel. Although there was space to sit down inside, she stayed out in the cold, quite literally hopping from one leg to the other with excitement. She only stopped when it occurred to her that people might think she was desperate for a pee. Her mind was racing, her heart pounding. He was real. He existed, and she had met him. He had touched her, so there was no way he could be imaginary or some sort of ghost. In fact, if she concentrated hard, she could still feel his touch on her arm from when he had helped her to a seat and then his hand in hers. The succession of magnificent buildings slipped past on either side of the Grand Canal, but she barely noticed them. The only image in her head was Rico and his amazing green eyes.

Such was her state of exaltation, she almost missed her stop. At the last minute she spotted the unmistakable façade of the hotel and pushed past the passengers coming on board to slip off just in time. She crossed the quayside and went in through the revolving doors just as Caroline was about to come out. Caroline took one look at her and held out a hand to steady her.

'Penny, are you all right? You look as if you've seen a ghost.'

'I have, Caroline, and he's real.' Penny saw the hall porter look up in surprise and she realised she was almost shouting with exhilaration. She took a few deep breaths and made a conscious effort to calm down, lowering her voice before continuing. 'I've seen him, Caroline, I've

224

touched him and he's a real person. His name's Rico and he's an artist. He's got amazing eyes and he's ever so nice and...' She realised she was babbling.

'What? Your pirate man? You've seen him?' Caroline's eyes widened. 'Where, when, how?'

Penny told her all about the scene in the Accademia and how she had finally met her mystery man. Caroline looked pleased for her, but still a little uncertain. 'That's amazing, Penny, and he's asked you out tonight?' Penny nodded enthusiastically. 'And you don't know where you're going? And all you know about him is his first name?' Penny nodded, less enthusiastically now. 'Are you absolutely sure you'll be all right on your own? Listen, Nick and I are supposed to be going to a place he knows over on Giudecca. I could get him to cancel the restaurant and I could come with you if you like.'

Penny shook her head vehemently. 'I wouldn't dream of it. I'll be fine. It's a restaurant, after all, and it's bound to be bang in the middle of Venice. If it were a private house or out in the sticks somewhere I might be a bit concerned, but this'll be fine. Besides, I'm sure I can trust him.'

'Well, if you're sure...'

'Yes, definitely.' Penny had absolutely no doubt about that. 'Now, you two lovebirds go out and enjoy yourselves. If I see the *Do Not Disturb* sign on your door handle later on, I'll draw my own conclusions.' She smiled as Caroline blushed red.

'Well, just do me a favour, will you, Penny? When you get back tonight, just send me a text so I know you're home safe.'

'Yes, mum.'

Up in her room, the first thing Penny did was to phone Olivia, to find out if she had decided to take the plunge and come across to Venice the next day, but there was no reply. She stared out of the window at the lights of Venice and knew she definitely wanted to talk to somebody else about her sighting of the mystery man. After a brief pause for thought, she called Jimmy. He answered almost immediately.

'Hi, Penny, how's it going? How's the double life treating you? Do you get two breakfasts? One for you and one for your employer?'

'Just the one, but talking of breakfasts, the food over here's out of this world. Anyway, listen, I've met my pirate man.'

'Oh, I say, how exciting! Do spill the beans.' She told him all about the chance encounter in the gallery and he evidently approved of Rico's technique. 'Couldn't have done better myself. Galleries are marvellous places for pick-ups.'

'It wasn't a pick-up, Jimmy. It was a chance meeting. Two artists in the same gallery at the same time.'

'Rubbish, he's been following you, that's what. I'm sure of it.'

'Of course he hasn't. It was just chance.'

'Whatever you say, sweetheart. But, either way, you've finally met him in the flesh.' He paused to giggle. 'Although that'll probably come a bit later on. So, tell me all about him. Is he as handsome close up as he first appeared? He hasn't got bad breath or hairy nostrils or anything?'

'He's got the most amazing eyes, Jimmy. Real emerald green. It's like staring at a cat. And, yes, he's a real hunk.'

'Mmh, sounds gorgeous. No chance of him being a little bit gay, maybe?'

'No chance at all, unless my radar's totally wrong. No, I think he's as straight as a die.'

'Pity.' Jimmy didn't sound too disheartened. 'Anyway, I'm so pleased for you, darling. After what that Owen did to you, you deserve a nice hunky man all to yourself. And fancy him being an artist as well! He certainly ticks all the boxes. And I bet it won't be long before he does more than just tick your...'

'Be that as it may, Jimmy, I'm going out for a few drinks with him and his friends. That should give me the chance to get to know him a bit better. I still can't get over the coincidence of seeing him all these times.'

'I still don't think it's a coincidence, but maybe that's just because I believe in love. Ah, a love story in Venice, how Shakespearian. Now, you will call me tomorrow and let me know how it went, won't you? And I'll be expecting a full description of him, warts and all. No, on second thoughts, forget the warts, just tell me about the good bits.'

'I'll call you tomorrow, but don't expect a blow by blow account of how the evening went.' She realised what she had said before she heard his giggle. 'No intimate details, all right?'

'All right, sweetheart. Have fun. I'll be thinking of you... or him.'

–

The *Ponte dell'Accademia* is a huge hump-backed wooden bridge and from the top, Penny found herself able to look up and down the Grand Canal in all its glory.

Even in the nighttime the views were spectacular. The magnificent *palazzi* all along the waterfront were each more beautiful than the other, and the constant flow of boats of all different sizes and types up and down this most famous of canals brought a vibrancy to the scene that she would have loved to capture on canvas. She took a number of photographs, in the hope that she might be able to use them in the preparation of a series of paintings when she got back home. She had only been there for a few minutes before she saw Rico running up the steps towards her and her heart leapt.

'Olivia, please excuse me for being late. I had to take a phone call just before I came out.' He came up the last steps and held out both his hands to greet her. He grasped her right hand in his and, even through her woolly gloves, she once again felt a tingle of excitement run through her. He shook her hand and then glanced back down the way he had come. 'Shall we go?' She nodded so he turned and led her off the bridge. As they walked, he explained. 'The place where my friends and I meet is just beyond the Rialto. It shouldn't take us more than fifteen minutes or so to get there, particularly at this time of year.'

'You mean because there are no tourists?'

He glanced across at her. 'There's never a time with no tourists, but this is definitely just about the quietest it gets in Venice. In mid-summer, it would take us twice as long.' He was right. The squares and streets they walked though were remarkably free of people, no doubt the freezing cold keeping many indoors. As they followed the narrow lane that was as close to a main street as Venice could provide, they chatted sporadically. For the most part, though, Penny just concentrated on committing her wonderful surroundings – and, of course, her intriguing companion – to memory.

The restaurant was just behind yet another church, situated in a narrow lane. Not for the first time, Penny found herself thinking of the logistical difficulties all businesses in Venice must face. Presumably everything was brought through the canals to the nearest point and then carried onwards by hand or by trolley. As she walked through the square in front of the church, she suddenly realised she recognised it from the previous night. After leaving the grappa café, she had walked home this way. In consequence, when she had seen him, he must have been within spitting distance of the restaurant. Maybe he had been on his way here. She looked across at him as they reached the restaurant entrance.

'Were you here last night?'

He looked surprised. 'Yes, briefly. I was out for a walk and I came to check if they had reserved a table for our group for today. Why do you ask?'

'I'm pretty sure I saw you, walking alongside one of the little canals.' She did a quick calculation. 'Just before eleven?'

He nodded. 'That's right. So you've seen me before, have you? Well, I'm very sorry, but I can't think how I could have missed seeing you. I normally have very good antennae when it comes to beautiful women. The first time I set eyes on you was this afternoon at the Accademia at precisely 6.24pm.'

Luckily they were still outside, so her blushes were hidden by the dark. 'You remember the time so exactly? That's amazing.'

'Some things you never forget.' She didn't have time to consider what that might mean before he pushed the door open and led her into the blessed warmth of the restaurant. It was a cosy place, with low, wood-beamed ceilings supported by brick arches, racks of wine bottles round the walls, and a smell of wood smoke in the air. It was almost full. There was a general hubbub of noise that rose as Rico led her towards a large table in one corner. His arrival was greeted by hoots of welcome from a miscellaneous bunch of people already sitting at the table. She and he squeezed into two free seats and he set about making the introductions. It occurred to Penny as he did so that she hadn't told him her surname and she had no idea of his. Somehow, this anonymity was really rather exciting.

'*Ciao ragazzi*. Can I present you my new friend Olivia? She's English, but she's done us the honour of learning our language.' He turned towards Penny and rattled off the first names of the other people round the table. Penny knew there was no way she would be able to remember them all so she just concentrated on memorising the names of those closest to her. These were a very pretty girl called Susanna with long dark hair and alongside her, a remarkable character called Fritz.

Fritz shook Penny's hand formally and immediately poured a big splash of red wine into her glass. 'Hi, Olivia, good to meet you. The name's Fritz.' He spoke to her in excellent English with just a slight German accent. What was remarkable about Fritz, however, was his hair. This was the first time Penny had ever seen a seventy-year-old man with a Mohican haircut. It looked almost as strange as the fur-trimmed jumper he was wearing, but Penny didn't bat an eyelid. She was no stranger to weird and wacky dressers. Many of the people she had got to know on the London art scene were as eccentric in their way as Fritz. She shook hands with both of them, slipped off her coat, hung it over the back of her chair, and addressed Susanna in Italian.

'Hi, are you an artist?'

The girl nodded. 'Yes, and you?'

Penny gritted her teeth, wishing she could tell the truth, and shook her head. 'Just an amateur, I'm afraid.'

Fritz laughed and joined in, this time in Italian. 'We're all amateurs here. There aren't many people who make a living out of painting these days.' His Italian was totally fluent and Penny was impressed. 'Apart from the caricaturists down on the waterfront.' He grinned. 'Or people making counterfeit banknotes.'

'Wow, you speak wonderful Italian.' Penny had never heard a German speak it so well. Fritz grinned at her.

'Thanks for the compliment, but that would be because I *am* Italian.' He explained. 'I was born and brought up in the mountains above Bolzano, to the north of here. It's Italy, but we all speak German as well as Italian. Anyway, *complimenti*, your Italian's pretty damn good. Tuscany by the accent.'

Once again, Penny gritted her teeth. It would have been such fun to tell them about her year working as an artist's apprentice in Florence, but now that she had opted for Olivia as an identity, she knew she had to stay in character. She thanked him and, as she did so, she felt Rico's hand on her arm.

'I see Fritz has already poured you some wine. What can I get you to eat?'

231

Penny liked the feel of his hand on her arm. He had now taken his leather jacket off and she was surprised to see him wearing a very smart jumper. Somehow, she had been expecting a big hairy pullover covered in paint stains. The wool adhered to the contours of his very fit body and she definitely liked what she saw. 'I'll have what you're having, but just not very much of it. I love Italian food and I won't fit into my clothes if I'm not careful.'

She saw his eyes flick down across her body and back to her face. 'I would say you've got a good way to go before that happens. Anyway, I'm going to have a plate of my favourite pasta, *bigoli in salsa*. Do you know it?' Penny shook her head. 'You'll have to trust me on this one. *Bigoli* are sort of big chunky spaghetti and the sauce is made with salted sardines and onion. It doesn't sound particularly appealing, I know, but it tastes really good and it's one of the specialities here.'

'I'll give it a try, but, like I say, a moderate portion.'

'And maybe some San Daniele ham to nibble as a starter?'

'You're the local. I'll put myself in your hands, Rico.' As she said it, she felt a delicious tremor of excitement. There was something very stimulating about being here with this very handsome, friendly, cultured man and yet not knowing anything much about him, nor he about her. She felt wonderfully relaxed, knowing she could pretty much say or do anything she wanted and nobody she knew would ever be any the wiser. As he removed his hand from her arm and turned to call the waiter, she laid her hand on his thigh and gave a little squeeze, telling herself it was just to attract his attention. He turned back towards her, his eyes glancing down to where her hand had landed, a little smile on his lips.

'You'd better get some water as well, Rico. If I spend all evening drinking wine, you might have to carry my home.'

'Well you did say you'd put yourself in my hands. Water, it is.' Reluctantly she removed her hand, but not before she felt his muscles tense.

It was a great evening. The company was warm, friendly and some of those around the table sufficiently outrageous to make her laugh out loud on many occasions. She spoke to Susanna about her work and learnt she was a sculptor who worked principally with marble. Penny didn't know a lot about stone sculpture and she was fascinated to learn that newly-quarried stone was much softer and more malleable than stone that had been lying around on the surface of the ground for centuries. She had never given that a thought before, imagining that stone was stone was stone. After a bit, she hit on the idea of inventing a friend of hers who was an artist and, by using her, was able to talk a bit more about the kind of stuff she was doing. She heard about the various exhibitions running at the moment, and Rico gave her a flyer advertising a brand new gallery with what looked like a fabulous collection of Renaissance works, opening later that week. She promised to do her best to go to as many of the exhibitions as she could fit in.

The ham was excellent, accompanied with fresh bread and olives and washed down with the local red wine. The pasta lived up to its billing and Penny found she had no trouble clearing her plate, even though the chef had clearly ignored her plea for a small portion. Too full for dessert, she ordered an espresso, as did most of the others at the end of the meal. This came with a bottle of grappa and a handful of shot glasses, but she shook her head, preferring to stay reasonably lucid, not least so as to remember this delightful evening in all its details. Beside her, the presence of Rico was very, very pleasant. He was a fun companion, very knowledgeable, but also a good listener. She told him as little as possible about her life, or that of Olivia, and she noticed that he said very little about himself as well. As the night went on, she found this ever more exciting; the notion of two anonymous people hooking up, like ships that pass in the night, somehow very stimulating.

She left the restaurant on Rico's arm well after midnight, having thoroughly enjoyed herself. They walked back towards St Mark's Square down darkened streets and narrow alleys. She hung onto his arm with both hands and loved the feel of his strength and his warmth against her. When they came to a little bridge, not dissimilar to the bridge where she had lost him the previous night, they stopped in the middle and she turned towards him, looking up in expectation. Her breath formed a white cloud in the air, barely illuminated by what looked like a centuries old street light. He dropped his head towards her, took her in his arms and kissed her.

It was fortunate that he chose to take her in his arms because there was a very real danger of her falling sideways into the canal as his touch once more destroyed her equilibrium. She reached her hands up and ran them across the sides of his face and on around his neck, catching his hair in her fingers. The kiss went on a very long time, but, even so, she didn't want it to stop. She pressed herself against him and loved every moment of it. Finally, they both came up for air. He raised his lips from hers and stared down at her, his eyes sparkling in the dim orange light. She could see he was smiling and she knew she was. There was no doubt in her mind as to what she wanted to do now. She wanted to go with him to his home and spend the night doing whatever felt right, knowing that their anonymity was preserved. She could say or do whatever she wanted and have no fear of recriminations in the morning.

'It's funny, Olivia, you've really surprised me.'

Penny looked up at him as he explained what he meant and as he did so, a cold, hard lump began to form in her stomach.

'I knew your father very well. I first met him a couple of years ago when he was over here buying a rather wonderful painting at auction. He was a charming man and we got on very well together. I was shocked to hear of his death back in the spring. I'm so sorry for you, Olivia. It must have come as a terrible blow.' Penny was still trying to come to terms with the fact that the anonymity in their relationship was purely on his side. She still knew nothing about him, but he knew all about her – or at least, he thought he did.

'I'll be quite honest, I'd heard some stories about your mother and you by extension, and neither of you came out of them too well. Stuck-up, arrogant and downright unpleasant were some of the words being used.' She felt his arms squeeze her to soften the blow. 'I'm sorry, but that's what I heard. And now I find that, apart from being stunningly beautiful, so beautiful that you took my breath away when I first saw you this afternoon, you're a sweet, funny, very intelligent girl without an arrogant bone in your body. So, Olivia, please forgive me for misjudging you. You couldn't be more different from what I'd been led to believe.'

'How long have you known who I was?' Penny's mind was racing.

'Maybe half an hour.'

She looked up and caught his eye. 'Half an hour?' She looked at him in blank incomprehension.

He nodded, a little smile on his lips. 'It was Gianni, the big guy with the beard and the earrings back there in the restaurant. You can't have missed him.' Penny nodded, remembering the giant on the far side of the table who looked like an Italian Obélix, even down to the blond pony tail. 'He recognised you. When we were at the cash desk, he showed me a photo on his phone of you with your father, taken here in Venice this time last year. Pity I didn't meet you back then.' He was still smiling, but Penny felt anything but happy.

So much for ships passing in the night. She now realised, with a sinking feeling in the pit of her stomach, that nothing more could happen between them. In fact, she had already, if unwittingly, done too much. Rico was now convinced that it had been Olivia who had abandoned herself in his arms a few minutes ago. In all probability Olivia herself was going to arrive in Venice the following day, looking forward to seeing a totally different man, and if she were to meet Rico, all hell would break loose. There was no way Penny could let herself take things to the next level with Rico, much as she knew she wanted to. She had to nip this developing

236

relationship in the bud before it got out of hand and caused all sorts of complications for her employer. With a very heavy heart, she stepped back, forcing him to release her. She steadied herself against the balustrade on the other side of the bridge and steeled herself for what she knew she had to say.

'I think I'd better get back to my hotel, Rico.' She saw the expression of surprise on his face. 'I've got a terrible headache and I need to sleep it off. Thanks for a lovely evening.'

A look of alarm crossed his face. 'Olivia, look, I'm sorry, really sorry.' He sounded very concerned. 'Those things I said, they were just things I'd heard from other people. You're not like that at all and I'm sure your mother isn't either. Oh, God, have I offended you?'

'It's all right, Rico, you haven't offended me.' Penny stepped towards him and kissed him softly on the lips, but retreated as she felt his hands reach for her. 'I just need to get back to the hotel. I'm afraid I have no idea where we are at the moment so if you could just point me in the direction of St Mark's, I'd better make tracks.' She did her best to ignore the expression, not only of bewilderment, but also of hurt, all too visible on his face. He looked like a little puppy who has been shut outside in the cold. 'This way?' She set off in the direction in which they had been heading. Behind her, she heard his footsteps and then felt his hand on her arm. His touch was still electric, but she couldn't shake the cold feeling of bitter disappointment that threatened to overwhelm her.

'Look, Olivia, please, I'm sorry, really sorry. Please don't go off like this.' Penny felt her heart breaking as she heard his tone. The emotion in his voice was all too evident. 'I've only just met you. You can't go off and leave me like this, please. Please, Olivia, I really want you to stay with me.'

'I'm sorry, Rico, but I have to get back.' Penny did her best to keep her voice as detached as she could and she steadfastly refused to turn towards him, afraid that his little lost dog look would melt her resolve. Inside, she felt awful. This chance encounter and the fantastic evening could so easily have been the precursor to something wonderful, but now it lay in ruins at her feet . From the sound of Rico's voice, he was every bit as gutted as she felt.

He tried on several more occasions to speak to her as they walked back through the maze of little streets, but every time she refused to do more than answer stiffly. At last they emerged into St Mark's Square, right at the feet of the illuminated Christmas tree. She vaguely remembered seeing a hotel just along the road from here and she led him to it. When they arrived at the entrance, she was relieved to see the lights still on in the lobby and a man sitting behind the reception desk. She stopped, turned towards Rico and delivered the little speech she had been working on for the last ten minutes.

'Thank you very much indeed for a wonderful evening, Rico. I loved meeting your friends and I'm very grateful to you for showing me a bit of real Venice.' She reached up on tiptoe and kissed him again. Although her intention had been just to deposit another light kiss, maybe even just on his cheek, she found herself pressing against him, her lips parting as she felt his arms reach around her once more. Then, taking a deep breath, she pulled back and broke away. 'Thanks again, Rico. I'll never forget tonight. Goodbye.' He must have heard the emotion in her voice, but she managed to keep the tears from falling.

She didn't give him a chance to respond, but just turned and walked blindly up to the glass door of the hotel and pushed, banging her head against it as she realised too late it was locked. The noise alerted the man at the reception desk and she heard a buzzing sound. The door swung open and she walked straight in, surreptitiously rubbing her forehead that had hit the glass, refusing to turn back towards Rico. She walked resolutely up to the counter. Realising that Rico was in all probability still standing on the other side of the glass door behind her, watching her, she knew she had to do more than just turn straight round and come back out again, so she summoned a weak smile for the benefit of the man at the counter.

'I was wondering if I could have some information about your hotel and maybe a copy of your price list. Might you have a room for tomorrow and maybe the next couple of days by any chance?'

The man reached under the counter and produced a colour leaflet along with a printed price list. He assured her that they had vacancies for the rest of the week, although from Sunday, the start of the Christmas holiday period, the hotel would be full. Penny kept her shoulders to the door and spent a couple of minutes pretending to study the leaflet and asking inane questions, until she felt confident enough to glance backwards. Rico had gone. She immediately felt two conflicting emotions. On the one hand, she felt relief that her masquerade had apparently worked and, on the other, a deep and lasting sense of loss. Rico was out of her life. The man who had made her go weak at the knees was no more. She was close to tears as she thanked the receptionist and went back out into the bare, frozen square.

She walked diagonally across the square, past the bell tower and out between the twin pillars bearing the statues of St Mark and St Theodore, the patron saints of Venice. She emerged on the waterfront. The street vendors with their carts of T-shirts, masks and postcards were long gone and there was barely a person to be seen. A couple came walking past her, huddled close together, probably as much for warmth as out of affection, as the bitter wind blew in across the water, cutting through Penny's gloves and coat. She screwed up her fingers and pushed her fists into her pockets, hunching her shoulders to try to protect her face. The wind brought with it a light sea mist and she felt moisture on her cheeks, running down her face like tears. Maybe they were tears.

She made her way along the quay, past the Byzantine beauty of the Doge's Palace, until she reached the hotel. She stopped at the door, took a few deep breaths, wiped her face with her gloved hand and then went in. The porter on duty gave her a smile of welcome.

'Welcome back, signorina. You look cold.'

She managed a weak smile in return. 'It's absolutely freezing outside.' Then, not having the strength to trudge up the stairs, she walked past the reception desk to the lift and pressed the button for the second floor. As she travelled up in the lift she composed a brief text message for Caroline as promised. *Home safe and well. X.* As she walked along the corridor to her room, she spotted a *Do Not Disturb* sign hanging from the handle of Caroline's room and she felt happy for her friend. But not for herself.

She went into her room and locked the door behind her. She didn't insert her key card in the slot, so the room remained in darkness. The night staff had closed the curtains, but after taking off her coat, scarf and gloves and dropping them on the bed, she felt her way across to the windows, pulling the curtains open so that she could stare outside into the darkness.

She stood by the window, her eyes stinging, still stubbornly refusing to let the tears run. How could it be that, just as her career as an artist was hopefully on the brink of taking off, her personal life could go so wrong? First Rick, then Owen and now, most painful of all, Rico. Tonight had been one of the most enjoyable of her life and yet, with just a few words, Rico had ruined everything. Of course it wasn't his fault. It was hers, for agreeing to pretend to be somebody she wasn't. If only the Obélix man hadn't recognised her, if only she had used her real name from the outset, if only she hadn't got involved in this increasingly complicated deception, playing the part of another person. She knew full well what her mother would have said if she had been able to talk to her about it, when it had all started, way back in September. 'It'll end in crying,' she would have said. And it had.

Penny stood there and watched the lights of a lone *vaporetto* as it made its way out from the quay and up into the Grand Canal, and did her best to think positive thoughts. At least she now had the confirmation that love at first sight existed, not just for other people, but for her as well. The thrill of his touch, the pleasure of his company and the overwhelming delight that had spread throughout her whole body during that long, passionate kiss told her, without a shadow of a doubt, that it had happened. The fact that she had now got herself into this insoluble mess of deception and lies couldn't obscure the fact that it was real. And, she reflected, if it could happen once, it could surely happen twice. She did her best to hold onto that thought and believe it but, deep down, she knew it was a forlorn hope.

She left the curtains open and made her way back across to the door. She felt for the slot and inserted the key card. The lights in the room came on, momentarily blinding her. She was standing there, blinking, when her phone started ringing. She glanced at the time. It was almost one o'clock, midnight in London.

'Hi, Penny, I haven't woken you up or anything, have I?' It was Olivia.

'No, in fact, I've just come in. I tried to phone you earlier but there was no reply.'

'Yes, sorry about that, but I've been out to the movies.'

'Really? Who with?'

'By myself.' Olivia sounded really proud. 'And I even went into the bar for a glass of wine first. So, how's everything over there?'

Penny really didn't know where to start so, to give herself time, she asked Olivia if she had made a decision about coming over to Venice. Olivia's reply was very positive and Penny felt a surge of pleasure, in spite of her depressed mood.

'Yes, I'm coming. I've done it. I've booked the plane for tomorrow. I should be arriving in Venice mid-afternoon.'

'Fantastic, Olivia, I'm so pleased.' And she was. This was excellent news and a definite sign that Olivia's troubles were sorting themselves out. 'I'll book myself into another hotel and I'll be out of the way for when you arrive.'

'But I still want to see you.' Olivia sounded genuinely concerned. 'I want to get all your news. There must be some way we can meet up without giving the game away.'

'I'm sure we'll think of something.'

'Are you all right, Penny? You sound a bit down. Nothing wrong, is there?'

Penny hesitated. It would have been nice to talk to her friend about what had happened, not least as Olivia was one of only two people with whom she could discuss this, three if she included Jimmy, but she felt too worn out to try. She did her best to sound more cheerful. 'I'm just tired. I think I'd better get to bed. I'll sort out a way for us to meet up and give you a call in the morning. Then I can tell you all about everything that's happened since I got here.'

'Is there much to tell?'

'More than you can imagine.'

Chapter 19

It took Penny a long time to get to sleep that night and she slept badly, tossing and turning, her mind constantly going over the events of that evening. On the occasions when she managed to drop off to sleep, she had a series of her regular dreams of Venice. But this time she was running through the streets, crisscrossing the maze of canals, looking in desperation for something or, more probably, someone. When she woke in the morning she felt jaded and miserable.

As she stood under the shower, she remembered her promise to phone Olivia, to tell her how the two of them could meet up without being seen. If it hadn't been so very cold here in Venice in December, they could have met up outdoors in any one of numerous places around the city, particularly down towards the area of the Biennale, where a park with trees, bushes and benches afforded ample opportunities for a clandestine meeting. The problem with meeting on a park bench, particularly in the dark, at this time of year was that the two of them would probably freeze to death within minutes. They either had to meet in the daytime, when the weak winter sun still offered some vestiges of warmth or they had to meet indoors in a dark or very isolated place. With thousands of tourists milling round, isolated places in Venice were few and far between, and with several hundred people from the conference knowing and recognising their shared face, the chances of discovery were substantial.

She was still thinking about this problem as she went up to the top floor restaurant for breakfast. She was surprised to find Caroline already there.

'Hi, Caroline, I thought you and your man would be having a champagne breakfast in bed this morning.'

Caroline looked up and grinned. 'He did the walk of shame an hour and a half ago. He's chairing a session on alternative energy today and he has to be at the conference…' She glanced at her watch. '…around about now.'

'So, how did it go? Did the lovely Doctor Nick live up to expectations?'

'The word you're looking for is *exceed*.' Caroline's face was relaxed and happy and, in spite of herself, Penny felt a touch of jealousy at her friend's happiness, as compared to the train wreck of her own life. The jealousy disappeared as soon as it had come, however, and she gave Caroline a big, genuine smile.

'I'm so pleased for you. You two took your time, but I'm so glad it's all worked out in the end.'

'Oh yes, and definitely worth the wait.' Caroline glanced up from her toast and gave Penny a quizzical look. 'Now don't get me wrong, Penny, you look as lovely as ever, but you do look a bit… weary. Have you been burning the candle at both ends? Maybe spending too much of the night with your pirate?'

'I wish.' The waiter appeared and Penny ordered a cappuccino. She waited until he had left before recounting the evening's events, and its bitter conclusion. As ever, Caroline was very supportive.

'I'm sure it'll work itself out. Just talk it through with Olivia. I got a text from her, saying she's decided to come over. You know that, too, don't you?' She glanced at Penny who nodded absently. 'By the way, kudos for that. Like I've said before, you should give up painting and take up counselling. You've pretty much got Olivia back to normal. Anyway, surely when she comes over you can talk it through with her and sort things out. The conference finishes at the end of the week and, after that, she'll be flying home. Now that she's resuming her role at the head of the Foundation, there's no longer any need for the deception. You can revert to being Penny again and you can see your pirate/artist man and explain everything to him. He'll understand, you'll see. And, by the sound of it, he'll probably like you all the more when he finds out you're a fellow artist, rather than a multi-millionaire.'

Penny didn't answer at first. Deep down inside, in a little compartment she had been trying to keep firmly locked, an uncomfortable thought. She waited for her coffee to arrive before opening up to Caroline.

'What if the kiss on the bridge was only prompted by the discovery that I was a multi-millionaire? He pretty clearly doesn't have a lot of money, what with his battered leather jacket and his bohemian friends. What if it was the discovery that the girl he picked up at the art gallery turns out to be super rich that decided him to make a play for her?' She reached for her coffee and took a sip to mask the sour taste in her mouth. Somehow, when looked at in that light, those wonderful minutes in his arms in the shadows of a Venice backstreet assumed a far less appealing aspect. Could it be that his interest in her had been, if not generated, then at least enhanced by the knowledge that she could be his meal ticket for life?

'Of course not.' Penny could hear the forced confidence in Caroline's voice. 'The fact is that he only found out who you are a few minutes before he kissed you. Up till then you and he had had a lovely evening and the subject of money hadn't reared its ugly head at all.'

'Yes, I know, Caroline, but I've been thinking about what you said about the few men in Olivia's life; you know about her not being sure whether they were after her for herself or her millions.' She caught Caroline's eye. 'Somehow I feel even more pity for her now. In my life up to now, all I've had to work out has been whether the men I've met have been interested in the contents of my brain or my pants. For somebody in Olivia's position, there's a third unknown in the equation.' She sighed and stood up. 'I'm going to get myself a plate of bacon and eggs. I need it this morning. Can I get you anything?'

By the time she had helped herself to scrambled egg and bacon from the battery of heated dishes along the breakfast bar, another unpleasant truth had occurred to her. She filled a glass with freshly squeezed orange juice and returned to the table. Caroline had finished her toast and was staring out of the window, an expression of deep contentment on her face. As Penny returned, the expression changed back to concern again. But before she could offer any more words of support, Penny pointed out the major stumbling block she now faced.

'Besides, there's a big problem. Even if I can talk things through with Olivia and we can come to some sort of arrangement that allows me to see Rico again and explain what's happened, the fact is that I still haven't got a clue as to how to go about finding him again.' She looked across at Caroline, a sense of deep frustration bubbling up inside. 'His name's Federico. He's Italian. He lives in Venice. He's an artist. And that's your lot. I don't know his surname. I don't know where he lives. I don't know a bloody thing about him.' She picked up her fork and stabbed angrily at the scrambled egg. 'He's gone, and that's that.'

'Surely not. What about the restaurant? I bet if you go back there and ask, they'll be able to tell you who he is or, if they don't actually know him, at least they might know some of the others in that group. Didn't he say this was a regular monthly thing? The blond giant, for instance? There can't be too many seven-foot-tall men going round Venice with blond pigtails.' She reached over and gave Penny's hand a squeeze. 'You'll see. Just talk it through with Olivia then go back to the restaurant. I bet they'll know.'

Penny nodded absently. Caroline was right, of course. The restaurant was the obvious answer. But first, she had to find a suitable place to meet Olivia. She dug into her plate of bacon and egg and found it excellent. The smell of bacon reminded her of her time at the Apocalypse Café. So much had changed since then, most notably the trio of men who had exited her life in swift succession. At least, she thought to herself, she still had Jimmy. He would know what to do. She decided to phone him later on to talk things through with him.

Before travelling over to the conference on what was in all likelihood to be her last ever trip in a water taxi,

Penny packed everything into the two suitcases and left them with Caroline. She filled a small bag with enough clothes to last her for two more days and, as she did so, she remembered the brochure she had picked up in the other hotel the previous night. She gave them a call and booked a room for three nights. On the way to the conference she checked in there and dropped her bag, so that at the end of the afternoon, she could seamlessly cease to be Olivia Brookes-Webster and revert to just being plain old Penny Lane. It gave her a funny sensation.

All the way over in the water taxi, she reflected on the fun she had had as Olivia. She knew she would never forget moments like the reception in the South-bank Centre with all those famous faces, her subsequent groping by Rafe Stinky-breath Kingsholme, her first ever flight in a private jet, the unbelievable luxury of the hotel or the feeling of having diamonds hanging from her ears that cost as much as a limousine. This brief interlude, apart from restoring her to a position of relative financial security and lifting her out of her rodent-infested previous existence, had also given her two really close girlfriends that she felt sure she would keep for the rest of her life. Her feelings at returning to the real world were genuinely mixed.

Before the first session started, she sneaked off to a corner of the beautiful cloisters and phoned Jimmy. He was on the morning shift at the café and she could almost smell the bacon as she spoke to him.

'Hi, Jimmy, it's me.'

'Hello sweetie, how's things? How did it go with your mystery man? You promised me details.' There was a momentary pause. 'But just don't tell me he's got a hairy back. If there's one thing I can't stand it's a man with a hairy back. Just tell me about the rest of him. Was he as hunky as you were expecting?'

'I never got to find out, Jimmy.' After glancing around to be sure the coast was clear, Penny told him all about their evening together and its disappointing end. Predictably, Jimmy was concerned for the man.

'The poor dear. How awful for him. There he was with a totally gorgeous girl in his oh-so-muscular arms, rubbing her juicy bits against him and then, just as he's getting his hopes up, slap bang wallop and she dumps him. By the way, when I say getting his hopes up, you know what I'm referring to, don't you?'

'I *always* know what you're referring to, Jimmy. But the fact is that I didn't have any choice. Besides, although I feel very sorry for him, it hasn't been a bundle of fun for me, you know. I hardly slept a wink last night.'

'You poor thing. But don't despair. Just you sit down with your evil twin and she'll be bound to let you tell him the truth. By the sound of it, you've pretty much reached the end of your contract now anyway, so the secret can come out.'

'I know, Jimmy, but first I've got to meet up with her and talk and that's not so easy. The one thing we don't want is for people to see us together. Nobody should ever know about this little subterfuge. Olivia has to be able to slip back into her job without anybody being any the wiser. The trouble is to find somewhere here in Venice where we can meet without being seen.'

They talked for a minute, Jimmy pitching suggestions at her and she shooting them down in flames, until he finally came up with a better idea. 'I've always found cemeteries good. People don't look at each other there; you know, respecting the grief of others and all that. Besides, you could wear a headscarf, a veil even. Isn't there a cemetery there you could go to?' The ramifications of Venice's situation in the middle of the lagoon suddenly hit him. 'Or do they all get a burial at sea there? Lots of decomposing corpses floating around can't be very sanitary though…'

Penny realised that he had indeed cracked it. 'The island of the dead. That's it, Jimmy. I was reading about it the other day. The island of San Michele is just one big cemetery and, even better, it's on the way from the airport to the hotel. I'll get Olivia to call in there this afternoon while the sun's still out and we can talk in peace and quiet. It should be pretty well empty on a cold December Wednesday.'

'And then you go and get your man, Penny. You deserve him.'

'Easier said than done, Jimmy. I don't even know his surname, let alone where he lives.'

'You'll find him. Let's face it, Penny, the universe couldn't really make it any clearer for you. He keeps walking into your life unannounced. You two just *have* to get together and you will. You'll be paddling your gondola along the Grand Canal and you'll bump into him. Just you wait and see.'

Penny couldn't help laughing. 'You don't really know how it works here in Venice, do you Jimmy? You don't paddle around in gondolas.'

'Well, canoes then. You know what I mean.'

Penny left the conference at half past three and took two different water-buses to get her to the island of the dead by just after four. She stepped onto the pontoon and walked in through the cemetery gates along with a handful of other people, all of them carrying flowers. For a moment she rather wished she had thought of flowers as extra camouflage, but nobody spared her more than a passing glance. As she entered the cemetery, she looked to her right, admiring the lovely old white church, one of the earliest Renaissance buildings in Venice.

She and Olivia had decided to meet by the tomb of Igor Stravinsky, one of a number of famous names to be buried here, and Penny easily found the gravestone. It was just a smooth slab with his name chiselled on it, alongside his wife Vera's. There were a number of bunches of flowers lying on the graves, along with notes, weighed down with stones. Out of curiosity, Penny glanced at one, but saw that it was written in Cyrillic script and replaced it. She had spent the princely sum of five euros to buy herself a black headscarf from an Indian man on the quay before leaving, and she had tied this over her head, concealing her hair. A further outlay of ten euros had brought a rather chunky pair of thick-rimmed dark glasses and she reckoned her disguise should be good enough to fool most people.

About ten minutes later, she heard the crunch of feet on the gravel path and Olivia appeared. Their eyes met and both of them had to struggle not to burst out laughing. Olivia, in an attempt to look anonymous and dissimilar to Penny, had unwittingly opted for an almost identical outfit, complete with dark headscarf and sunglasses. The net result was that they still looked like twins, in spite of their disguise. The good news was that their faces and hair were suitably hidden and here, in this part of the cemetery, there was nobody to be seen. Olivia came across to the grave and deposited a bunch of flowers on the tombstone before straightening up and coming across to give Penny a hug.

'Penny, hi. So good to see you again.'

Penny kissed her on the cheeks, genuinely delighted. 'And me, Olivia. Congratulations on doing it. I'm so, so pleased you decided to come.'

'So am I and so's my stepmum. She called from Antigua to tell me she's having a great time and feeling really good. She sends her love.'

Penny felt a real sense of satisfaction, knowing that Olivia's stepmum was regaining her own happiness. 'Who's looking after Gilbert? He'll be missing you.'

'He'll be fine. Janice spoils him rotten and Arthur walks him to the pub and then feeds him crisps. He'll probably be ten pounds heavier by the time I get home.'

Together they walked across to a stone bench in the sun, situated beneath a centuries-old yew tree, and sat down side by side. Penny glanced around cautiously, but there was only a gardener way over to one side, well out of earshot. 'Have you left your stuff in the water taxi?'

Olivia nodded. 'He's waiting out by the pontoon. He'll take me round to the hotel once we've had a chance to catch up. So, tell me all about it. You definitely sounded a bit down last night. What's happened?' An expression of concern appeared on what little of her face was still visible. 'It's not about Jonathan, is it? He hasn't cancelled our date tonight or anything, has he?'

Penny was quick to reassure her. 'No, nothing like that. He'll be waiting for you in the lobby at eight o'clock or even earlier. By the way, when I saw him the other night he was wearing a jacket, collar and tie, so I imagine you should aim to look a bit smart tonight.'

Penny saw Olivia smile. 'I'm not just going to look smart, I'm going to look so blooming good, his eyes'll pop out of their sockets. Anyway, so what's happened?'

Penny told her all about her chance meeting with Rico at the Accademia, their evening together, and then the discovery that he knew who she was, or so he thought. She ended up apologising. 'I'm really sorry, Olivia, I shouldn't have gone out with him. I forgot my job, I'm afraid. Hopefully I managed to nip things in the bud, so you don't need to worry about finding yourself with a hairy artist knocking on your door, hoping you'll fall into his arms once more.' Penny tried to sound as upbeat as she could, but she didn't fool Olivia.

'Oh, Penny, you should've told him! It wouldn't have mattered. I'm feeling good now, really fine. There's the conference tomorrow and I'm really looking forward to it, and to seeing a load of people I know again.' She reached out a gloved hand and caught hold of Penny's. 'This is all Miles's fault, isn't it? I told him there was no need for a written agreement between us, but of course, just like all lawyers, he had to dot the i's and cross the t's and put the fear of God into you. I'm so sorry, Penny, it's my fault you've lost him.'

'Of course it's not, Olivia. You know what they say about mixing business with pleasure. Anyway, if by some miracle I do find him again, you're sure it's all right with you if I tell him the truth?'

'Absolutely. Tell him whatever you like.' Olivia glanced around, but they were still alone in that part of the cemetery. 'But how are you going to go about finding him?'

Penny didn't have an easy answer to that one, but she knew where she was going to start.

—

Penny spent the best part of half an hour wandering around the island after Olivia had left, the sombre mood of the cemetery matching her own. Finally, as the setting sun dropped to the horizon in an orange ball, she took the *vaporetto* back to Venice, taking the precaution to get off a stop further on than normal, so as not to alight directly in front of the hotel where Olivia had now taken her place. She made her way through the narrow streets back to St Mark's square, the temperature dropping like a stone as darkness fell. As she threaded her way through shoppers and tourists, she spent a good bit of time looking in the shop windows for a present for Jimmy. He had always been so very supportive and, of course, his agreement to keep silent about their charade was invaluable. The answer came to her just as she was approaching her new hotel. She spotted a shop that described itself as *The Home of Artisan Leather*. In the window were exquisite wallets, bags and cases, all looking beautifully soft and smooth. She went inside for a look around.

Doing her best to think of what Jimmy might want, she remembered that he usually carried a canvas shoulder bag. She found the perfect replacement in a chestnut brown leather satchel, complete with retro brass buckles and a padded shoulder strap. She felt sure that Jimmy would appreciate this and she added a matching wallet as an afterthought. The present took a sizeable chunk out of the thousand euros she had got from Olivia, but she knew he was worth it.

Her room on the top floor of the new hotel, while very different from the luxury of her previous room with its views across the lagoon, was comfortable and clean, with free wifi, and the view from the window over the roofs of Venice had considerable charm. As soon as she got in, she dumped her stuff and stripped off her Olivia clothes. The impeccable linen blouse and the mohair jumper disappeared into the little wardrobe, as did the designer jeans. She ran herself a bath and poured in the contents of one of the bottles she had picked up in her previous bathroom. Within minutes, the water was invisible under a dense cloud of bubbles. She climbed in and lay back, feeling like Cleopatra in her bath of asses' milk. As she closed her eyes, she did her best to think happy thoughts.

She was definitely, genuinely, happy for Olivia, who now looked as if she was really back on her own two feet. She was also happy that Mrs B-W appeared to be emerging from the cloud that had struck her too. She was immensely pleased and grateful to have had the opportunity to visit the amazing city of Venice, not least as everything she had been hearing at the conference had made it ever clearer that Venice was desperately threatened by climate change. And she was extremely happy, and grateful, that Olivia had insisted that she would be paid a thousand pounds a day for the next two days, even though she was just going to spend the time cruising around the outlying islands of the lagoon. Not many people got to do that and even fewer got paid that kind of money for doing it. Yes, she told herself as she lay there, feeling the tickling of the bubbles as they exploded against her nose, she had a lot of things to make her happy.

Unbidden, however, the spectre of Rico appeared before her. In fact, his image was so powerful that for a moment she felt a sensual thrill run right throughout her body. Oh, she thought to herself, to have him there with her. She found herself remembering things he had said, little things about his voice, his face, those amazing eyes. She remembered the warmth of his thigh against hers at the table and then the feel of his arms around her and his lips upon hers out there on the little bridge. There was no doubt in her mind that the way she thought of him was different from any man she had ever known, and that included Rick and Owen. Of course, she told herself, that was the problem with this love at first sight thing; it wasn't just for a few seconds. It happened and then it carried on happening, hopefully for a whole lifetime. And now, in all likelihood, in spite of what Jimmy had said to try to cheer her, she really had lost him forever. Would she ever see him again? She closed her eyes and let her head sink below the surface, the water washing away the tears that had sprung, unwanted, to her eyes.

When she emerged from the bath, she had regained her resolve, and she knew what she had to do. After an embarrassing hiatus when the hairdryer in her room didn't work and a replacement had to be found, she finally set out from the hotel into the cold winter night at about eight o'clock. She was wearing jeans; not designer jeans, but her normal jeans, and with thick tights underneath. She had a woolly hat pulled down over her newly washed hair, and a hefty scarf wrapped round her neck. In consequence, she felt pretty confident that nobody from the conference would recognise her if they should spot her as she set off through the backstreets in the direction of the restaurant.

Within fifteen minutes she was lost once more. Time and time again she would follow a narrow lane, only to find her way blocked by a canal or a dead end. She was forced to turn left and right into ever smaller alleys so many times that she lost all sense of orientation. It was, therefore, with a certain amount of relief, a good while later, that she emerged on the eastern side of the city on the waterfront, looking out towards the isle of the dead.

She stood under a street lamp and studied the map she had got from the hotel. Even though she could see she was on the shore of the lagoon, it still took her five minutes to work out where she was and where she had to go. Finally, after a bit of a struggle, she made her way back in the general direction of the restaurant until, mercifully, she came across it. She heaved a sigh of relief that only lasted until she read the notice on the door. It translated as *Closed on Wednesdays*. She stood by the darkened windows and growled, 'Bugger, bugger, bugger.' But it didn't help.

After a few minutes, she turned and set off again. Within a few minutes she managed to find a familiar sight. It was her grappa café and it was open. She went in and was greeted as an old friend by the man behind the bar whose name, she now knew, was Leonardo.

She spoke to him in Italian, always glad to have the opportunity to practise.

'Hi, Leonardo. I came back to see you.'

'And you're very welcome. You still look cold. What about some grappa?'

Penny shook her head. 'I'd better not, thanks, but I'd have a hot drink if that's possible.'

'Of course, what would you like?'

'Could I have a cup of tea, English-style, with a drop of cold milk?'

'Of course, and maybe a sandwich or a *focaccia*?'

Penny spent half an hour there, doing her best to get over her disappointment that she hadn't been able to find out about Rico. She even considered asking Leonardo if he knew him, but just enquiring whether he knew a tall man with a black beard would have sounded very lame and would no doubt have achieved nothing in a city of a quarter of a million people, excluding tourists. She ate a warm *focaccia* with a roast vegetable filling as she drank her tea and the whole lot cost less than a small beer in her previous hotel. She left there just before ten and managed to navigate her way back to St Mark's Square successfully. By now she was feeling very tired after her broken night: she was back at the hotel and in bed before eleven, wondering how Olivia and Caroline were getting on with their dates and what Rico might be doing, wherever he was. Mercifully, she didn't lie awake too long as tiredness overcame her and she fell into a deep sleep.

Chapter 20

Penny woke up feeling warm and comfortable. She had been dreaming of Venice again, but this time it had been a dream of magical islands and hot summer sun. She had been effortlessly sculling her own gondola across the lagoon when she had spotted Jimmy sitting in a canoe. He was carrying his new satchel in one hand and with the other he was pointing in the direction of a man standing on the shore of a tiny island. The man had a mass of unruly black hair and she could see the outline of his beard, but his face was turned away from her. She tried her hardest to row towards the shore, but the current kept pushing her away, closer and closer towards a rocky reef. Fortunately, it was at that point that she woke up.

She glanced at the time and was surprised to see that it was already well past eight. Of course, she told herself, she was effectively on holiday today but, even so, she was surprised that she had slept so well and for so long. No sooner did her mind clear, however, than the warm comfortable feeling was replaced by a sense of melancholy that not even the prospect of a day on the Venice lagoon could shift. She was still lying there, unwilling to get up and launch herself into the day when her phone started ringing. It was Olivia and it soon emerged that she had some amazing news.

'Hi Olivia, how did it go with Jonathan last night?' Penny settled back against the pillow.

'It went brilliantly. We had a super time and we talked and talked and talked. And part of what we talked about was you, Penny.'

'Me?'

'Yes, I told him all about how you've been standing in for me over these past few months and he was truly amazed. He had no idea at all that you weren't me.' Penny could hear her giggle. 'He even confessed to having enjoyed the kiss you gave him so much he couldn't sleep for thinking of me.'

'It was only a teeny weenie little kiss, but I'm glad if it helped.'

'Well, I gave him a considerably longer kiss myself later on, so he went off very happy indeed. Anyway, Penny, listen, are you interested in a job?'

'A job? I thought you were back in business.'

'And I am, but it's not that sort of job. Listen, Jon's father's crazy about art. He and my father were very close friends and I know they even talked about setting up a gallery together. Anyway, since Daddy's death, that's what Jon's father has done. He probably told you they have a charitable foundation, sort of like ours.'

'He did, and he said the new gallery was here in Venice.'

'That's right. Anyway, they're looking for an assistant curator. The right person would need to have an art degree, preferably postgraduate, and be fluent in Italian and English. Well, I immediately thought of you. What do you think? Interested?'

Penny sat bolt upright in bed. She had been planning on existing on the proceeds of her work for Olivia at least until she could see the success or otherwise of her Piccadilly show. If her paintings started to sell well, then she hoped to make it as a professional artist. If, as was more likely, she only sold a few or, God forbid, none at all, she had no doubt that she would have to seek a "proper" job in order to support herself. But a job in a gallery here in Venice?

'Olivia, that sounds awesome.' And it really did. 'The only problem's my show coming up in January. I would probably need a bit of time off to go back to London for the vernissage and to see how it's going, maybe even do a few press interviews if I'm really lucky.'

'I thought of that and mentioned it to Jon – he wasn't bothered. In fact he was very impressed to know that you were exhibiting your own paintings. The gallery here opens its doors to the public tomorrow night, but that exhibition's going to run until Easter. He says he could easily spare you for a few weeks in January. So, what do you think? Does it appeal?'

'Yes, yes, it does. It appeals very much indeed. Wow!' Penny's melancholy had been chased away in a flash. She got up and pulled the curtains open, looking out onto the roofs, most covered with white frost. In fact, as she stared outside, she saw a few little snowflakes in the air. It didn't need the sight of a row of pigeons, feathers puffed up to twice their normal size, sheltering on the window ledge directly opposite her hotel, to realise that it was going to be another extremely cold day, far from the tropical conditions of her dream. She returned to the matter in hand. 'So what should I do? They'll want to interview me.'

Olivia gave Penny Jon's phone number. 'He said I should speak to you first thing and he asks you, if you're interested, to ring him straight away.'

'Fantastic, Olivia, I will. Thank you so much.'

'No thanks needed. So, what's your plan for today?'

'Well, I'll see what Jonathan says. By the way, his name's Carstairs, isn't it?' She heard Olivia agree. 'Once I've seen him, I'm planning on taking that tour of the outlying islands you recommended.'

'You'll love it. And what about your mystery man? Did you manage to contact him?'

'The restaurant was closed last night. I'm going to have to try again today.'

'Well good luck with it. I'm sure it'll work out. Will you ring me this evening to tell me how you got on with the daytrip, the job and of course your pirate man?'

'Of course. And thanks again, Olivia.'

After she had rung off, Penny dialled the number Olivia had given her. As she heard it ringing she had a sudden moment of panic. What should she call him? As a potential employer, it should really be Mr Carstairs, but as her friend's boyfriend and a man she had also kissed, then Jonathan would appear more logical. She was still weighing up her options when she heard his voice.

'Hello.'

'Um, hi, hello, it's Penny Lane calling. You know, Olivia's friend.'

'Penny, hello. Thanks so much for calling. First of all, my congratulations on the splendid job you've been doing for Olivia. You had me totally fooled.' There was a momentary pause during which Penny found herself wondering if he was going to comment on the fact that she had kissed him. Quite probably he was thinking along the same lines as his voice sounded more than a little sheepish as he carried on. 'Yes, totally fooled. Anyway, has Olivia told you about our new project?'

'The gallery you mentioned to me on Monday?'

'That's right, and has she mentioned that we're looking for somebody to work alongside the curator? Well, if you can spare the time to come along this morning, we'll both be there and we could have a little chat about your background and experience.'

'Of course, thank you very much.' A thought occurred to her. All her smart clothes were packed into suitcases in Caroline's room. 'I'm afraid I'll just be in jeans, though, as I've left most of my clothes in the other hotel.'

She heard him laugh. 'Yes, Olivia told me the subterfuge extended all the way to your wardrobe. Anyway, don't worry about that at all. Come as you are, we'll be delighted to see you.' He gave her the name and address of the new gallery and they agreed to meet at half past ten that morning.

After putting the phone down, Penny had a sudden thought. She felt through the pockets of her jeans and, in the back pocket, she found the leaflet Rico had given her about a new exhibition opening that week. She had slipped it into her pocket without doing more than casting a quick glance over it and only now did she see that the name of the gallery was the Carstairs Gallery. There was a website address and, as she was searching for it on the internet, she suddenly realised that there was a chance she might meet Rico there. She resolved to go to the opening the following night, whether she got the job or not. This might be an even better way of getting back into contact with him than asking at the restaurant. Her spirits rose even higher.

As she slowly perused the website for information about the new gallery and the exhibition, she phoned Caroline. She explained about the job interview and broached the subject that had been worrying her. 'The thing is, Caroline, if they offer me the job, it'll mean me coming to live here in Venice and that means moving out of your place. I don't want to leave you in the lurch. Is that going to screw things up for you with the mortgage?'

'Not at all. I'll be sorry to lose you, but, to be totally honest, I somehow don't think it's going to be long before Nick and I start thinking about moving in together.'

'Things that good between you and him?'

'Things are just amazing between us.'

'I'm so, so pleased for you both. Well, if you're sure, wish me luck.'

'You don't need luck. You'll nail it.'

As she settled down to study the website, Penny found she was humming to herself.

—

The new gallery was housed in the most amazing Renaissance palace right beside the Grand Canal. As a place of work it looked truly remarkable. Penny arrived just before half past ten and walked up three steps into the stunning entrance hall. The floor was a complex mosaic of pink and white marble, worn smooth in places by the passage of countless feet. Massive stone columns supported a ceiling made up of huge oak beams, between which were strung steel wires studded with ultramodern LED lights. Right in front of her, as the glass doors slid silently apart, was the base of a column supporting a naked torso without a head, perfectly sculpted out of the finest Carrara marble. Penny stopped to admire it for a moment before turning towards the reception desk. A girl was standing behind the long counter and she looked up with a smile.

'Good morning, signorina, how can I help? The exhibition doesn't open until tomorrow.'

'Hello, my name's Penny Lane and I've got an appointment...' A voice from behind interrupted her.

'Penny, how wonderful to see you.'

She turned to see Jonathan running down the stairs towards her. 'I saw you on the screen.' He pointed towards a bulbous lens at ceiling height. 'Security has to be tight here. The artworks on display are irreplaceable.' He smiled across at the girl behind the desk. 'It's all right, Carla, I'll look after Penny.'

He came across and shook her hand and then led her back up the stairs towards the first floor. He kept glancing across at her and smiling. Finally he clearly couldn't hold himself back any longer. He stopped just before the top of the wide marble staircase and turned towards her. 'It's absolutely amazing just how similar you are. Are you sure you and Olivia aren't estranged twins or something like that?'

Penny grinned. 'I've got a friend who thinks that, but I think it's just coincidence, and a bit of smoke and mirrors with hairstyles and fingernails. We are very similar though, I must admit.' Her grin broadened. 'I had you fooled, didn't I?'

He blushed. 'Yes, you certainly did. Anyway, come and let me present you to Enrico. He's our curator.' Penny followed his outstretched hand up the stairs and paused at the top to wait for Jonathan. He guided her towards an open door on the left, gave it a little tap and led her inside. 'Enrico, please let me introduce you to Penny. She's interested in being your right hand.'

An elderly gentleman with a shock of white hair looked up from his desk and dropped his pen onto the documents he had been reading. He stood up and came around to greet her, removing his reading glasses as he did so. As he reached her he shook her hand and gave a little bow of the head. 'Enrico Innocenti. How very good of you to come and see us.'

Penny answered in Italian and, as she did so, she was turning over the old gentleman's name in her head. It suddenly came to her. She gave him a big smile. 'Professor Innocenti, it's a privilege to meet you. Your work on Venetian artists of the Renaissance pretty much wrote my MA thesis for me.' She glanced across at Jonathan who was looking on amiably. Sensing that he wasn't following the conversation, she translated into English. 'Professor Innocenti's books are world famous. I'm so excited to meet him.'

The interview took place partly in English and partly in Italian. By the end, Penny knew she would love to work with Professor Innocenti, here in this amazing place. Jonathan, it turned out, was only here for a few days to see that the grand opening tomorrow went well and would only be popping back from time to time to check that everything was going smoothly. Penny wasn't sorry. Somehow, after the intimacy of her first meeting with him, when he had clearly been besotted with her, albeit thinking she was somebody else, she knew it would be weird to work with him on a daily basis, knowing that he had strong feelings for her sort-of-identical twin. As it was, this sounded like a perfect solution.

Professor Innocenti asked her a number of searching questions about her MA studies and she had to rack her brains to remember some of the names and dates but, all in all, she thought it went pretty well. He was fascinated by the study she had made of Olivia's Bosch triptych and she promised to send him a copy of the article. He was very interested in her upcoming exhibition and insisted upon her showing him some photos of her work that she had on her phone. He studied them reverently, zooming in and out of the pictures, lavishing as much attention upon them as if they were priceless historical canvasses, before pronouncing his judgement upon them.

'You have considerable talent, Miss Lane. I think you will go far.'

She blushed red, awed to receive praise from such an exalted source. Finally, Jonathan asked her if she would mind taking a seat downstairs in the entrance hall for a few minutes so that he and Enrico could have a little discussion. Penny made her way back downstairs again, really hoping she would get the job.

The receptionist, Carla, offered her a coffee and Penny accepted gladly. A quick telephone call and two minutes later a waiter appeared at the door with a tray. Carla explained that the café across the road was very obliging and always happy to deliver. Penny was impressed. With espresso coffee just a phone call away, she knew she would have to watch her caffeine intake if she did come to work here.

As they drank their coffees, they chatted in Italian. Penny asked her about the palace itself. Carla explained as much as she knew. 'To be honest, I only started two weeks ago and there's been so much to do with getting the exhibition set up and making the arrangements for tomorrow night's vernissage party, I haven't had much time to find out all about it. I believe Jonathan said the building dates back to the fifteen hundreds.'

Penny nodded. That sounded about right. 'I wouldn't be surprised if parts of it were even older. This floor, for example, is stunning. I wonder if it might not even be early medieval. Who owns this place? Jonathan and the Foundation?'

Carla shook her head. 'No, they lease it, I think. It belongs to some old noble Venetian family. And you, Penny, are you from an old noble family in England?'

Penny laughed. 'No, dead common I'm afraid. I'm an artist and I've been working in a café for the last couple of years, trying to make ends meet.' She glanced round at the unbelievable decorative refinement of the palace and reflected upon the difference between it and the Apocalypse Café. She decided that, sooner or later, if she did get the job, she would have to get Jimmy to come over and see it for himself.

A few minutes later, the phone on the counter rang and Carla told Penny she had been asked to return to Professor Innocenti's office. Feeling really quite nervous, she walked back up the stairs, but she needn't have worried. Professor Innocenti was waiting for her with a sheaf of papers and the offer of a job.

'Jonathan has been called away for a video conference, so let me tell you what we're offering, in the hope that you will accept our offer and take the job. Personally, I would be delighted and proud to have an artist of such talent working with me. And a Renaissance art historian as well!' He went on to outline the terms and conditions of the job and Penny was pleasantly surprised to hear the salary. She knew that accommodation would be her biggest expense here and in all probability, she would have to do as so many did and live on the mainland in Mestre or Marghera and commute by bus or rail to work. Even so, a quick calculation confirmed that she should be able to live on what they were offering and even maybe start saving a little every month. When he had finished explaining everything, repeating that it was perfectly all right for her to take time off in January for her exhibition in London, she gave him a big smile and said yes.

'Professor Innocenti, I'm delighted to accept the offer. I can't imagine a more wonderful working environment, and the idea of working for you is too exciting for words.'

They decided that Penny would start work at the beginning of January, so that she had a little time to make all the practical arrangements before then. The first person she called when she emerged from the interview was Caroline. It was almost half past eleven and she hoped to catch her during the mid-morning break at the conference. She did.

'Hi, Penny, how did the interview go?'

'Hi, Caroline, that's what I'm calling about. They've offered me the job and they want me to start in early January. Are you sure that's okay with you?'

'Of course it is! Oh, Penny, I'm so pleased for you.'

'It's really a perfect job for me and it's in such an amazing place. I can hardly believe it.'

'What's on the programme for the rest of the day? Drink yourself insensible on prosecco, maybe?'

'No, I'm staying sober today. I'm off to the islands and I want to appreciate them and remember them. The prosecco can wait. And please, can you tell Olivia the good news and say that I'll give her a call this evening?'

'Of course. By the way, you'd do well to phone her before eight because she's out with Jonathan once more. It sounds as if those two are really hitting it off.'

Even through her happiness at having got the job, Penny felt a little wave of remorse that everybody around her seemed to be finding love while all she had done so far was to fall in love and then immediately trample all over it. She did her best to rise above such sentiments. 'I'm really happy for her, and for you, Caroline.'

Caroline knew her well by now. 'You'll find him, Penny. I know you will. But, for now, just celebrate the job. As for your man, things will work out, you'll see.'

—

Penny's head was still filled with conflicting emotions, part joy, part sorrow, when she got on the water-bus bound for Murano. The sky had cleared a bit, but tiny little flakes of freezing snow landed on her cheeks as she stood in the open central section of the boat, determined not to miss anything as they headed out past the isle of the dead. The wind had died down completely and the water had a smooth, almost oily texture as the ferry sliced through it. The lagoon was a grey green colour, quite unlike anything she had seen anywhere else. She took a number of photos, leaning precariously over the side so as to catch the bow-wave, and vowed to incorporate this into a painting some time soon.

The ferry deposited her on the island of Murano and she went for a longer walk round, to see what it looked like in daylight. It was lunchtime by now and the touts were already at the doors of the restaurants, doing their best to inveigle tourists into their establishments, but Penny already knew where she wanted to go. She made her way back to the same little restaurant where she and Caroline had eaten on the first night and ordered a plate of rabbit stew with polenta. Presumably the rabbits weren't from the island, as everywhere she looked appeared to be built up and industrialised, but they tasted wonderful.

After another excellent meal, she visited the amazing Byzantine-style basilica, quite plain on the outside, but wonderfully ornate inside, with a mosaic floor that recalled the floor in her future place of work. From there she went to the other main church, San Pietro Martire, to admire the paintings by such legendary names as Veronese, Bellini and Tintoretto. A friendly local told her that most of the other churches and historic buildings had been destroyed, first by the French, and then the Austrians, who had occupied much of this part of Italy in the eighteenth and nineteenth centuries. The glass business here had totally taken over the island and although she knew that there were some amazing artists working inside the factories, the overall appearance of the island, while still attractive, was more industrial than cultural. She left the island on the ferry to her next port of call, Burano, feeling a little let down with the views, although the rabbit stew had been memorable.

Burano, on the other hand, was spectacularly different. Where Murano had been industrial, Burano was an artist's paradise. The houses vied with each other to be the most colourful on the island and the interplay of powerful reds, greens, yellows and blues was stunning. She took numerous photos, knowing that she would come back here again and again during her time in Venice just for the sheer pleasure of walking around this little gem of a place.

It was while she was taking a photograph of the perilously leaning bell tower that she had an attack of déjà vu. Just before the bell tower was a lace shop and, as she was lining up her shot, a tall man emerged from the shop and set off away from her, down towards the end of the road and the lagoon. He had a wild mass of dark hair and a black leather jacket. It could have been a sequence from one of her dreams. As he glanced to one side, she spotted the beard. She almost squealed with excitement, crammed her phone back in her pocket and set out after him at a run. Had the universe really given her another chance? This time there was no canal between them and she caught up with him well before he reached the gardens at the waterside.

She ran up behind him and called out breathlessly to him in Italian. 'Rico? Is it you?'

The tall figure turned back towards her in surprise and held up his hands, his pale blue eyes looking at her quizzically. '*Wie bitte?* Is there a problem?'

Penny stopped dead, her face aflame with embarrassment. All she could do was to shake her head and apologise to the German man for troubling him. As he walked off again, she went across to a bench and sat down, giving her racing heart time to recover, while trying her best not to snort with frustration and annoyance at herself.

While she was sitting there, she got a phone call from her parents in Devon. She had phoned and left a message on their answer phone that morning, after the interview, and now she hastened to give them the good news. Her mother, predictably, was concerned that her little girl was going off to live abroad, while her father, equally predictably, sounded delighted that she had finally got a job that would give her enough money to live on. She confirmed that she would be flying back to London in two days' time and then she would travel down to spend Christmas with them on Tuesday. Her mother asked about the weather in Venice and then went on to tell Penny that this December had been the wettest in Devon for half a century. Penny looked round at the winter sunlight that was now beginning to break through the clouds and knew that she was going to enjoy herself here and, surely, sooner or later, she would be bound to meet Rico again. The thought cheered her immensely.

–

Early that evening, Penny phoned Olivia and gave her a rundown of her day, thanking her profusely for putting her onto the gallery job. Olivia sounded delighted for her.

'That's wonderful and it gives me a perfect excuse to come over to Venice again this winter to see you.'

'I'm really looking forward to it. In fact, I'm going to start looking for accommodation tomorrow. I expect I'll end up living on the mainland like most people.'

'Well, it's only a few minutes in on the train and then it can only be a fifteen minute walk down to the gallery. Speaking of which, I imagine you're planning on going to the inauguration of Jon's exhibition tomorrow night?'

'Yes, but so are you, aren't you? We can't really turn up together, though, can we? To be honest, Olivia, under normal circumstances I'd just stay out of it and let you go, but if I can't get hold of Rico through the restaurant, that's going to be my last hope of seeing him again.'

'Of course, you must. But I don't see why we can't both go. Jon said it starts at six and he's going to be tied up with speeches and things for the first hour or so. Why don't you go along at the start and then drift off an hour later, hopefully arm in arm with your pirate man? Send me a text when you've left and I'll turn up in your place and voila! Nobody will be any the wiser except you, me and Jon.' She giggled. 'I'll warn him that it'll be you for the first hour. I wouldn't want him to sweep you into his arms and start kissing you.'

'So it's reached the sweeping up and snogging stage, has it?'

'Very definitely. A good bit more than snogging, to tell the truth.'

'Well, good for you, girl. And, yes that's a great solution for tomorrow night if you're happy with it. I'll be there from six to seven and I'll text you as I slink out of the door.' A thought occurred to her. 'Hang on though, should we maybe wear the same outfits? People might find it a bit weird if you do a quick change act midway through the event.'

'Of course, you're right. And, much as I'd rather he did, I'd better tell Jon not to act too affectionate towards either of us, so the curator and any other staff who know you won't start thinking you're having an affair with the owner.'

'So, what outfit? A dress presumably, and fairly smart.' She had been wondering what to wear, caught between trying to stay as casual as Rico always was and, at the same time, wanting to show her new employers that she knew how to dress up smartly for a champagne reception. Now the decision was being made for her and she was secretly rather pleased.

'Well, how about the cream Chanel dress? Did you bring it with you to Venice?'

Penny smiled. This was the cocktail dress that had so inflamed the desires of Rafe Kingsholme. 'Yes, it's in a suitcase in Caroline's room.'

'I'll ask her to drop it round to you tomorrow morning. And you'll need the same shoes as me, too.' Penny could hear the excitement in her voice. 'What fun. I always did love dressing up.'

'That's brilliant, thanks. I'll look forward to seeing Caroline in the morning. Enjoy yourself with Jonathan tonight.'

'Oh, yes, I'm sure I will.' Olivia's voice became a bit more serious. 'And, Penny, I do hope you find your man.'

So did Penny.

–

At seven thirty Penny left her hotel, in search of the restaurant where she and Rico had spent that lovely evening. This time she managed to navigate her way there without getting lost and she was delighted to find it open. She went in and took a good look round, but didn't immediately recognise anybody. A waitress she hadn't seen before showed her to a table in one corner, from which she could survey the whole scene. A group of men came in and sat at the next table and she felt their eyes on her, but they didn't interest her. Her luck began to change as an elderly waiter appeared with a menu for her. She immediately recognised him as one of the waiters who had served the group table the other night. She ordered a small carafe of prosecco and waited for him to return to take her order. When he did so, she leant forward and lowered her voice.

'I was here on Tuesday night with a group of friends, artists. We sat at that table over there.' She saw him nod. 'I'm trying to get hold of one of the men, his name's Federico... Rico. Do you know the man I mean, tall, dark hair and a beard?' Just for an instant she saw what might have been a shifty look on the waiter's face, but just as quickly it passed and the man shook his head.

'Alas, signorina, I don't know the man you mean. We often get artists in here. I think I remember the group you were with, but I'm afraid I can't help you. Now, what can I get you to eat?'

Having had a hefty lunch, Penny just ordered some of the wonderful San Daniele ham and a salad. The waiter nodded, reached down and poured some of her wine into her glass and then left. Penny watched him go, turning over in her head whether he maybe knew more than he was telling. But, she asked herself, if that was the case, then why was he doing it? Was it just natural Venetian solidarity in the face of yet another tourist? More worryingly, did Rico make a habit of bringing random girls to this place? Was the waiter under instructions not to divulge his identity in case of recriminations? She couldn't help thinking that it really was a bit strange that Rico hadn't told her anything at all about himself. Had she just been destined to be another notch on his bedpost and then discarded? It was a distasteful thought.

Irritably, she tore open a packet of bread sticks and nibbled one for something to do, fighting with her sense of frustration and annoyance. Unless she spotted another familiar face here in the restaurant to ask, she now knew that her only realistic chance of catching up with Rico again would be tomorrow night, if he came to the inauguration of the exhibition for which he had given her the leaflet. If she didn't see him there, then that would be that. She would be returning to London the following morning.

Her meal was delicious, although the disappointment of not finding out about Rico and now her other doubts as to his true intentions rather spoiled the overall effect. She didn't stay long. After finishing her salad, she asked for the bill and left. It was barely nine o'clock, so she went for a walk before returning to her hotel. She managed to get herself to the Rialto Bridge, crossed it and headed round to the west of the Grand Canal, an area that was totally new to her. It was even colder tonight than previous nights and in spite of her woolly gloves, even with her hands tucked in her pockets, her fingers were still frozen. She stopped in a café near the surprisingly large open space of Campo San Polo and ordered a hot chocolate. It wasn't as good as the one she had had with Jonathan, before her true identity had been revealed to him, but it certainly cost far less. She stood at the counter in the long, narrow bar, listening to a group of Canadian tourists discussing their plans for the next day and gave serious consideration as to what she, herself, was going to do.

Tomorrow would be Friday, and effectively her last full day in Venice. Most importantly, she needed to find somewhere to live from January. She could always stay in a cheapish *pensione* at first if necessary, but the sooner she found somewhere the better. She resolved to call in at the gallery the next morning and ask Carla if she knew which agency, website, or local newspaper to consult. Apart from this, she needed to do some shopping for Christmas presents for her family back home in Devon and then she still had a load of galleries to visit. At least, she thought to herself, seeing as she would be back here to start work in less than three weeks, she could always catch up on the ones she missed in January. She made a list in her head of all the places she wanted to go and realised that it was going to be a very full day. And then, of course, in the evening, there would be the opening of the Carstairs Gallery and maybe, just maybe, the chance to see Rico again.

And if she did see him, she wondered, staring down at the chocolate in her cup as she warmed her hands around it, what would happen? The thing was that there was no guarantee everything would work out fine, even if she did see him again. If he turned out to be a gold-digger, the discovery that she wasn't after all a millionairess would no doubt hammer the final nail into that particular coffin. If she had just been intended as a casual pick-up and a one-night stand, she knew she no longer wanted just that, even though the idea had had considerable appeal two nights ago. The fact that she couldn't shake him from her head told her that this was something very different, something unique in her life so far. Grudgingly, she had to admit to herself that it was looking very much like a serious attack of love, at least as far as she was concerned. As for the way he saw it, well, that was the big unknown. There was also the fact that she had lied to him about her identity. Even if his feelings towards her were more than just materialistic or carnal, he might with some justification feel miffed that she hadn't been straight with him from the outset.

She signalled to the barman that she would like to pay. As she went back out into the cold, she shivered, but it wasn't just because of the sub-zero temperature.

Chapter 21

There was a knock on Penny's door next morning. It was Caroline, carrying a bag.

'Here, you have to make sure you're looking your best for when you see your mystery man tonight.' She handed it over to Penny, who took it gratefully.

'It's not *when*, but *if* I see my mystery man. Anyway, thanks, Caroline, and do thank Olivia. That's really nice of you. Come in and tell me how it's all going with Nick.'

Caroline shook her head. 'I can't, I'm afraid. I've just realised it's Christmas next week and I haven't done any shopping. I'm hoping to find some shops open now before I head over to the conference. Anyway, things with Nick couldn't be better. And I summoned up the courage to tell Olivia about me and him yesterday and she sounded very pleased for us.'

'That's great. And I'm like you about the Christmas shopping business. I'd completely forgotten until yesterday. I'll maybe see you in the shops.'

Penny went straight to the gallery that morning and had a long chat to Carla. She came away with a list of places she could contact about accommodation, fortunately, a number of them online, so she could continue the hunt from the UK over Christmas. She bought a couple of papers and called into three agencies. The upshot of her investigations was that, as expected, the only flat she could hope to rent here in Venice with the funds at her disposal would be minute, without any hope of space to paint. In consequence, she knew she would have to look for somewhere on the mainland. She walked up to the station and took a train to Mestre, a journey of only a matter of minutes, and was relieved to find a number of agencies, all of whom claimed to have accommodation available. Needless to say, as Christmas was only a few days away, their advice was to wait until she came back in January, take temporary accommodation for the first few days, and then look around. Penny accepted their advice.

She returned to Venice after lunch and managed to buy Christmas presents and see a couple of the exhibitions on her list. It was a very busy day and she hadn't had time for lunch so, as she made her hesitant way through the paved streets in her high heels just before six that evening, en route to the Carstairs Gallery, she stopped for a quick coffee and a croissant in a little bar. The look she got from the barman when she undid her coat was reassuringly admiring, if a little lecherous, and she felt pretty confident that she wasn't going to look out of place among the great and good of Venetian society who had doubtless been invited to the opening night.

When she got to the gallery, shortly after six, the event was already in full swing. She was waved in by a smiling Carla who had pinned her hair up and was looking very elegant in a little black dress and heels. Penny was reassured that her decision to dress smartly was the right one. At the top of the stairs, she found

Professor Innocenti in a dinner jacket, a carnation in his button hole, welcoming guests to the exhibition. When he spotted Penny he made his way across to greet her. He took both of her hands in his and gave her an admiring look. 'Good evening, Penny, you look enchanting.'

'Good evening, Professor Innocenti. I was just thinking how smart you were looking as well.'

'Penny, hi. I'm so glad you could come.' Penny turned at the sound of the voice to find Jonathan at her shoulder. He, too, cast an approving glance across her. 'You look stunning, I must say.'

Professor Innocenti had been captured by another couple so Penny was able to lower her voice and give Jonathan a conspiratorial grin. 'Afraid it's just me in here for now, but Olivia'll be coming at seven.'

'I know, she told me all about it.' Just then he spotted somebody over her shoulder. 'Do please go on in and look around. I look forward to hearing what you think of the exhibition. You'll have to excuse me now; I've just spotted the British Ambassador who's come all the way up from Rome to be with us.'

Penny walked into the huge first floor exhibition room and paused at the door. The very first thing she saw, right in front of her, was a massive painting of Venice, unmistakably by Canaletto. As she stood in silent appreciation, a waiter glided up with a tray and offered her a glass of champagne. She took one and then moved on into the room, partly looking at the artworks, but really very much on the lookout for Rico. All the women were dressed to the nines and she in no way felt out of place in her frighteningly expensive Chanel number. All the men were wearing suits or dinner jackets and there was absolutely no sign of a battered black leather jacket or, indeed, a tall man with an unruly mop of dark hair. Her hopes began to fade. A sense of disillusionment gradually began to settle upon her as she realised that her last chance of seeing her mystery man again had come and gone. She took a big mouthful of champagne, reflecting that her new job might, at least, indulge her in her newfound taste for the expensive stuff, but it didn't help.

She worked her way around the room full of priceless treasures, unable to fully appreciate their beauty because of the cold void of disappointment that had formed inside her. She was standing in front of the magnificent portrait of Flora by Titian, on loan from the Uffizi, when she heard a voice.

'Good evening, Olivia, I've been hoping so very much that you'd come.' The voice came from behind her, but she would have recognised it anywhere. She wheeled round with a delighted smile that changed to one of amazement when she saw him. The mass of dark hair had been seriously trimmed by a very good hairdresser. The scruffy beard had been removed and was now reduced to sexy stubble on his cheeks and chin. His tall, muscular frame was now clad in what looked like a silk dinner jacket that screamed good taste and expense. He looked even more drop dead gorgeous than normal and she felt the now familiar unsteadiness in the knees that his appearance always caused. He was smiling back at her somewhat nervously. 'This was my only hope. I had to see you again. I even went back to that hotel of yours and asked for Olivia Brookes-Webster, but they had no record of you.' He suddenly looked very serious.

'Listen, Olivia, I've got to talk to you. I'm so, so sorry I offended you. Please let me explain and maybe you'll be prepared to forgive me.'

Penny was literally speechless. He looked so very unlike what she had been expecting. Gone was the unkempt, bohemian look, to be replaced by elegance and affluence. She found it hard to process. However, although muddied by his changed appearance, her feelings at seeing him again, when she had truly believed all hope had gone, were close to ecstatic. With a considerable effort, she cleared her throat and addressed him.

'Rico, I'm so very, very pleased to see you.' Her voice almost cracked with emotion. 'No, you didn't offend me, yes, we've got to talk and, yes, I really am at that hotel, just not registered under that name. There's so much I've got to tell you.' At that moment, a waiter appeared and murmured something into Rico's ear before withdrawing. Rico nodded and looked back at Penny.

'Will you do something for me, please, Olivia? Can you just stay here and not budge for ten minutes or so? I'm afraid there's something I've got to do.' He gave her that same nervous smile. 'You won't go off again, will you?' She shook her head and he left her there. Suddenly, as her eyes focused on the Titian again, she saw it with new eyes. The girl in the painting had hair almost the same colour as hers, and her enigmatic look away from the viewer was tantalising, not least as she was near naked. As she studied the picture, her head was spinning. He was here, Rico. She had found him and the only thing she couldn't get her head round was the way he had changed so markedly from casual to formal in appearance, even though his smile had still been unmistakably his.

She didn't have to wait long for the explanation. She heard somebody tapping on a microphone and the noise level in the room suddenly dropped. She turned to find Jonathan standing on a low podium at one side of the room, ready to give his welcome speech. On one side of him was Professor Innocenti and on his other side, to her considerable surprise, was Rico.

'Ladies and gentlemen, I'm delighted to welcome you all to the Carstairs Gallery, part of the Carstairs Foundation, created by my grandfather back in the nineteen-sixties. It was always his intention to set up a gallery here in the incomparable city of Venice, to create a space where quintessentially Italian art could be show-cased. And now, at long last, this has come to fruition. We've been extremely fortunate to have been able to find as the home for our new galley this magnificent Renais-sance palace, owned by my good friend Prince Federico di Valdastico.' He turned towards Rico. 'Would you like to say a few words, Your Highness?'

Penny's amazement was then compounded as Rico took the microphone and started to speak in near-perfect English. Up until now she and he had only spoken in Italian together, and she had had no idea he was so very fluent in English. And then there was the fact that he was a prince. As she vaguely listened to him talking about how worthwhile a cause the Carstairs Foundation was, and how happy he was to have this amazing exhibition housed in his property, a terrible realisation began to dawn upon her.

He was a prince. She was a nobody.

He obviously believed she was Olivia and, as such, a person of similar social standing. So, far from Rico being a possible gold-digger, the only person trying to punch above her weight here was Penny herself. And when he found out who she was, or rather, who she wasn't, that would be that. Yet again, she found herself bitterly regretting entering into this charade. Her mum would have been oh so right. It would, indeed, end in crying. And the person doing the crying would be her.

She looked round. Rico was still speaking, now in Italian, thanking all the civic dignitaries who had come along to the opening, and his attention was directed towards a group of sober-looking men in suits at the far end of the room. Slowly, so as not to attract attention, Penny slipped backwards through the crowd until she was able to disappear behind the screen upon which the magnificent Canaletto was hung, and make her escape down the stairs. She knew she had to get out, to avoid putting Rico, and most probably Jonathan, in a most embarrassing position when her true identity was revealed. What, she wondered to herself, would he think when Olivia herself appeared and positioned herself on Jonathan's arm? Penny was quite sure she didn't want to be around to see that.

Remembering that Olivia would be arriving to take her place in less than half an hour, Penny told the cloak-room girl that she had to pop out and she would be back shortly. She retrieved her coat and rushed out of the main entrance, not even waiting to put it on. Only when she was several streets away did she stop in the light of a street lamp and pull the coat on, wrapping her scarf tightly around her neck. Her breath formed clouds in front of her face and she wished she had brought her woolly hat. Remembering what she had told Olivia, she pulled out her phone and sent a two word text, *Gone. Penny.* She retrieved her gloves from her pockets and pulled them on before setting off, blindly, into the Venetian night.

As she walked along a succession of narrow, stone-paved streets, she couldn't miss the fact that, in spite of the cold, there were more people about. It gradually began to dawn upon her that it was not only a Friday night, but the Friday night before Christmas. In five days time it would be Christmas and she would, by then, be back in the UK with her mum, her dad and her sister's family. She would not, however, be with Rico. She would never again be with Rico. In spite of the sparkling Christmas decorations everywhere she looked, in spite of the evident happiness of the majority of people she met, she felt alone and sad. She had found him, she had lost him, and she had found him again – only to discover, a matter of minutes later, that he had once more to be torn out of her life.

She walked round in circles, losing track of time, barely aware of her surroundings, her eyes passing over the incomparable beauty of Venice without registering what she was seeing. It was only much later, when she found herself on top of the humpbacked *Ponte dell'Accademia,* where she had met Rico barely three days earlier, even if it now felt like a lifetime ago, that she stopped and took stock. She went over to the wooden balustrade and rested her elbows on the rail, looking down onto the dark waters of the Grand Canal. Behind her, a street vendor was flying little luminous helicopters, but she ignored them and stared down into the shadows. To one side were the red and white posts that marked a landing stage outside a stunning ochre palazzo flying the flags of Europe, Italy and Venice from its façade. A water-bus was chugging down towards the open lagoon and all around there was a magnificence, a stunning beauty that finally managed to break through her depression. She took a deep breath of freezing air and mentally shook herself.

No, she told herself, she didn't regret taking on the job of replacing Olivia. First and foremost this had brought her two new friends. Second, it had allowed her to sample a lifestyle she could never otherwise have afforded and, third, it had allowed her to come here to this magnificent city of art and culture. The beauty of Venice shone through, defying her to be too downhearted at losing the first man who had ever turned her knees to jelly. She gazed around in silent appreciation of a place that was unique in the world and living perilously closer to disaster with every high tide. She was glad she had come to Venice, no matter what.

Her reverie was interrupted by her phone. She pulled it out and checked the caller ID. It was Jimmy from London.

'Hello, Jimmy, if you've phoned to cheer me up, you've timed it just about right.'

'Oh, sweetheart, didn't you find him?' He sounded truly sorry for her and she felt a warm wave affection for him.

'No, Jimmy, I found him all right. It's just that it turns out he isn't who I thought he was.'

'So what? Let's face it sweetie, you aren't who he thinks you are either.'

'I know, Jimmy, but, you see… it turns out he's a prince.'

'He's a what?' She could imagine the expression on Jimmy's face.

'A prince. Prince Federico of Valsomething or other.'

'Blimey. So that makes you Cinderella, I suppose. But, to be honest, I didn't think there were princes and princesses in a place like Italy. Isn't it a republic?'

'I've no idea, Jimmy. All I know is that the man I fell in love with is way, way out of my league.'

'Don't be ridiculous. Those days are long gone. Look at Princess Kate for instance.'

'No, it's not going to happen, Jimmy. The man owns a palace! Why would he want somebody like me?'

'I'll tell you why he would want you, why I'm sure he does want you. He wants a sweet, kind, caring, funny girl. He wants one of the most gorgeous-looking girls I know and the most talented artist I know as well. So you aren't a princess. Who cares?'

'When he finds out who I really am, he'll care, Jimmy. I'm from another world.' She glanced at the time and was amazed to find it was almost nine o'clock. 'And he'll definitely know by now. No, Jimmy, the best spin I can put on this affair is the whole "better to have loved and lost than never to have loved at all" thing. Who said that? Shakespeare maybe?'

'Tennyson, Alfred Lord Tennyson. Who says I'm just an uneducated waiter, eh?'

'Not me, Jimmy, and you know the other thing you are? You're a star. You're a lovely man and I'm really lucky to have you as my friend.'

'Well, listen to your friend now. All right? I'll speak slowly so you can understand. Go back and look for your pirate prince once more. If he's going to dump you because you haven't got your own castle or palace or whatever, you need to hear it from him. It's not fair of you to prejudge how he might feel about you. Give the poor man a chance, would you?'

'I'd be wasting my time… and his.'

'Then waste it, for crying out loud. But you've got to hear it from him. If you really think I'm a good friend, then listen to me and go back and hear him out. You might be surprised.'

'All right, Jimmy, just for you, but…'

'You won't be wasting your time, believe me.'

Penny dropped the phone into her pocket and made her way back down the slope and off the bridge. She knew her way from here to the gallery; it barely took her five minutes. However, as she reached the gallery, she was unsurprised to see the lights out and the doors locked. The party was all over and everybody, including Rico, had gone. She stood there for a few moments, unsure what she felt. On the one hand, being unable to see and talk to him as Jimmy had instructed was disappointing, but, on the other, she knew she was relieved she didn't need to go through the embarrassment of what would, she felt sure, be rejection.

She set off back to her hotel. As she passed restaurants and bars, now mostly packed with people, she toyed with the idea of stopping for something to eat, but her appetite had deserted her. Instead, she decided she might as well go home and go to bed early. St Mark's Square was still cold and dark, but tonight there were certainly more people to be seen, walking round enjoying themselves. She took a final look at the massive Christmas tree with its bright lights and then went down the road beside the basilica to her hotel. When she walked in the door, she got a surprise.

'Thank goodness. I thought I'd lost you again.' She stopped dead. It was Rico, waiting in the lobby. 'I came here and did what I should have done the other day. When they told me they had no guest with the name Brookes-Webster, I should have done what I did tonight. I asked them if they had a very beautiful English girl with shining chestnut brown hair and grey eyes, who spoke really good Italian. They knew immediately who I meant so I've been waiting. So, I understand I have to call you Penny now?'

Penny still hadn't got a clue what to say. She just stood there, stock still, staring at him. Slowly, part of her brain started to react again. 'You know my name?'

'Jonathan and the real Olivia told me all about your little bit of play-acting. Very convincing by the way. The thing is, you weren't the only one. I owe you an explanation and an apology.' He glanced across at the receptionist, who was trying not to look as if he was listening to their conversation, and then dropped his eyes to his watch. 'Have you got time for a little walk?' Penny nodded blankly, still unsure what was going on and what she should be saying or doing. She let him take her hand and lead her out into the street once more. Once outside, he kept hold of her hand as they walked back into St Mark's Square. She didn't mind.

As they walked across the square they didn't speak. She was still trying to come to terms with the fact that he had tracked her down and, apparently, didn't seem to mind the fact that she wasn't Olivia. A few minutes past the square she realised they were heading back to the gallery. He squeezed her hand and looked across at her. With her killer heels she wasn't much shorter than him. 'I've got wine and cheese at my place if that's all right.'

She nodded her head, still unsure of her voice.

His place, it turned out, was the top floor of the palazzo, above the exhibition. The entrance was down a narrow alley to the left of the building and she saw that the alley finished at a wooden landing stage on the Grand Canal. The door was a massive, carved oak affair, with nails embossed into it. They walked into a spacious hallway and up a very fine white marble stairway to the second floor. He opened the door and led her inside. He flicked a switch and a single lamp came on, giving just enough light for them to make their way past a huge settee to the window. When they reached it, she stopped in awe. The view onto the Grand Canal and across to the ancient buildings on the other side was incomparable. She stood there, eyes ranging over the scene before her, and she knew this was one of the most amazing views in the world. She felt him come up behind her. His arms reached gently round her waist and pulled her towards him. She felt his lips on her neck and then she heard his voice.

'I'm sorry for deceiving you. I didn't mean to, but it's just a sort of self-protection mechanism I have. My friends all know it, even the waiters in the places I go know it. I don't like the bright lights and all the para-phernalia of celebrity. I would have wriggled out of tonight's event if I could have done. I'm much, much happier if people just think of me as Rico. That's all I ever want to be. Will you forgive me?'

His lips touched her earlobe and she almost collapsed backwards. Her whole body felt more alive than it had for months, years. She kept her eyes on the canal and took hold of his hands in hers as they clasped across her waist. Then she, too, apologised.

'So you know the story now? I didn't want to deceive you either. It's just that I was employed to do a job and the job involved me changing into somebody else. But I've changed back now. I'm Penny, I'm an artist, I live in London and I'm very pleased to meet you.'

She felt his arms rise to her shoulders and then he very gently turned her towards him and kissed her. She kissed him back and pressed herself against him, her heart soaring. After the kiss, he crushed her into his chest and she heard his voice again.

'There's something I've got to tell you.' He sounded unexpectedly hesitant. 'Three days ago, in the Accademia, the strangest thing happened when I saw you, Penny. It's never happened to me before. The very first moment I set eyes on you, the very first glimpse I had of you as I came into that room, I just knew somehow.' He paused and she felt him take a deep breath. 'Like I say, it's something I've never encountered before. The only way I can explain it is that it was love at first sight. Yes, I know, ridiculous, isn't it? But that's the only way

I can describe it.' He paused again. 'This is the moment you burst out laughing.'

She raised her face towards him, his eyes shining back at her in the light reflected off the glass of the window.

'Love at first sight? No, I'd never dream of laughing at something as serious as that.'

Acknowledgements

A big thank you to Fiona Wilson, book reviewer extraordinaire, for reading this book and encouraging me.

Warmest thanks, also, to Michael Bhaskar at Canelo for believing in me as a writer.